Nurren's Folly

H. Hotri

iUniverse, Inc.
Bloomington

This is a work of fiction. All of the characters, names, incidents, organizations, and dialogue in this novel are either the products of the author's imagination or are used fictitiously.

iUniverse books may be ordered through booksellers or by contacting:

iUniverse
1663 Liberty Drive
Bloomington, IN 47403
www.iuniverse.com
1-800-Authors (1-800-288-4677)

ISBN: 978-1-4502-7578-1 (sc)
ISBN: 978-1-4502-7579-8 (ebook)

Printed in the United States of America

iUniverse rev. date: 12/30/2010

For E.H.W.

Prologue

The old, dusty saloon harbored the usual afternoon patrons quietly tucked in their corners, numbly passing the time with their daily diversion. Without warning, the doors flew open as if a hurricane had blown in, and a haggard man dashed into the establishment and ran straight to the bar, slowing only in the last few steps. He was the retired runner, the three-time Olympian. Hero. Ultimate record holder. History's best athlete. His claim to fame was astonishing; he had never lost a race since high school, from the hundred-meter sprint to the marathon. No one could outrun him. New words had sprung up around him, such as *staffling* and *unstaffable*. But no one recognized him here. Or if they did, no one showed it or cared. They completely ignored him and his loud entrance.

Staf Nurren stood at the bar with both hands on the counter as if for support. His heavy breathing slowed from frantic gasping to panting, and he looked around with a scared, bewildered look. He scanned the left side of the room with wide, yellow-brown eyes, barely noticing the man in the shadows with the wide-brimmed black hat. The smoke and darkness hid all his features. Smoking was still allowed here, and the man seemed to be taking advantage of it, probably with a large stogie, judging from the large red end penetrating the darkness like a neon light.

A threesome was playing cards near a dirty window; they were two empty tables from the black hat corner. They ignored him too. The blinds let in only enough light to make out vague shapes. The tables in the middle of the bar were empty. On the other side, a pair of older, wrinkled men with sweat-stained shirts sat alone. One was extremely skinny, and his baggy clothes accentuated his thinness.

The other, the exact opposite, had a large paunch stretching his shirt to limits. A few buttons around his midsection were unfastened to allow room for the expanse within. The other customers were involved with their own whispered discussions, but Staf became acutely aware of their occasional glances his way. He was clearly not a regular here and did not belong.

Staf finished looking around the room, returned his gaze to the bar, and then looked down at the dirt as if his upper body was too heavy to support. His greasy brown hair hung in loose clumps down his face.

"A beer, and make it quick," he quietly stuttered, saying it quickly between gasps. *Quick* clearly didn't mean anything to this barkeep; he was busy drying a glass and slowly put down the towel and went to the draft. Staf barely noticed this. Years earlier, he would have insisted on a cold glass from the fridge instead of a warm, freshly washed one. In truth, the glass had not been washed at all; the barkeep was merely wiping out the previous contents. He rarely washed his glasses.

He stared at Staf with beady, suspicious eyes as if angry at the request and filled the glass without taking his gaze off him. He made sure there was lots of foam. He was the type of bartender who kept a loaded shotgun somewhere behind the counter, although he probably didn't need to use it; he was a fairly large, muscular man, with long black hair neatly gathered in the back.

With no pretense of politeness, he slammed the pint on the counter in front of Staf, allowing some to spill over the lip and run down the side. This was not a bar for friendly chitchat, and there would be none with this bartender. He silently made it very clear that he didn't like strangers, or anything different from one day to another, for that matter.

In a clear, deliberate tone, he demanded three dollars. English spoken, dollars demanded instead of Mexican pesos.

Staf didn't recognize how cheap this beer was as he straightened himself up and slunk a hand into his pants to get out some money. He put twenty dollars on the counter instead of handing it to the bartender. Staf was lost in thought and not really at the bar anymore.

He was slightly above average height. He had a slim build, but strong and wiry. He looked as though something had taken a tremendous toll on him, and although he looked his age, the hidden toil made him look older and more haunted than the average thirty-year-old. He did not look like an athlete. He did look like someone who had been running a lot recently, but not in an Olympian sort of way. He looked like someone on the run.

As he stood at the bar with a slight slouch, the corners of mouth drooping down, he projected the image of a tragic tourist who had gone through a horrible vacation. The state of his attire alone blended in quite well with the bar. There was fear in his wide eyes, and if you looked into them, you might be too afraid to ask what the problem was. He looked manic, and as he started to control his breathing, nerves took over and his hands began to shake. He drew himself up to the bar and took a deep breath.

A sudden clack pierced the silence. Staf spun around instantly, not quite knocking over his pint but still spilling half the contents on the bar. The bartender hid his fury and made no attempt to get to the spill. Staf was on high alert. His breathing quickened again, and he looked around the bar, frantically trying to find the source of the noise. After two scans, he finally realized that he had overlooked two people playing pool on a beat-up table in another dusty part of the bar. He caught sight of them just in time to see the next shot and hear the next clack. The sound, even though expected, still made him jump. He fumbled for his beer without looking at it and, unable to find it, took a quick glance at the counter and snatched it so he could keep an eye on the room. No one seemed to notice or care about him.

As his hurried looks came to the old men, the door slammed, causing Staf to spin around again, nearly spilling the rest of his beer.

The bartender's fury rose higher. It took every ounce of energy within him not to reach for his shotgun. He weighed the effort of trying to hide the corpse against the joy of reducing the world's population by one imbecile and decided to wait. For the moment.

Staf finally got to drink the mouthful that was left in the glass and placed it on the counter and asked for another. The bartender, with grinding teeth, slowly came over, refilled the glass, and slammed it on the counter more deliberately than before, without spilling any. The foamless top remained smooth.

"Eight dollars," he demanded, cooling his rage a little with the amusement of making this dolt pay for his recklessness. He almost smiled.

Staf didn't notice the price change. He reached into his dirty pants and pulled out another twenty-dollar bill, which he placed near the first one, again without looking at it. He kept scanning the bar and noticed that the two old men were staring at him. Staf stared back while raising the glass to his mouth. He was about to take a drink from his refill when he heard the faint sound. His heart started to race again, and the fear in him caused it to beat in his ears. He held his breath and strained his hearing. Nothing. Just as he was about to let out his breath, he heard it again, unmistakable, closer, and getting closer all the time. It was like the clip-clop of a horse. The sound was unmistakable to him, and although he tried to believe that it was impossible for it to be here that quickly, he would not allow himself to think otherwise.

He recalled the tremendous pain. The fiery, skin-peeling pain of the first meeting—the introduction, where he had learned what would happen if he was ever caught. It had felt like hot coals behind his eyes, a hatchet notched to the hilt in his skull, and grubs chewing inside his head. It was the fear of Hell. He threw down the glass and ran out of the bar.

Chapter 1: Young Staf

Young Staf Nurren liked to run. He was born running. He crawled fast and then ran fast, bumping into everything as a toddler, unable to control himself. As a young child, tag was his favorite game, and he equally liked being it and not it. When he was it, he would pick someone to chase, always one step behind, an arm outstretched just on the verge of touching them. If they slowed, he slowed. Always a step behind, his hand just a breath away, until the victim was exhausted. Then he would chase someone else.

He did the same if he was not it. He would leave himself vulnerable and then run, only he would always be a step ahead until the reverse victim got tired and gave up.

As he got older, he decided to prove himself and went to the state track and field championships. He was certain that if no one in his town could beat him, a faster runner couldn't exist. After all, he always ran, and no one else was like him.

He lost every race. Not by a lot, but he lost decisively. Not a single medal. He had thought that no one else liked to run and run endlessly. But there were Stafs in every neighborhood across the city, state, and country. That's when he realized that it would not be easy to do well in running; he would have to work. Work very hard.

The drive home was glum. His cheery parents couldn't console him. Competition woke in him, and that's when he decided to train in high school.

Staf joined the track team, and to his horror, he didn't qualify—too many other, quicker Stafs. At practice they put a tremendous amount of work into training, work that Staf had never done. It wasn't fun like tag. He persisted in coming to practices but never went to any track meets. So he also joined the football team for extra running.

Young Staf Nurren shot off the line the second the ball was in the quarterback's hands. He flew across so quickly, his opposite had no time to react. He was in the open. As had happened already many times during the practice, his heart raced. An easy touchdown, he thought. He turned and noticed his continuing good fortune. No one was near him. Grant had joined Joel and double-teamed Chester, who was the perennial team superstar. It never occurred to Staf that they covered Chester out of necessity. Wide open. He was wide open for the umpteenth time this practice. He ran and looked back. He continued to run and look back. He ran some more and looked back again for the ball that didn't come. The ball that never came. Ever. It used to, a few times in the first practice. It came, and he missed it. Gradually, as he missed it, dropped it, or fumbled it, the ball came less and less. Now it never came. But he didn't care. He was part of the team, and he was going to catch it sometime; he was always going to be ready to catch it.

Chester broke away from the pack, easily caught a short toss from the quarterback, and shot off. There was no need to run to the end zone; the conclusion was foregone. The play stopped. Staf was already in the end zone, waiting for the *never-ball*.

They quickly assembled back on the line as the coach threw a flurry of words. Staf made it halfway back, but they started the next play without him. No need to wait; they never threw the ball to him anyway. But for him, practices were better than games. During practice, he was actually allowed on the field.

After practice, the team squeezed through the door into the changing room, and Staf was somewhere near the back of the line. He kept quiet, knowing that if he said anything, he would draw attention and then be the butt of endless jokes and badgering. That had happened last practice, and he hadn't forgotten that lesson.

"Try to catch this," they had said and tossed his clothes around the room. The clothes ended up in the shower to laughs and guffaws.

The following day at track practice, Coach Saunders decided to let Staf run the four hundred meters at the upcoming meet. Staf saw this as a sign to devote himself completely to running, so he retired from his short pigskin career.

It was late afternoon, and Staf had been at the track all day. It was the first track meet of the year, and it was taking place four hours away from Bakersfield on the outskirts of Los Angeles. The team had taken a bus early in the morning, and Staf had waited all day for the four hundred–meter run to take place. He lingered with the team, enjoyed lunch, watched runs, and cheered. He did not feel that the four hundred was his best event, but no one else wanted to run it. Had someone wanted to, Staf would likely not have been at the meet.

Staf was in the outside lane of the staggered starting line and therefore ahead of everyone else. It was like getting a head start, he thought. Since it was only high school, no one had starting blocks. They were on the start line, and after a quick look behind, he watched their posture for the start of the race. Staf bent down and struck a similar pose.

The gun went off, and Staf shot off the line. Everything was a blur as he exploded down the track. He wondered if anyone could see him, or if they could only see a quick flash go by. Surely with this head start and the speed he was keeping, he was already guaranteed first place. Probably a high school record. Around the first corner, the runner in the next lane was passing him. Staf was surprised and made an effort to speed up. It didn't work.

Oh well, he thought, second place wasn't too bad for a first run. A quarter lap later, Staf was watching all the other runners from behind. As he rounded the last corner, the cheers indicated that someone had won the race. By the time Staf crossed the line, people were already packing up and leaving. The timekeeper had left too. After catching his breath, he found the standings. He didn't know what DNF meant and decided to look it up later rather than ask anyone. It was probably not a good acronym.

The topic during the bus ride home was whether or not Chester from the football team had slept with cheerleader Jenn. It was a welcome diversion from his forgettable debut.

During a previous bus ride, the football team had had time to develop nicknames for him: Gaff, Stiff, Fluff.

The track team, being more individual, generally didn't use nicknames; however, after one particular practice when he had dropped the baton several times during the relay, they had started to call him Stumble Staf, which had since morphed into Fumble Stumble.

On this bus ride, Staf was prepared for the worst, but the antics of Chester and Jenn fortunately left him anonymous.

Staf walked home and daydreamed about track meets. The roar of the crowd. A packed Olympic track. The hundred-meter sprint. Staf sets a new record. Receives the gold medal, hand over his heart for the national anthem. Ticker tape parade. A meeting with the president. Then he was home.

"How was school?" was the usual greeting from somewhere in the kitchen quickly followed by "How was the practice?" from somewhere on the couch in the other room. Today was no different. He mumbled some quick okays and went to his room. No need to talk if they had forgotten that today was the track meet, not a practice.

Later that afternoon, Staf played basketball with his friend Jake outside with the net over the garage.

"DNF means 'do not forget,'" said Jake. "It's a subtle message not to forget about the fair tomorrow. It also translates as 'do not sleep in.'" Jake missed a lay-up. "Are you going to keep going to meets?"

"I dunno," lied Staf. The real answer was that he just loved to compete for some reason. It never occurred to him to quit. He missed an easy basket. "I could try for a DQ next time. 'Don't Quit,' right?"

"You need to find something you're a bit better at. Something that comes a little easier, something to build on. But don't pick basketball. Too bad sleeping isn't an event," Jake said as his shot bounced off the rim.

Staf barely nodded. "It beats coming home and watching TV," he said, and then he quickly added, "or playing boring basketball in the driveway."

Jake promptly made a three-point shot and said, "Remember, 9:00 a.m., sharp!"

Chapter 2: Trip to the Fair

Staf was soundly asleep in his room when there was a sudden noise. He was used to ignoring noises in his house, from his family's morning rumblings to the outside noise of neighborhood traffic. It disturbed an erotic dream of Amy, so he quickly dozed off again, trying to continue it.

The wind rustled slightly at the second-floor window, and the usual tree branch occasionally scraped against it. He vaguely heard his mother call out. He opened half an eye, saw nothing, heard nothing more, and dozed off again. Suddenly, there was a rattling; he woke to find an eyeball in his face. He jumped

"What the heck!" he exclaimed and then recognized his mom. She stood back with her hands on her waist.

"Jake's here. Apparently you are supposed to go to the market or something, and you aren't even up yet!"

"Jake!" shouted Staf as he bolted up and looked at the time. "Shit!" he blurted and instantly apologized to his mother for the profanity, which she took lightly, considering his age and the fact the he was late. She made a frown anyway.

He jumped out of bed while she left his room (satisfied that he was getting up), and he somehow jumped into some clothes and ran downstairs.

"Just a sec Jake," he said, barely entering the room, "I have to hop into the shower."

Jake rolled his eyes, but he knew this was inevitable. Besides, the Nurrens would give him some coffee, which he wasn't allowed to have at home.

6

Staf had a thirty-second shower, hopped out, and dried himself quickly. He grabbed some clothes from the not-too-smelly-yet pile and was downstairs before Jake had taken his first sip. It didn't surprise anyone, although Jake had secretly hoped that he would have time to finish the strong cup.

They made their way down the front steps of the house and turned right on the sidewalk, continuing down the tree-lined street to the end. It was a nice, late-spring day, just warm enough to start putting away jackets, although everyone kept one around just in case.

The trees were green with fresh leaves, and the start of the summer canopy over the road was well under way. A light breeze made it a very comfortable day, perfect for the market.

A few blocks away, the houses gave way to a commercial area, starting with older houses converted into dentist, lawyer, or accountant offices. Another block, and they morphed into the more conventional square buildings with big glass fronts and apartment units above. The buildings also started to get taller. They were three blocks from the market.

Jake suddenly took a turn down a dark alley.

"Wrong market," said Staf sarcastically.

"Just humor me," said Jake as he stopped, took off his packsack, opened it, and dug out a wrapped book. It was wrapped in newspaper, as Jake and Staf had done frequently over the years. "Happy Birthday, dude," he said, trying to be genuine but cool in a teenage boy sort of way.

"Shit," apologized Staf, suddenly embarrassed by his slight anger at the diversion to this alley and became humble as he received his first birthday gift; he had forgotten what day it was. He tore off the paper and opened the book to reveal a small disk enclosed in a case. The cover was plain, and the title was *Cougars on the Prowl*.

"Gee, thanks," said Staf, trying to sound enthusiastic.

"What's the matter?" replied Jake, smiling.

"Nothing at all," came back Staf. "I like documentaries." He forced a smile.

7

Jake punched him in the shoulder. "You're thinking of the wrong type."

Staf got mad. "What other type of cougar …" He trailed off as he realized the answer to his own question and let out a long "ohhh."

Staf looked around with an immediate inclination to be embarrassed to be caught with something like this. After realizing that no one was around, he slowly developed a grin. This was his friend, his best friend, the only person who knew what a sixteen-year-old boy would want. He thought about the useless rubbish that he was going to get later today from his parents and sister.

"And, my naïve friend, be sure to hide it, but not too well," said Jake. "Be sure that if *someone* needed to find it, they could." He winked.

Staf had no idea what he meant by this. There was no way he was going to let anyone in his house catch him with this. It was going between the pages of one of his books on his shelf.

"And now, the pièce de résistance," said Jake, trying to sound French, and he brought out a small, mysterious envelope. It looked like a wrapped business card. Staf took it and examined it, and a sly smile came across his face, although he had very little idea what it was. If the previous one was a teaser, this would be even better.

He opened it to reveal a driver's license. This didn't make sense; he hadn't passed his driver's test yet. His look of confusion and disappointment betrayed him.

"You freak!" shouted Jake, and he paused, savoring the moment. Staf still didn't understand and looked up, baffled. Jake continued. "It's freaking bogus ID. You're twenty-one today, not sixteen!" He punched him in the shoulder. Staf didn't get it. Jake rolled his eyes and let out a deep breath. "You bonehead, keep it handy just in case we find ourselves in a bar, somewhere, sometime, like, maybe today?"

Staf suddenly got it and laughed. Jake laughed with him. It was going to be a good birthday.

They continued out of the alley and down the main street of Bakersfield, en route to the large parking lots where the festival was taking place. Jake got distracted by a group of girls on the other side. He nearly hit a lamppost as he walked, craning his neck. As he turned his head to follow the girls and check out their butts, it reminded Staf of the head-turning scene in the Exorcist. But track was on his mind. The next meet of the season was coming up, and he had convinced the coach to give him a shot at the hundred-meter sprint.

He noticed a large billboard, a picture of a car ad with the words "Get what you want now!" emblazoned below it in large red letters. They stuck out in his mind. At the same time, a sudden gust of wind rustled some leaves along the side, which startled him out of his daydream. *Get what you want*, he thought, and remembered his dream of Olympic gold medals.

A sign from the Pentecostal church at the corner read "Ask and you shall receive", and he silently mouthed the words, "I want to be the greatest athlete of all time", and almost felt embarrassed at having the audacity to hope for something so big with his limited talent. He noticed more leaves rustling in a little circle and thought he saw some shadows dance in another alley, but when he turned his head, they stopped.

They passed various stores with insignificant things: a furniture store, a ladies' clothing shop, a shoe store. He thought the lights flickered ever so slightly as he passed the cosmetic store. He slowed a little without drawing Jake's attention, and his eyes were drawn to a new fragrance called Dare. Silly, he thought. *Dare to go for what you want*, he mused to himself and then saw the small ad advertising the new product, and his heart almost skipped at beat as he read it: "Dare to get what you want."

Ridiculous, he thought as a cold feeling gripped him, and the shadows danced more bravely in the corner of his eye, disappearing if he tried to look at them directly. He was slightly superstitious and sometimes believed that if he paid attention, there were subtle signs pointing to paths or routes to take in life.

"What's up?" asked Jake.

Staf just shrugged it off and continued on his way. The fog in his mind cleared a little as he noticed a source of light across the street in another alley and a pale young woman (or was it a young man?) with large, heavy-lidded eyes, plainly dressed but out of place. She had shoulder-length hair, just the right length to be long for a man or short for a woman. The light didn't have a source. She stared at him with unblinking, innocent eyes, which he wasn't used to, and he looked away briefly, casually looking back again every few steps to verify that she was in fact looking at him. Soon they were around the corner, and he didn't see her anymore.

Weird, he thought, but he had an intense feeling of foreboding. His birthday, he figured. And it was always weird at the festival's flea market.

They walked quietly, taking in the scenery and watching more girls along the way. Suddenly Jake grabbed Staf and dove into a doorway. Staf saw a sign above the doorway (a beer sign) that said "Get it now all in a glass." He shuddered for no reason.

Staf squinted through the smoke and recognized that they were in a bar. But the hair stood up on the back of his neck, and he thought he recognized the shadows that had been following them show up on the walls of this pub. Jake led him to the bar stool, where he sat down with his best impression of a regular.

"Two Coronas," ordered Jake, trying to sound bored.

The bartender stood there unimpressed, arms on his hips. He was clearly the owner of the bar and very experienced.

"ID," he demanded, bored but surly and direct.

Staf produced his neat envelope from his pocket and gently handed over his new, unblemished driver's license. Jake scoffed at his amateur friend. Staf realized his mistake as he watched his friend dig out his wallet with great inconvenience and fumble around for his driver's license, which was hidden in his supposed pile of credit cards and other wallet stuff. Jake then casually made some small talk with Staf, ignoring the bartender while the ID was being checked.

The bartender was no fool and took an extra look at their cards, particularly Staf's, and after looking at them with a very skeptical glare, he handed them back. Staf noticed the slightest grin on his face and a barely perceptible glint in his eyes. Jake knew they were in and relaxed a bit. Staf was still on edge. Two Coronas appeared in front of them.

"Ten bucks," demanded the bartender, and as Staf was about to sloppily count his change, Jake produced a quick ten. Trying to sound normal, he requested two limes. Staf wondered what that was for but instinctively kept his mouth shut, although his face betrayed him. The bartender picked up this slight mistake and gave him another glance but ignored the slip, happy to play the game with these kids. The cops were all at the flea market anyway, or handing out speeding tickets. Furthermore, some of his customers were at the market's beer tent.

As the bartender wandered away, Jake proudly yelled out "Cheers!" and they clinked bottles. Staf took his first sip of his own beer. He knew what it was going to taste like; he had snuck a sip or two at home from half-empty bottles after parties that his parents had hosted. But this was his beer, and it tasted great, coldly slithering down his throat. The shadows danced again in the barroom corners.

Two hours passed, and without realizing it, Staf and Jake started to sit just a little more comfortably at the bar. Although not regulars, they sat with a very slight slouch, not caring about who else was in the bar and not surprised at the variety of beer and drinks available to choose from. Either the novelty had worn off, or they had had a few drinks and didn't care anymore.

"We should get going to the market," said Staf, suddenly realizing how much time had passed. Another patron ambled up to the bar to the right of Jake and ordered a draft.

"But we have lots of time. Besides, it runs tomorrow too," said Jake. The older man to the right of Jake fumbled in his pocket and brought out a handful of change and started to count it out on the bar.

"But there is track practice tomorrow afternoon, and you know I have to get ready for the hundred meters."

Jake was obviously frustrated again at his friend, who was constantly daydreaming about sports. "I know," he said. "This is where I tell you again that it's just one practice, and you lecture me about how every practice counts."

The man next to Jake had to fish into another pocket to find more change. Miraculously, none fell on the floor, although one coin wanted to escape and started to discretely roll along the bar, only to be caught by the patron, whose fat fingers protruded from fingerless, worn-out gloves.

"Would be great to be a star and not have to work for it," said Staf. "Not only for that, but for anything. One year older. That dream had better become apparent soon."

"One year older, eh?" Mumbled the hunchbacked patron, embarrassingly loud for Staf. He smiled at them, showing missing teeth among the blackened ones that remained. He was elderly, but it was hard to tell exactly how old. He was short, as if stooped with old age. His face was wrinkled, and he had messy, greasy hair.

Staf and Jake remained silent, hoping to communicate that this intrusion was not wanted. The patron came over nonetheless and leaned into Jake and Staf. His breath smelled like rotten fish. Staf and Jake had an immediate impulse to lean away and possibly make for the door, but they didn't want to ruin the pretense that they were old enough to drink. They wanted to continue this ruse despite their juvenile birthday talk. They ignored him, hoping he would go away. Staf was acutely aware that the fellow had a wandering eye, and it was therefore impossible to tell who he was looking at.

"How would you lads like to get into a little something? Shall we say, uh, an opportunity?" and he proceeded to pull up a stool, and it was clear that he intended to join them.

"Actually, we were just about to head out the door," put in Jake as he sloshed back the last of his glass. The patron turned his head to Jake, but Staf noticed that one eye still looked at him.

"Well, suit yourself, but let me tell you something." His voice suddenly became a whisper, and he leaned in so they could hear. Staf and Jake instinctively leaned in too, forgetting the odor of his breath until it was too late. Instinct told them to leave, but they were drawn into the conversation.

"I know a way," whispered the patron, happy to have their attention and noticing that their desire to leave had diminished a little (after all, they could have been out the door already), "to cheat the system, if you will. One chance, and not a moment to lose." The patron stopped and looked at them both. They were interested but not convinced. He looked around the bar as if to make sure that no one was nearby to hear this absolutely top secret information. The shadows stopped dancing on the wall.

"I know a way," he repeated, "and the timing couldn't be better. But I'll need you guys to show me some interest." He paused and looked back and forth at each of them solemnly and sincerely.

"You have my interest," put in Staf quickly, destroying the air of mystery the patron was trying to create.

"You have mine too," added Jake, a slight grin on his face, glancing at Staf in mild amusement.

"I'll need a little more than that," continued the patron, a slight frustration betrayed in his voice and a different look in his eyes. Neither Staf nor Jake could tell who he was talking to.

"Okaaay," Staf said. "I am really, really interested." This pissed off the patron, who gave up the game.

"Just buy me a fucking beer, and I'll give you the directions." There was a pause of understanding.

"Can't," replied Jake casually. "It's his birthday and my treat, and I'm tapped out."

The patron grumbled and ground what was left of his teeth as he perched on his stool, hunched, still leaning into them. His hands shot out from under his coat like a jack in the box, and he held Staf and Jake's arms and drew them in closer. Through his clenched teeth, he hissed, "Then take this advice seriously and to heart. Go the market now, and find the chocolatier. Ask specifically for an almond cashew ball, just one." He paused for effect. They were still seated perfectly so that one eye was focused on Jake and the other on Staf. "Then go exactly ten stalls down, to the apothecary."

"The what?" interrupted Jake. The patron looked like he was going to slap Jake. They were a little scared of him with his sudden, icy grip on their arms. They felt paralyzed but not with fear. Something else held them in place.

The bartender caught sight of the small commotion and showed interest. The patron noticed this and leaned in more,

"I'm going to tell you this once, and only once. And you, idiot, do you know what a pharmacy is?" Jake barely nodded. "Same goddamn thing. Go to the ..." he paused again, as if to challenge Jake "... apothecary and ask for Azra, and tell her you have an appointment with the dentist and need a good toothpaste. Make sure she sees you eating the almond cashew ball. She will give you a prescription." Staf was acutely aware that the one eye on him seemed to penetrate past his natural barrier to people; he couldn't look away anymore.

"You know the toy store in the square?" He gave them an opportunity to reply if they wanted, although Jake was probably going to stay quiet now. "Go to the back door, knock exactly three times, and enter. You have one hour from"—and he suddenly let go—"right now."

The trance was over, and Staf found he could look at his friend again. The shadows started to move again in the corners. But the patron leaned in once more with his fish breath fresh in their nostrils and said, "Remember, this a chance of a lifetime. Miss it, and another will never ever come up again."

The bartender put down his towel and started to walk over to them when the patron suddenly got up and loudly said, "Besides, you have nothing to lose," and hobbled to the other end of the bar without looking back.

"Just a sec," said Staf, surprising Jake, and to the bartender he said, "One more draft." He had sort of felt sorry for the fellow, clearly down on his luck and needing a break. Jake resisted the temptation to intervene. The bartender stopped and looked back at the patron and then back at Staf, and with the slightest shrug, he went back and produced a tall glass of cold beer. The patron, on hearing this, slowly turned, a devilish grin coming to his face.

"Thank you, lads." He comfortably came back to their table, but he didn't take a seat. He stood, reached for his draft, and took a long swig. He leaned toward Staf and whispered something into his ear. It was clearly quite a message, because Staf's face registered interest, and then shock, and then fear.

The patron, when finished, nodded at Jake with a quick wink and took his leave. He went to the back of the bar and disappeared into the smoky dark.

"Whoa," said Jake after a second. "Let's get outta here." Just outside, Staf made a right, while Jake made the left.

"What's up?" asked Jake, noting the different turns they had taken. "We can go to the market tomorrow; it will be a better day."

"Well, it's just around the corner. We have a few minutes. Let's just check it out."

"No way," replied Jake. "That guy is setting us up. I'm not going anywhere he sends us."

"Let me investigate it. I want you to come with me to the door, and if anything happens, well, you can be my witness, okay?"

It sounded easy enough, so he quickly agreed. He was intrigued with the events and wanted to see how this mystical journey was going to go. They walked up the road, and as they approached the market, the streets became busier with people, strollers, and dogs on leashes.

It was late afternoon, and people were starting on their way home for the end of the day to make late dinners, tuck in tired kids, and relax after a long outing to the annual market. The walk was tough, because they were going against the general flow of people. It also felt like a slight breeze wanted to push them back.

Staf was aware of a feeling, a torn one; he felt he should turn around and leave, but he also wanted to see what would happen. Anything to help him at the track meet.

Gradually, they got their bearings and made it to the area where the wooden stands and faded dirty awnings indicated temporary shops. The flea market.

The area was organized in layers and sections. A few stalls of clothes, a few stalls of shoes, a few with fruit, all grouped. They crisscrossed several aisles, and Jake started to protest about how long it was taking to find their destination. Staf gave in. It seemed like they were wasting time.

They were in a quiet aisle with few people and were about to leave. Then they saw him: the chocolatier. He had a small stall with glass cases instead of walls outlining his square space. He was a tall, dark-haired man dressed in a white baker's outfit complete with a white cap. He was busy over a large copper drum, mixing with a wooden spoon while he allowed a thick syrup to ooze slowly into the concoction. The chocolatier's stall was obvious and stood out from the rest. Staf wondered how they could have missed it.

Staf immediately set about searching for almond cashew balls. There was quite an assortment: cherry blossoms, marzipan drops, caramel squares, all with dark, white, or milk chocolate. Jake was casually searching the other glass counter.

The chocolatier noticed them and, dusting his hands on his white apron, came over with a bright smile and twinkling brown eyes. He reminded Staf of a taller version of Mario from the Mario Brothers video games.

"What can I help you with?" he asked through his mustache in a deep, friendly voice. Jake stopped searching.

Staf, however, didn't look up, and still peering in the counter, he said, "an almond cashew ball."

The stall grew dark. Staf didn't notice the smile vanishing from the chocolatier's face, the pause in his step (or maybe even a step back), and the friendly gleam disappearing from his eyes. Shadows formed in the corners of the case, and Staf was acutely aware that they were the same sorts of shadows he had noticed earlier.

He saw the glass slide open from the back and watched as a hand slowly went into a corner behind the coated strawberries and a delicious looking ball of nuts and chocolate emerged. It went into a small paper bag. Reaching for it, he noticed the scowl and fearsome face of the chocolatier. He threw the bag at Staf without saying a word and returned to his copper bowl. It occurred to Staf that he hadn't paid for it, but he was suddenly afraid of this man. He fished into his pocket to get his wallet as Jake came to his side.

"I think I'm going to get one of those wafers," he mumbled quietly to Staf, aware of the sudden tension around them.

Staf was about to offer some money when the chocolatier looked up from his work with a menacing sneer and wide eyes. He continued working, getting his hands dirty. Clenched teeth made the corners of his jaw twitch. This was a signal to Staf and Jake to leave at once, which they did.

Staf stopped. "Sir, do you know where the apothecary is?"

The chocolatier ignored him. He dropped the large spoon he was working with and disappeared behind a curtain without looking at them. The abandoned concoction in the bowl sat there in need of attention.

Staf shrugged and continued to wander the flea market. It did not seem like the Chocolatier was going to come out while they were there.

In the copper bowl, the syrup bubbled and turned brown. A crack appeared on the surface, and white, sticky, grubs wriggled out, feasting, squirming, and multiplying instantly.

"That was a little off," said Jake. "What the heck is going on here? I thought this was going to be some sort of fun joke or game. Like a treasure hunt, or hide and seek." He said it suspiciously, but it was clear he was starting to get intrigued by this too. Jake was the more daring of them, always looking to do something out of the ordinary. He was no longer in the mood to go away and come back tomorrow. He was ready to find this druggist or apothecarist or whatever it was.

Staf was aware of the change. He slowed and recalled that they were on a time limit.

"We had one hour from the bar, right?" He looked at his watch. Forty-five minutes had passed.

"Let me have a look at that chocolate nutty thing," demanded Jake.

Staf, intrigued too, opened the bag. It looked normal.

"Let's have a taste." Jake made an attempt to grab it. Staf quickly withdrew the morsel, knowing his friend was joking but not wanting to let the game get too far.

"Not a chance!" he said, and he started off again to find the apothecary.

It was hopeless. There was none, or no such thing. They decided to split up, noting which section they would find one another in later.

Jake bolted down the next row to the right, Staf turned left, and there it was, exactly ten stalls down. It was so obvious that he wondered how they could have missed it earlier.

This stall was slightly bigger than the chocolatier's, with 'Apothecary' clearly written in large red letters above it. A woman sat in a chair behind the counter on one side reading a paperback. Staf ran up to the counter excitedly.

"Yes?" asked the slim, attractive brunette cheerfully, feeling his enthusiasm without looking up from her book. She put down the paperback and looked up with large brown eyes.

"I'm looking for Azra," he said with a big smile.

The woman hesitated, the smile faltered, and with curiosity, she replied, "Yes, that's me." She cocked her head to one side and appeared to be evaluating him.

At once Staf said, "I have an appointment with the dentist, and I need some toothpaste."

"Do you now?" said Azra, drawing the words out slowly, deliberately, all humor vanishing from her face. As before, the stall grew darker. Azra noticed this, and a slight shiver shook her. Staf was really beginning to wonder about these shadows. Something inside him was sending a warning.

Azra studied him. Staf waited, expecting a prescription. Then he remembered the almond cashew ball, produced it from the bag, and took a bite.

There was an amazing explosion of sugary taste in his mouth as the chocolate melted and mixed with salt and nut oil. It was heavenly. Or maybe devilish. Something extraordinary.

Azra's face paled, and her eyes widened so much Staf though they might fall out of her head. She ran to a drawer and quickly scribbled something on a paper. She thrust it out to Staf without looking at him. As he slowly took it, she withdrew her hand immediately and disappeared behind a panel at the back of the stall.

Staf was shocked. Was this change in moods just a giant joke? It started to bother him. How could all these people know each other well enough for it to be a good joke? Clearly they were at the market to sell their wares, not because of some elaborate scheme to humor him with a treasure hunt on his birthday.

He snapped out of this short trance and looked at his watch. He had three minutes left. But there was a bonus; he knew where the toy store was located. It was not part of the market but one of the stores that bordered it.

He ran down the lane, wondering about Jake. He didn't have the time to get him. He found the front of the toy store and briefly looked up to see if there was anything unusual about it today. Noting nothing different, he turned to run to the back alley. He almost ran into the pale glowing androgynous person he had seen earlier. Staf wondered how he could have failed to notice her approach. She looked at him with wide, innocent eyes.

He ignored her and ran down the back alley. As he turned the corner, he had to slow. This was an area he hadn't seen before, and he didn't realize how much this looked like a typical, dingy, dark alley. Several overflowing dumpsters lined the wall. Garbage and old newspapers were strewn everywhere. It smelled like old garbage too.

Something crawled and squeaked along the dark wall, and a rat's shadow cast a flickering, distorted cameo on the red bricks.

He easily found the metal door that served as the back entrance of the store, which was probably used for deliveries. It had one light over it. He ran to it and figured he had less than a minute left. As he looked at his watch, he knocked loudly three times and watched the seconds tick down. He was twenty seconds early by his reckoning. Nothing happened. Staf tried the door. It was locked.

"Hmmm," he said out loud to himself. He stood back and looked up at the door, the alley, and at his watch again. Maybe he had been mistaken. Everything else had seemed to work like clockwork he mused, impressed with his play on words. He took another long look and decided to go to the front again to get his bearings right and maybe look for another door.

As he turned, he noticed the light above the door flicker. The door clicked open and remained slightly ajar. Staf stopped, held his breath, and looked around. Nothing but garbage and newspapers. An unseen bird crowed. It was late in the afternoon now, and the sun was setting quickly. It was suddenly quiet. No shadows danced. No rats crawled along the wall.

He faced the door again, reached out, and opened it. The inside was complete darkness. He couldn't see anything; the remaining light outside could not penetrate the wall of darkness behind the door.

Staf took a quick look down the alley, hoping to spot Jake. He wasn't there. He looked through the door again and was ready to close it and leave. Then he remembered the track meet. He remembered the hundred-meter sprint. Somewhere in this darkness was the possibility to be a better athlete. What were the risks? Was there a personal danger? He felt there was.

He looked down the alley again and saw the radiant young woman. She was slowly shaking her head, and she held out her hand. She was still glowing, like a beacon in the dark lane. She started to walk towards him.

He thought about the bar patron, the chocolatier, Azra, and this ghostly woman haunting him. It was a day for meeting weird people. He wondered what was next. He looked into the darkness and took a hesitant step in. His foot disappeared but found a floor. Fear went down his spine, and the hair stood up on his neck. He took a deep breath and then another step.

Darkness. Nothing but darkness. He could still see the square outline of light behind him where the door was, but there was no light coming into this room. He looked about the room and thought he could make out one faintly burning lightbulb to his right. He took five steps toward the lightbulb. The door gently closed behind him as he stepped forward. He noticed this and noted how similar the feeling was to the horror movies he sometimes watched. Doors closing for unknown reasons (or from unseen forces). He told himself to leave, just like he would tell a character in a movie. And just like in the movies, he didn't leave.

He turned back to the light. It was much brighter now and lit up the whole room, which was small, with plain, painted brick walls. It was cold and clammy.

He heard another door open and turned slightly to see a tall man wearing a fine, well fitting, neatly pressed black suit. If this was a friend of the patron in the bar, they were like complete opposites. He had short, neatly trimmed hair and was clean shaven.

He approached Staf deliberately, purposefully. There was an aura of professionalism about him, of no-nonsense business. Staf felt confident and at ease that he was in the right place. He also felt a little more assured that his current situation might have something to do with track and field and not horror. A clean, professional man seemed more related to running than hunchbacks, chocolates, and prescriptions.

As the man approached, his expression did not change. He was plain and regular looking, with black hair matching his black tailored suit.

"Hello, Staf," he said and extended a hand, which Staf took. The stranger had a firm handshake. They regarded each other for a moment, after which the man, clearly wishing to get right to the point, said, "I hear that you are here to improve your athletics." It was a statement more than a question. Staf merely nodded. "He can help you with that." Staf wondered who "he" was. The answer came without needing to ask.

"He is like a magician of sorts," came the vague answer. "He can give you, shall we say, empowerments, that can help you." He studied Staf.

To Staf, this sounded like a teaser. Something to get him interested. The rest came soon enough.

"He can come up with a mixture, an elixir, to help you become an all-star athlete." Staf's heart skipped a beat. The magic words *all-star* and *athlete* had been spoken. This fellow had a calm and deliberate way of talking that evoked trust and confidence. He paused again for effect.

"Do you have any questions?" he asked.

Staf stood with lots of questions whirling in his mind, but he couldn't articulate one.

"In short," continued the mysterious man matter-of-factly, "my employer will offer you what you want, in exchange for commitment."

This caught Staf's attention immediately, and his tension and heart rate rose. He spied the door and made a quick step toward it. The man calmly stepped out of his way.

Staf took two more steps, reached for the handle, and waited. The escape was too easy. If it was this easy, then it couldn't be that dangerous, he thought. Maybe he could get more information. An educated and informed decision would be best, he told himself, trying to alleviate his mounting fear.

Another thought came to him. If he ever wanted to be a professional athlete, something crazy and outlandish like this would be the only way of doing it, considering his limited talent. It suddenly seemed plausible. He had come this far today, and he didn't want to close the door to this opportunity without finding out more.

The man remained silent as Staf stood at the door. He waited patiently as Staf turned around and took a hesitant step back into the room.

"Well, that is a confident start. Most people are out the door already, as you almost were," he said calmly. "So have a seat and let me tell you all you need to know."

Staf recalled that the room had been empty, but as the man motioned him to sit down, he looked back and noticed a comfortable chair behind him. It had not been there during his initial desire to leave. He looked up again and noted an ornate desk between him and the man, who was now sitting in a high-backed chair. Staf was immediately worried that he had already committed to something he wasn't sure of.

Sensing this, the man said again in a calm, deliberate voice, "Don't worry, nothing will be done today; it is his policy to always wait a minimum of twenty-four hours. And a maximum of seventy-two," he quickly added. "My name is Rial, and I am one of his agents. Like you, I had an ambition that I could not achieve alone. I arranged a meeting with him in a similar fashion as you and made my arrangement. I am now under his employment and am afforded additional powers and duties, as are most of his business associates. And as you may one day be." He paused to let it sink in.

"May I propose that for your benefit, you may pick six events, and will win every race you enter for those events. No one will outrun you. This will last for thirteen years. Three years to complete high school, four to complete college, and an additional six before your new job starts. That's thirteen years, and only thirteen," he emphasized, and leaned forward to drive home the point. "How you handle those years is up to you. At the end of thirteen years, you will retire, come under his jurisdiction, and serve his purposes as an agent." He paused again. "Any initial questions?"

Staf asked the first question to come to mind. "Do I have to sign in blood?"

"You watch too many movies," the man replied with a slight laugh. "You will, however, be expected to conduct yourself in a professional, intelligent manner." He sensed the confusion in Staf and added, "You will basically have a job like mine." He gave a curt smile. It quickly vanished.

He studied Staf. "The agreement is simple. I doubt there can be many more worthwhile questions. As already mentioned, you have between twenty-four and seventy-two hours to decide. There is, of course, no consequence to passing up this opportunity. However, should you accept it, you will be required to meet with him personally. I will help you with that. You may leave now."

Staf didn't know what to do or say. This had taken him by surprise. In the morning, it had been just another day, some nice birthday presents, a bar, beer, and a humorous treasure hunt for chocolates and toothpaste. And now this. He had hundreds of questions swirling in his mind, but he couldn't get hold of any.

He looked at the door, ready to leave, and then back at Rial. He was standing again, the desk and chair gone. He held out his hand with a piece of paper in it. Staf stood up awkwardly and took the paper. It was a business card. The name Rial was neatly printed in fancy black Gothic font in the middle with a phone number beneath it. Nothing else was on the card.

Rial offered his hand. Staf fumbled as he shook it. Rial motioned him to the door. Staf turned to leave, mildly registering the fact that his chair had also vanished. He finally grasped some questions. Most importantly, how did Rial know that Staf was interested in running? He turned and discovered that he was alone in the room. Once again, the only light came from the lightbulb in the corner, and it was growing dimmer. Staf slowly opened the door and stepped out of the darkness into the early evening.

"There you are!" exclaimed Jake, who had apparently been studying the door. "I've been wondering where you were. Funny, I tried this door and it wouldn't open." He stepped forward. Staf let the door close. "Wait!" he said and dove for the door just as it closed.

Staf still had the handle turned, and realizing his friend wanted to have look inside, he opened it.

"There's really nothing to see in there."

Staf and Jake stood stunned, looking at a solid brick wall. There was no need to explain to Jake that there had been a room there, as he knew quite well his friend could not open a door and come out of a wall. They walked home in silence.

Chapter 3: Jake's Story

They arrived at Staf's house in time for dinner. Jake liked the informal atmosphere at the Nurren house. They were all very different from one another, yet they all seemed to belong, and Jake felt he belonged too. It was always a bit sad to leave and go home. He had a lot of fun with the Nurrens.

Today was another fun dinner at Staf's house, and as Jake slowly shuffled home, kicking the odd fallen leaf or stone on his path, he reflected on his sixteen years.

He was the proverbial good student. He always studied, was rarely up past ten, and spent most of his waking moments finishing projects due weeks in the future.

On this particular walk, he pondered how different he was from his friend. Staf was smart. Almost a genius. He rarely studied and got excellent grades. His projects were usually done at the last minute, late the night before they were due, in desperation. He recalled last year's science fair.

Jake had prepared for months and had actually started the year before. He initially proposed the project to his parents, carefully applying their suggestions. Then he studied the traits of resilient plants, obtained some specimens, and grew them in the most hostile environments he could create. He then compared them to plants surviving in the poles and deserts. He even researched the preliminary results of studies conducted at Chernobyl.

He composed a twenty-page report on how these plants survived and discussed how they could be most beneficial on future colonies on other planets. He went on to hypothesize how these might be the kinds of plants most likely to be found indigenous to other planets.

Ms. Spencer was impressed. She had never seen such a professional, thorough, and complete project before and was sure he was going win the state contest. He would have a serious chance at the national competition. She asked him if he was going to work for NASA. The thought of it was incredible. He had planned on becoming a lawyer, a very practical, sensible, logical career. But the thought of science and NASA seemed exciting and adventurous. At the time, he seriously thought about looking into it.

Then Ms. Spencer saw Staf's project. Clumsy, dopey, genius Staf. On the day before the science fair, Jake walked to school with Staf. Their projects were due tomorrow, and Staf, of course, had forgotten. He saw a plane flying overhead and got an idea. He daydreamed in English about a project, read a book on planes during lunch, pretended to play football after school, and then went home and made a miniature jet engine out of Coke cans that ran on fermented vegetation and powered a lightbulb. His five-page report outlined the simplicity of turning organic waste into power, solving both the garbage and electricity crises. It even explained the benefits of increased production of alcohol in general. And then there was a line about back-up power from the liquor store that cost Staf a few marks, but he didn't care about that.

On the walk home after the fair, Staf joked about the dual benefit of powering colonies on other planets and having alcohol too. Jake fumed at the slight to his project. But he would have picked Staf's project for the county finals; it was more fun.

They both won the science fair and earned spots at the county finals. Staf didn't go. He had other things to do—running, most likely. Jake happily went alone.

As Jake turned the last corner on his walk home, he continued to compare their differences. Staf was naturally smart; things came easily and quickly to him. Jake worked his ass off in school. Staf was uncoordinated. Jake was not. Far from it. Jake fondly recalled his first week of high school. The only week of fun he could remember.

He had his parents' reluctant permission to try out for the football team. The equipment felt natural, the plays simple, the running easy. The ball, whenever he caught it, seemed to stick to him. No one could touch him when there was some space. One person came close: Chester, who was one year older than Jake and last year's star player. Chester had a good first practice too, but he was not like Jake. For Jake, it was natural. They were evenly matched in practice, except for one play. Chester slipped ever so slightly as Jake dodged his tackle, and as Chester chased after him, everyone noticed how the space between them grew. Everyone noticed, but no one talked about it.

At end of the week, Jake's name was on the team. A starter. Receiver . It was going to be a good year. That practice was the best part of his first high school year. Jake recalled coming home from school that evening.

"There's no need to practice more," his mother said, "one practice a week is good enough."

"Can I have one practice and one game next week?" asked Jake. "There is a game on Thursday."

"I don't think so," replied his mom, "but I'll ask your father later during dinner."

Dinner that evening was quiet as usual. Jake sat at the table playing with his peas like a child, waiting for the topic to come up. The silence was disturbed only by clanking forks and the slithering of knives through a light roast. Occasionally one squeaked on a plate. Worst of all, Jake could hear everyone chew. The mushing of food around mouths, mixing with sloppy saliva, eventually turning into a squishy sound, and then the swallow. Gulp. It was like a small bomb. Then another clink, squeak, squish, gulp. The more Jake tried to ignore it, the louder it got.

"So, Jake," his father finally said, breaking the rhythm, "your mother tells me that you want to devote all your time to football now."

Careful, thought Jake. *He's prodding you. He knows very well that two hours on two days is not devotion. Don't take the bait.* He felt like a cautious animal avoiding an obvious trap. He calculated his response, making sure that he had a fresh load in his mouth that he could deliberately chew and buy time to formulate a response. It also let him feign thoughtfulness and deliberation.

"It might seem that way," said Jake, "but we have had a very slow week—no assignments. It's all basically a review of grade eight, and classes are devoted to helping others catch up." Jake was buying time. Try to get to play just one week at a time. Get the okay to play this week; work on next week later.

"What do you think, Ellen?" his dad asked. Jake's heart skipped a beat. This was approval. This meant his dad was giving his permission but didn't want to show it. He was the denier, the no-man. When he meant yes, he always let Ellen actually say it.

His mother was still another hurdle, but an easier one. She also knew that by deferring to her, Levin had already consented. But she couldn't come straight out and say it.

"Well, I don't see the harm," she said to Levin and then turned to Jake. "As long as your grades are not affected, and absolutely not more than one per week, game or practice. Except for this week," she quickly added and nodded to Jake and then Levin approvingly.

Take it one week at a time, thought Jake.

They silently went about chewing, squeaking, squishing, and swallowing the rest of the meal. Jake kept his eyes down. He didn't want any more discussion; it could ruin what he had already accomplished. He was exploding inside. He held it in during dinner, feigning boredom as if football were an insignificant matter.

After wolfing down the rest of his plate, he hurried up to his room so that there would be no opportunity for his parents to change their minds.

He called Staf. "I'm playing next week!" he calmly whispered on the phone. Staf was genuinely happy for his friend. He confessed that he had never known Jake liked football.

Ever practicing, Staf was on the list of substitutes. There was no order in the substitutes. They were listed alphabetically, but they were certain his performance earned him a spot at the bottom of the list.

Then came Monday's practice. Jake played better and more naturally than before. The coach spent a lot of time with him, Chester, and the quarterback, reviewing specific offensive plays. He never missed a catch, never missed a tackle, and got tackled only once, by Chester, when he almost threaded his way to a first down. It was a great play; Jake was praised for making it through most of the wall and Chester for reading the play and stopping a touchdown. The teamwork was fantastic. Everyone praised the players. The coach was looking very confident, and there was a lot of smiling and checking clipboards and cheerful profanity instead of anger.

On Tuesday, Jake got the results of the grade eight material review. In math, he got 99 percent, by far the highest mark. It was the only A in the class. The next highest mark was a 74 percent. Jake was beyond elation. He was finding high school more than easy, and he was on the football team. Things were going extremely well. Maybe too well, he thought cautiously.

He left his paper on the usual place on the kitchen counter and went out back to find something to do—rake some leaves, play some basketball, ride his bike.

He was in his room when he heard Levin drive up. He heard the car park. There was a very long pause, a few minutes. Then he heard the car door open and close.

That took too long, thought Jake. *That means he's in a bad mood. Stay out of sight.*

There was another long moment, and he heard trudging footsteps to the front door. It opened slowly.

An extremely bad day, possibly one of the worst ever.

He heard the slow removal and thud of his father's shoes; the long, heavy sigh; and the slow walk to the kitchen.

Good, my test paper will lift his spirits, Jake thought. He was an only child and knew the impact his small triumphs had on his parents. He heard some murmuring in the kitchen as his parents had a light talk, and then he heard his name called.

Jake came down instantly into the living room and sat at his spot on the couch opposite his dad's customary recliner.

"I noticed your test on the kitchen," said his father. Jake tried, as usual, to read his dad, trying to judge moods and then evaluate his responses.

Levin was a noted lawyer, one of the best in the State. Jake always had to think about what he was going to say and listen very carefully. That was why Jake wanted to be a lawyer; he was getting used to it. Watching people, evaluating, judging, saying the right thing, and most importantly, thinking before talking.

His father's response opposite him was ambiguous. Was his bad day still on his mind? Had the good test raised his spirits just a little, Jake wondered.

"The test was a breeze," said Jake immediately, a small modest smile forming on his face. "By far, I was the best in my class. Aced it! The teacher said the next highest mark was a 74 percent. It was incredibly easy." Jake couldn't hide his pride, and his face beamed.

The silence was stark, and he suddenly realized he had talked too quickly. He had talked with too much emotion and pride. His smile wanted to fall, and he had to work to keep it up.

At length, after a long, disappointed look, his father spoke. "I hardly think you would be proud of it. Jake, it's a 99 percent! Why wasn't it 100? This was a review! This was material you should already know! Are you feeling okay? How could you possibly be proud of less than 100 percent on material you already know? Don't tell me you are already forgetting last year's material. Don't lower your standards. You have to keep them very high. I didn't get to where I am by setting the bar low and settling for anything less than 100 percent. Jake, you have to ..."

Jake stopped listening. He sat there, bubble burst, embarrassed, stupid. He knew the speech, the general gist of it. The hard work, the this, the that. He focused on the picture on the far wall. It was always a good distraction. *Gathering Nuts* it was called, an old oil painting by a Canadian artist from sometime in the 1800s. Two young girls sitting in a field with a few nuts that they had gathered that day in their aprons. The nuts were clearly not important; there weren't many. They were deep in conversation. One was a brunette, serious, eyes cast down with a distant look, revealing something, probably a secret. The other, fair, looking up at her, excited, interested, listening to the secret revealed. He guessed that idly gathering nuts is what you did in the 1800s. But they looked content, and he was jealous of them. Jealous of a pair of girls in a painting.

"… and that's why we are going to have to suspend this football thing. Clearly, it's too much of a distraction. It's affecting your schoolwork. You understand, don't you, Jake?"

This was not really a question; there was only one answer.

From somewhere, Jake replied, "Of course," and tried to make it sound like it really didn't matter. "I'm sure I'll be able to make up lost ground." He said it with a hint of sarcasm that he thought might go unnoticed. But his father's eyebrows lifted, so Jake had to backpedal. "Football is really not my thing; it was just something I got into with Staf as part of the excitement of the beginning of school. I was sort of just changing my mind anyway."

The lie was painful. He had to spit it out and feign sincerity while he was a tempest of anger and rage. Bottle it up as always. A lump formed in his throat, and slight wetness started to sting his eyes. He had to think of something else and get out fast. You never cry in front of your dad. Never. Never ever. And double that for Jake's dad.

He continued to put up his pleasant front and nonchalantly left the room and went upstairs. The lump subsided as more rage took over. He should have known. The veiled temporary permission, waiting for a good reason to take it away, something that he could turn into a life lesson. He had underestimated his father again and was blinded by the thought of getting a little joy. He walked into his room, collapsed on his bed, and shouted at his dad into his pillow. He vented long and hard, and his throat hurt.

But at this moment, he hated his teacher most of all.

"The paper had no errors," the teacher had explained, "but I don't believe in perfect marks. Therefore, with the help of the English teacher, I found a grammatical error and deducted one mark on your math test." She had been sitting at her desk, and she had rolled her eyes up at him without lifting her head so that the glasses on her nose were pointing to the paper, and she had looked at him over the top of the lenses, as if that increased the authority with which she spoke. It had also made her look old.

Jake, always practicing to be a lawyer, had been tempted to engage in a debate, but he picked his battles carefully, and this one was not going to be worth it at the start of the year.

But now, at home, this teacher's imposing philosophy had completely ruined high school.

Jake sat in his room and came to terms with his life. He was not going to have a childhood. His parents were going to sacrifice it for a head start on the rest of his life. He was beyond being sad for it.

Jake composed himself and came downstairs. Thankfully, it was the same quiet dinner, except that his throat was sore and there was rage behind his eyes. He avoided looking at his parents and was glad there was no talk.

But that had been a different dinner than the one he shared today at Staf's house. An informal, comfortable, delicious pizza among close friends instead of an alien family.

And now it was a peaceful spring evening, and young Jake was on his way home. It was like returning to a coffin.

Chapter 4: Staf Succumbs

Staf couldn't concentrate at school. He had Rial's business card with him and looked at it frequently. He explained to Jake what had happened and showed him the card. They agreed that it was best to stay away from this mess. At the very least, it looked like something illegal was going on. At worst, something unknown. They didn't talk about the unknown part, but imagination allowed for terrible consequences.

The track meet was a short after-school event with the closest four schools. Staf ran the hundred meters. He had lower expectations, and he did come in last place; however, because of the short race, it looked like he ran well, unlike the previous four hundred meters. They also allowed him to participate in the relay. He ran anchor because he was less likely to drop the baton with only one handoff. And he didn't drop it. But he squandered the lead his team had developed, and made it another close last place. His team was nevertheless supportive.

At home, Staf looked at Rial's card again. It haunted him. He was about to rip it and throw it away, but then he suddenly reached for the phone. He dialed it quickly, before he could change his mind. Rial answered the phone before it rang.

"Hello, Staf," said Rial without an introduction. "I take it you have decided to accept the opportunity?"

"Yes," replied Staf quickly, still afraid he would change his mind.

"Get your shoes on and go outside," Rial replied curtly and hung up.

Staf felt obligated to comply immediately and went outside. Rial was in front of his house, standing by a large black car. He opened the passenger door for Staf and went to the driver's side. Staf had no time to hesitate. He got in.

During the drive, there was no small talk. Staf was given instructions, and he tried to pay attention, still unsure he wanted to go through with this.

"All of these instructions are important, so listen very carefully. When you get to his door, knock precisely three times. When the door opens, enter immediately. Do not speak unless spoken to. Do not delay. Sit down when told. Do not ask questions. Do not look at him. Most importantly, do not back out once you are inside. Any thoughts on the agreement?"

Staf was prepared for this part. "I want to be the fastest runner, swimmer, and skater, jump the highest, aim the most accurately, kick the farthest, and hit the hardest both with racquets and baseball bats. I also want to never miss a tackle, and to be untackleable."

They were going downtown, but not to the toy store.

"I can tell you right now that won't work. The deal is to be the best at one thing, one sport only."

Staf didn't have to think about it. "Running. I just want to be the fastest runner. Fastest ever. I don't want anyone to be able to catch up to me."

Rial responded in a monotone. "Okay. He will arrange for you to be the fastest runner. Uncatchable. In up to six running events for a maximum of thirteen years, as we discussed. How you use that skill is up to you. Running from a tackle, running from fans, running the bulls, or running from the law." Rial glanced at him.

That was almost an attempt at humor, thought Staf.

He considered the proposal. It was a lot less than he had wanted, but then again, wasn't one good enough? There were lots of running events. He would need some breaks to do other things. "What do I have to do for this?"

"After thirteen years, you will have a new job. You will be employed by him and basically do what I do for the rest of your life."

It looked easy enough to Staf. A nice car. Nice suit. Fame. Fortune. They entered the parking lot of a strip mall that had a men's clothing store. The mall was busy, and all the spots were taken except for one in front of the clothing store's main doors. Rial got out and went to the door. Staf didn't know he was supposed to follow until Rial paused at the door and looked impatiently back.

Staf jumped out and ran in, wondering what kind of a boss worked at a men's clothing store. *Maybe mafia*, thought Staf.

A salesman immediately ran to Rial, and after a short discussion, he motioned for Staf to follow him to a changing room in the back. Staf waited there, and the salesman returned with an armful of neatly folded clothes. A suit, shirt, socks, and even underwear. Staf was astonished to find that they fit perfectly. He had become accustomed to trying on several items to find the compromise between his tall height and skinny teen physique. This new suit fit like nothing he had ever tried on before. It fit like a glove. Comfortable, too. He put on polished black shoes and admired himself in the mirror. This deal was starting to sound and look very good.

Rial was waiting for him outside the changing room. He looked him over and indicated to the salesman that he was satisfied. The salesman look relieved.

"Come this way," he ordered Staf and led him to the back of the changing room area. He opened a door and motioned Staf forward. As Staf entered, Rial loudly whispered to him, "Remember what I told you."

Staf suddenly realized he was going to see the boss right now, but he wasn't mentally prepared. He went through the door with a blank mind.

He found himself in a dim hallway. There was barely enough light to see where he was going, so he inched forward with his left hand on the wall. It reminded him of the toy store's back room. He carefully walked forward to an ornate, ominous wooden door that was easy to see despite the limited light. It was intricately carved with fine figures. A closer look revealed delicate scenes of half-wolf, half-human beings hunting, killing, or maiming other animals.

There was a dark feel about the door. Staf was afraid to touch it, as if it might bite him, or worse.

There was a knocker in the form of a large bull with a ring through its nose in the middle of the door. As instructed, Staf carefully raised the ring and let it fall three slow, deliberate times. Silence. Nothing happened. He waited, wondering if he had done something wrong according to Rial's precise instructions. As he reached for the handle again, he heard a snap, and the door creaked open. It opened an inch, so Staf had to push it.

Old, dusty cobwebs resisted the door, but Staf easily pushed passed them. He wondered why this door would have cobwebs and why it was so mysterious. For the first time since this adventure began, he wondered why he didn't know about this office. He knew everything in this small town.

The door silently opened to reveal a large dark room with stacks of books on all the walls, shelves reaching up into darkness. At the end of the cavernlike room, which was lit only by candles and torches on the wall, was an immense black desk in front of a huge fireplace. The red light around the fireplace hinted at a very hot fire, but no flames were visible.

Behind the desk sat a tiny, skinny figure draped in a black cloak. Its features were hidden by a black hood, which resisted all the light from the nearby candles and torches. Staf couldn't see a face.

There was a long red carpet leading to the desk. He looked down at the carpet and could see small images moving in it. Battles between dragons and knights, with knights losing and being eaten or burned alive. Wars between men, skewering, and decapitating. There were images of torture and death. There were stretching wheels, bodies being torn apart, ligaments snapping and springing out of ripped flesh. Iron maidens let loose a flood of blood. Staf noticed blood all over the red carpet. He thought it was possibly made out of it.

None of the blood splashed onto Staf or marked his shoes, and he took a subtle glimpse behind him and found no footprints on this live carpet.

As he continued the long walk to the desk, he also noticed people screaming at him. His heart went out to them, and he was afraid to walk on some. People were being impaled on pikes. Others were tied down on guillotines, desperately screaming at him, begging him to stop.

He bent over a scene of a man screaming in terrible pain as he was being stretched. Agony reflected in his eyes as he called out to someone, anyone, maybe a god, to intervene. Staf wanted to reach out and release him from his bonds, but the scene suddenly appeared two dimensional in the carpet. He stood up, and continued to the desk, glued to the stories on the carpet. He wondered what sort of stories qualified for this magic carpet. They were not good stories, and he feared that his would be in there too.

The stories evolved into rape, murder, strange mutilations, and other scenes of more modern torture. He wanted to look away from the images but couldn't, like a bystander passing a car crash.

Halfway to the desk, his attention was drawn to a baby in the embroidery. A bald infant, probably only a few months old. He was shrieking in such a manner that Staf could almost hear the desperate cry. Something moved off to the side. It was a dark, caped man with a cleaver. The baby was sprawled helplessly on his back and was shrieking so intensely that his eyes were closed shut, squeezing tears out through the sides so that they slid down his head toward his ears. Staf looked in horror as the caped man raised his arm above the baby, slowly and deliberately. Was he going to attack it? Staf instinctively started to reach out to grab the cleaver, but it was only a moving image on the carpet. The cleaver made a shadow on the baby's body, and Staf could sense the hooded figure's preparation to make a quick, solid blow. Staf renewed his desperate bid to grab the cleaver, but his fingers slid by uselessly. He tried to close his eyes and look away but couldn't. The baby's eyes were still closed, screaming in unknown pain. Suddenly, the shadow fell and severed the child's arm. Blood sprayed on the infant's face. At the same time, the crying stopped. The eyes opened wide in shock and intense pain, looking directly at Staf. The eyes slowly shut again, tighter, and the mouth slowly curled into a crooked, horrible scream. The shadow of the cleaver slowly reappeared over the left arm. Staf tore himself away. Bile rose from his stomach and started to work its way up his throat. He leaned over and tried hard to swallow it. The battle between throwing up and swallowing continued for a moment, and he finally calmed down by telling himself that it was just an image on a carpet. Somewhere, he knew something like this had happened before. He didn't want to be here anymore. He was only halfway to the desk, about twenty strides in, so the walk back up shouldn't be that long. He stood and looked around and noticed, as he tried to ignore the vile taste in his mouth, that he was directly in front of the desk.

The darkness increased around the desk despite the large lit candelabra overhead. Shadows flickered in all the corners; maybe reflections of the candles, but it seemed there were more. Other dark forms scuttled about, mysterious things that could be insects and rodents but were not visible except for vague outlines, squeaks, and screams.

The desk was an ornate, intricately detailed wooden frame. Inside the frame was complete darkness, darkness so deep it looked like a black hole. The legs looked like tree trunks with branches spread out to create the frame. There were scenes carved into the frame just like the door. But to Staf's relief, the figures did not move like the ones in the carpet.

The desktop was a void. It might have been a window into darkness or maybe nothing at all. Staf couldn't see anything through the desk on the other side, such as the figure of the boss or the flameless fireplace, so he assumed something had to be there. The black desk was clear, smooth, and flawless. Staf was afraid to touch it for fear of leaving some kind of mark or getting sucked into the void.

The small, cloaked figure of the boss was hunched over it, apparently writing on something in the void. Bug screams and chirps came from somewhere nearby, but nothing was visible except for reflections in the candlelight. Whatever the boss was, he took little notice of Staf as he approached. The black hood hid his face, and his clothing seemed oversized, unlike Staf's new, well-fitted suit.

Staf stood at the end of the desk, fearful and silent. He looked around casually. He marveled at the bookshelves that lined the entire corridor he had entered. They seemed to reach into an invisible abyss above. Invisible heights, voids in the desk. Huge corridors in small buildings. This place seemed full of endless paradoxes. He wondered if he was in an underworld right now and shuddered.

He noted that there was only candlelight and no windows. This was not how he recalled the outside of the building; it seemed to have many windows. The air was damp and still.

"Sit," was the sudden whispered command that echoed throughout the corridor. The quiet words made his skin shiver. The bugs stopped moving and sat too. A bird flying overhead immediately perched on a bookshelf.

Staf, remembering his coaching, only looked slightly behind him, noticed a chair, and immediately sat. The chair was solid wood with red lining and cushions. The arms were engraved in fierce-looking griffons, and he was afraid to look at the red cushions because they might hold scenes similar to the carpet. Or worse.

The bugs relaxed and started scuttling about again. He heard them but couldn't see them except for the black shell of a beetle that scuttled under a bookshelf to his left. Apparently it joined some other beetles, and a high-pitched sort of bug argument erupted. Another high-pitched squeal put an end to the argument. *An ominous omen,* thought Staf as he focused on the figure in front of him.

He tried to peer into the hood that draped the head to see the face, but he could not penetrate it despite the light from the candles. Then he remembered Rial's rules. He felt the sweat start to permeate his shirt, and beads formed on his forehead. The beast in front of him continued to scrawl. Staf noticed that there was a small crystal ball slightly to the right of the desk that had a dim, barely perceptible glow.

"Do you like my crystal ball?" asked a friendly voice, sending a slight echo down the hall. Staf had the impression that the voice could be thunderous if it wanted to. He wondered if the question was directed at him. He had been told strictly to speak only when spoken to. He was unaware of anyone else in the room. He took a deep breath, and as a bead of sweat started to create a river down his temple, he started to form tentative words. The bugs all went silent again.

Staf became aware that there were spiders in their webs in front of some of the books in the cases. Some were larger than others, although they were all generally big. He tried not to look their way. Normally a person can sense eyes on him, but spiders are rumored to have eight eyes, and he could feel many octets of eyes on him like an insect audience in a stadium.

The form in front of him grew impatient at his hesitation. The temperature rose.

"It's nice," squeaked Staf, sounding as quiet as the bugs in the room. The temperature fell back to the normal heat. More sweat formed on his head, and a bead trickled down from his armpit. He sensed a large wet spot forming there. The small figure stopped. Staf still couldn't see its face, although there seemed to be cold gray eyes there somewhere.

"Any questions on the agreement?" asked the kind voice as the figure leaned back in its chair. The creaks in the chair sounded like screams. Staf dared not guess who or what image was in the chair and was reminded again of the scene in the red carpet. He fought another gag.

"Thirteen years of being the fastest ever?" Staf thought something was missing. He quickly added, "Then I will be your employee." He laughed nervously, which he immediately regretted. *Wait,* he thought, *something doesn't feel quite right.* Was there something he had forgotten? The cloaked figure behind the desk didn't move. There was something else. The temperature began to rise. The spiders in their webs became restless, the beetles scuttled a little faster into corners. A hot silence hung in the air. Staf was not unaware of this, and his fully sweaty body tensed. What was missing? The number six seemed to figure prominently.

"Uh," he stammered, inciting a hidden rage in the thing before him. "Um." A wave of heat hit him as two slight red glows gradually formed where there might be eyes in the hood. The figure behind the desk grew in height and in bulk. It was now slightly larger than an average man.

"Uh, six events only?" Staf phrased it as a question, hoping this would ease the tension and temperature. The red eyes faded back to gray and disappeared in the hood. The form was small again, the size of a child. The spiders relaxed in their webs, and the beetles and other bugs slowly re-emerged from under the bookshelves. Black birds started to circle again above, disappearing frequently in the abyss.

"Sign, then drink," said the form nicely as it sat back making the chair moan. There was no room for small talk here. He realized why the agent had briefed him so thoroughly. But he still felt unsure about something. His dad was a good negotiator, and Staf had often observed him, meticulous about contract details. "Never leave anything out," he remembered his father saying over and over again. Now, more directly in front of him slightly to the right, a large mug, presumably filled with something, had joined the crystal ball on the desk, and directly in front of him was an elaborate piece of paper with an empty pen.

Staf sensed that this was the real thing and not some kind of joke, which had been in the back of his mind. He had heard of these elaborate jokes before and had vowed never to allow himself to be a victim. This did not fit the picture, but then again, that's how it's supposed to look. He looked at the wooden pen. Odd, he thought, that he hadn't noticed it as he sat down. But there seemed to be a lot he didn't notice, like the chair that had appeared behind him the moment the boss had commanded him to sit.

With nervous, sweaty, shaky hands, he picked up the pen. His mind raced. Was this it? Was he going to be the world's fastest runner? The best athlete of all time? What was the condition again? He tried to search his excited and unfocused mind for the right idea. Unstoppable? It didn't sound right. Unbeatable? Too broad.

The temperature rose some more, but the boss's eyes stayed hidden. They weren't red yet; that was a good sign. He thought about the deal and picked up the pen, scared to show any hesitation. He wanted to read the paper in front of him and leaned slightly forward over the large document. He scanned it. It had fancy calligraphic writing, some large and some small. He could easily make out his name, but the name of the being in front of was elusive. As he gripped the pen and looked closer, trying to distinguish his rights and his debts, he noticed the number six written three times at the top. That seemed to be in the right place. He caught the word uncatchable, which was the correct word he had been trying to remember. This relieved him. To avoid angering the being, he moved his hand as he quickly read the document.

There was a sudden prick in his finger, and he felt the warm liquid of his blood enter the pen. The prick was not painful, but it appeared to allow a lot of blood to flow into the pen.

Shit, this is going to be signed in blood, he thought. He had been betrayed by Rial. He had specifically asked him about this, and Rial had denied it. Then Staf recalled how Rial had answered. It had been something like, "You watch too many movies," which really wasn't a denial. But he had been cleverly deceived, and he was furious. He slowed his movements so he could quickly read the whole complicated document with its flowing letters. He was frustrated, because if it had been written in plain font, he would have been through it by now.

He decided that he was not going to sign the document. Staf turned and looked at the exit. It seemed a long way off, but he figured he could reach it before the boss could get around the desk. He would be able to get out before it was even close to him. The temperature rose. The boss stopped doing whatever was occupying him and raised his head. Staf could not make out a face in the small hood but could see the faint glow of light red eyes with deep black pupils.

The glare was piercing, and a sudden headache nearly made him buckle to the floor. His knees felt weak, and he had the sensation that his skin was starting to melt off. Numbness of impending pain began to creep all around him, hovering just away from his skin, which was about to melt away. The onset of pain made him hold his breath, and he sensed immense power in the air. He felt his heart had stopped beating. He winced, and as if the act of closing his eyes took him away from the spell, he felt instantly better. He put his hands on the desk to stop himself from toppling over. He still held the pen, which was full of his blood now. The hall was extremely quiet. No bugs moved, no birds flew, even the air stayed still. He started to breathe again. But as much as he breathed, he couldn't get enough air. Everything was stagnant and still. He opened his eyes, sweat dripping from his forehead, and made a very conscious effort not to look at the boss. The figure spoke again. It spoke quietly yet sternly, but the sound echoed like a shout throughout the room and quietly bellowed in his ear, just short of creating another mind-jarring headache. He resisted the temptation to look at the boss.

"Is there a problem?" There was a long pause. Staf's mind raced. He was in deep trouble here. He needed to get out.

He thought again about the distance to the door. It was about twenty steps away. A quick run would take seconds. He made up his mind: he was going to get out; this wasn't the deal. It was some kind of trap. He held the pen near the paper as though he was about to sign.

Then, without warning, he turned and ran.

He ran like never before, like his life depended on it. He had taken twenty steps before he even started to breathe. He was lightning fast. He focused on the door, focused on getting there, and focused on moving his feet fast. Invisibly fast, as if he had been released from a slingshot, still accelerating. He had taken about twenty steps and should be almost there. Just a few more steps. He reached out to the door. It was still there. It looked the same. It wasn't as close as he had thought, so he ran impossibly faster. He took shorter, quick steps instead of longer bounds. He started to breathe quickly. Another thirty quick steps. The door was still out of reach. His legs started to complain; they couldn't keep this up. The bookcases on the side zoomed past, but the door didn't get closer. Seconds later, he was gasping. His sprint turned into a sloppy, clumsy, flat-footed trot. He couldn't get enough air in his lungs to meet the demands of his legs. They were tired too and could no longer move as fast as he wanted. He reached out for the door, but just like he had always been in his childhood game of tag, it was out of reach. He fell to the red carpet.

Red blood started to creep up his arms. Some of the figures started to run away from his hands. Others, the evil ones, moved toward his hands and readied their weapons. The red dye climbed past his wrist, and his fingers seemed to sink into the carpet and change texture and color to match it. To his horror, he was becoming part of the carpet. He tried to move his hands away but couldn't. The pikemen poked his fingers; a farmer came over with a pitchfork and stabbed his thumb. A chainsaw started to cut a path through his index fingernail.

A fierce red glow burst from behind him, but he was stuck to the carpet and couldn't turn to see it. The crows cawed mercilessly, and the rats and insects screeched and squeaked with incredible noise, coming out of the crevices and casting long red shadows. The fierce glow came suddenly, and then the heat hit his back in an intense wave. Breathing the hot air became impossible. He could hear heavy breathing from behind as a huge shadow interrupted the red glow. It was impossibly large, monstrous, and he could feel it breathing on his back, each breath creating another wave of heat. Sweat was pouring out of him and trickling down into his soaked shirt and suit, and several drops fell from the tip of his nose. There was a deep growl behind him and then a deafening voice.

"Is there a problem?" A wave of heat accompanied each word, burning into his back. He was trapped. The red on his arms reached his elbow. His wrists were in the carpet. The looming shadow behind him scared the pikemen, farmer, and chainsaw away from his fingers. Staf didn't know what to do. There was no way out of this. It was impossible to get out of here without signing the document. He would have to sign it or else become part of the torture in the carpet.

Panting, Staf started to speak, and he just made up the words as they came out of his mouth.

"Why no, sir, there is no problem at all." He gasped for air. The squeaks and caws echoed. He couldn't think. His mind raced from one thought to another. He couldn't concentrate and looked at the blood pen in his right hand embedded into the carpet. "No, sir," continued Staf, "the pen merely slipped out of my hand, and I just had to come down here and pick it up." He closed his eyes. The squawking and chirping stopped. Silence.

He prepared for impending pain, waiting for something sharp to pierce his back. He was afraid to open his eyes in case he was already a character in the carpet. He tensed.

The breathing behind him subsided. The air returned from scorching to hot. He cautiously relaxed his back and slowly opened his eyes. His hands were no longer in the carpet, and the red dye was gone. He pulled himself up and turned. He was still in front of the desk, as if he had run in place. The figure behind the desk was massive, like a wall of muscle, but Staf had no idea how large it had really become. The eyes were maliciously red.

His hand shook uncontrollably as he reached out with the pen, and just as he was about to write his name, his hand steadied, and he neatly wrote "Staf Nurren." As he wrote it, he swore he would find a way to get back at this rotten deal. He would get back at Rial, the boss, and the patron at the bar. That oath would be as binding on him as was his blood signature. He swore revenge with such vigor, determination, and malice, that he felt like a new person.

He recalled the flea market and the looks on the faces of the chocolatier and Azra. He would have looked the same for anyone going down this path. But the contract was signed now. They were locked in a deal, and his fear diminished. But not completely.

"Drink," commanded the beast. It was now too big to sit in the chair. It had appeared small and talked quietly to entice him to enter the corridor. It didn't need to hide anything now.

Staf knew this drink was not going to be good. In order to avoid getting hung up on it, he grabbed the mug and drank. He swallowed quickly to avoid having anything linger in his mouth. Chunks floated down with the mixture, some of them soft. In the last mouthful, something crawled into his mouth. Staf gagged, and reached into his mouth. The thing rapidly crawled to the back of his mouth and forced its way down his throat. Staf reached into the back of his mouth. He didn't care if he threw up, this thing was not going down his throat. Its hairy legs tickled his throat, and hooks clung to the back of his mouth despite Staf's gagging. He felt it walk down his throat and swim into his stomach. Staf slammed the mug down on the desk.

"Leave now," ordered the being.

Screw this, thought Staf, and he put the pen in his pocket. The air crackled with energy. Staf obediently turned and casually walked down the corridor. Nineteen steps brought him to the door, and he sensed incredible power being restrained behind him. He opened the door and stepped through, and it shut solidly behind him. He was outside in the toy store alley instead of the men's clothing store, but that transformation didn't shock him anymore.

He checked the pockets of his soaking pants and pulled out a handful of sand stained with blood. He walked home, wondering how close he had come to disappearing forever.

Chapter 5: Staf's New Skills

At the next track practice, Staf was anxious to try out his new abilities. He was going to astound the coach and have his revenge on his teammates. Staf was relaxed but energetic as he lined up with some of the other team members. His legs were burning to run; he felt warm, stretched, electric. His heart was already pumping fast. His body felt light, as if his legs had nothing to lift. He was breathing deeply without panting, fuelling his blood with oxygen. He stared down the line and imagined himself as a bullet; he was going to run like he had been fired out of a gun. He felt like a drag car waiting for the green light. While other teammates loitered half-heartedly on the starting line, Staf was completely focused.

The gun went off. Staf exploded off the line, and the race was over before he had started. He took several strides to slow down, and turned. The hurdlers stopped stretching, Sam crashed into the high jump bar, and Kevin's javelin went no farther than a toy lawn dart. All was quiet; the team gaped. The run wasn't timed, but he had easily won. The coach came over.

"Nice run, Staf! Where did that come from? Keep up the good work!" Staf beamed and tried to ignore his teammates' stares as if it had been an average run. He silently enjoyed the moment.

They did some other drills, exercises, and cool-down stretches. Staf was ecstatic.

For the next three practices, Staf found the warm-ups, drills, and practice runs a breeze. He didn't notice coach Saunders timing him methodically. He ran several races and did phenomenally. The rest of the track team responded enthusiastically. They were starting to believe they had a state champion in their midst. Possibly even better.

The coach called him into his office for a post-practice meeting. *Fantastic*, thought Staf. This was his chance to find out the events for the upcoming regionals. The winners would move on to the state finals and then qualify for nationals either independently or representing the state.

Staf knocked on the door and entered the disheveled office. Papers and forms were strewn all over the desk and floor. Pictures hung crookedly on the walls. There was scattered equipment— missing mouth guards, a broken helmet, a lonely shin guard without its partner. It reminded him of his bedroom, and he liked it.

"Sit down." ordered coach Saunders. Staf sat, waiting for the good news, although the atmosphere was unpleasantly reminiscent of his meeting with the boss.

"You have had some very good runs lately." Staf beamed. "I took special note of your times today, and they are phenomenal. My methods are not precise, but they are around state—and possibly national—standards." He looked at Staf. He was hard to read. He rarely smiled, and on the special occasion that he did, it looked insincere. Staf merely nodded. Coach Saunders was unusually serious. Actually, he was always serious, but no one took him seriously. But it felt different right now. He had a concrete, serious face that showed no softness. Staf was worried.

"Staf, I'm concerned."

That doesn't sound good, thought Staf. He noted the coach studying him. He wondered why.

The coach stared at him like a predator, watching every move, every twitch. Staf cracked his knuckles, and the coach moved his eyes to the fingers without moving his head. The eyes returned to Staf, and the studying continued.

"I've coached for a dozen years, and I've seen runners come along. But not like that. I had the misfortune of coming across two runners who had taken drugs to improve their performance." He paused and tried to read Staf, who sat there emotionless.

Staf felt deflated, and fought the instinct to look guilty and maintained eye contact. He didn't want to hear the next part. He knew what was coming. He had tried too hard, made it look too easy. He should have done it gradually, he chided himself. Saved it for the important runs. There had been no need to impress everyone at practice. He continued to listen to Saunders while his mind raced for options.

"You're taking something, Staf, and I want to have nothing to do with that. You might win some races, but my morals and philosophy are to work hard and play hard. With integrity and honesty. I won't have a student dishonor the school and my reputation by cheating." The words hung thickly in the air. Staf held his breath, and he didn't have to wait long for the hammer.

"I had high hopes that you could participate in the hundred-meter race and put in a personal best from hard work, but I don't think you can run a fair race anymore. Therefore, I am suspending you from this team."

Staf was numb. He had put a lot at risk to get to this point, and he needed to find a way out.

"Look, Mr. Saunders, I have always been a runner, all my life." He realized that sounded silly coming from a teenager. "I haven't taken anything." He thought about it. "They have tests for those kinds of things, don't they?"

"Tests can be inconclusive. Steroids can be masked."

"What is masking?"

The coach peered at Staf. It was unlikely that he had gone to these extremes. He studied him for signs of unusual growth, abrupt changes in appearance, aggression. He found nothing.

"There are other types of drugs and techniques, such as blood doping and growth hormones. But I am most worried about the side effects. There can be some serious health problems. Physically and mentally."

"I feel fine," replied Staf, and then realized that wasn't the issue here. "I'll take the tests. All of them." Staf wondered if the stuff he had had to drink would show up on a test, but he had to take this chance.

"No need to. I've already made up my mind. You are off the team," replied Saunders bluntly.

"But that's not fair," protested Staf desperately. There was no way he was going to take this easily. He felt like he was drowning. "I should be able to take some tests and prove it. There is no reason why I should be removed from the team on suspicion or a hunch. Tell me what tests to take. Tell me where to go for the tests, and I'll have them all done."

Coach Saunders thought about it. He was all about sportsmanship, fair play, personal development. Staf had a point. He was sure that something irregular was up here, but he had no proof. Staf seemed sincere.

"Go to the Westside Clinic, and have them test for these." He searched a pile of papers. Then he dug in the desk drawers. Giving up, he opened his laptop, printed a form, and handed it to Staf. "You can come to practices, but I won't let you run the regionals until I'm satisfied you are clean." He ordered Staf out of the office.

For several minutes after Staf left, Coach Saunders sat in his chair and thought about what he was doing. He had seen enough, even in high school, to know about cheating techniques. He was still interested in a college coaching position, and if he wasn't imprisoned to his teaching salary, he might even work internationally. To do that, he might have to look the other way when it came to drugs in sports.

He was all for high levels of protein in a diet. It was one of the simplest ways to build muscle mass. Creatine increases energy and muscle growth. Perfectly legal.

There were many other minor techniques that were legal for high school. Painkillers to mask pain and train beyond thresholds. Antihistamines to improve breathing. Excessive caffeine as a stimulant. He wasn't concerned about that. The improvements in Staf's running did not come from inhalers and a cup of coffee.

He walked to his car. Years ago, a friend had snorted cocaine before a tennis match. He was able to get to shots easily, because everything had seemed to move in slow motion. The friend was also warned by the umpire for conduct because he couldn't stop laughing at his opponent.

Drug use happened in high school, but he had watched Staf very closely today and studied him in the office. Staf was not on a recreational drug.

He found his car unconsciously and drove home on autopilot; he wouldn't be able to recall anything about the drive.

Next on his list were anabolic steroids. Testosterone and others. Symptoms would be increased muscle mass, excessive hair growth, premature balding. Also aggression. Staf was a scrawny kid. The most aggression he had displayed was a plea to take the drug test. Steroids would be used in cycles. His body would try to catch up, increasing and decreasing testosterone production for balance. This would be most hazardous for a growing teen in high school. The urine test would uncover that. But would Staf have time to mask it? Drink lots of water. Vitamin C. You need forty-eight hours for that. There were also products out there that worked in less than three hours. Masking agents that bound to the evidence in your system and keep it there just long enough to pass a urine test. These could also be detected, and indirectly pointed to steroids. Staf wouldn't be that knowledgeable. You needed a high-level coach for that. Staf could also supply a false sample, but the clinic would have safeguards for that.

Human growth hormones? They had recently found a way to detect it in blood tests. Beta Blockers? No mediocre high school student would need a medicine used to relax arteries for heart attack victims. This was just a high school track meet. That would be for very advanced national and international sprinters needing every little edge to shave off tenths of a second. Staf wasn't close to the fastest in the school. Until three days ago.

Coach Saunders arrived at home and was still troubled. He hoped for Staf's sake that he was wrong.

Chapter 6: The Third Track Meet

Staf's results came back in time for the regional track meet. All parameters were normal. The levels of testosterone were normal for a sixteen-year-old boy. There were no signs of masking agents like hydrochlorothiazide. Blood counts were normal. No unusual HGH levels. Certainly no sign of beta blockers.

Staf earnestly handed the results to Coach Saunders and offered to take additional tests trackside if needed. Saunders accepted the results and asked to see him after school. He needed time to think about it. In truth, he needed to consult other experts, including a colleague at LSU. What troubled him was that if drugs had been used in the quantity required to help Staf win a race, the results would have been screaming at him. They weren't. Tampering? Not likely.

Coach Saunders decided to let Staf run the events. All events. He consulted State officials, presented the results, and offered to let them make their own tests and assessments. In fact, he requested that testing be mandatory at the track meet. Then, trusting Staf's integrity, he advised them to ensure their timepieces were correctly calibrated to accurately evaluate Staf's new records.

In practice, Staf was acutely aware of Coach Saunders's continued scrutiny. Staf's body continued to feel electric on the starting line, like a dog straining on a leash. Training was easy. In fact, Staf had to make it look hard. That was obvious too. He clocked sprints at less than full potential. But he was consistent. Coach Saunders noted no obvious signs of tampering. Staf kept a low profile and successfully stayed under the radar.

Three weeks later, they were at the regional qualifiers. Staf held back again and barely qualified in all events. Another week later were the state finals. Staf held back again and set new records in the hundred meters, two hundred meters, four hundred meters, fifteen hundred meters, and three thousand meters.

Chapter 7: The Coach's Perspective

It was very late in the night, and coach Saunders decided to walk down to the pub. It was a treat after a very busy, very successful year. After all these years, he had finally won a state gold medal in track. He had won several bronzes before. A few silvers. One gold. Never five golds. Never five new records. Never the team trophy. All because of one person.

Tirelessly, every year, he put together a hopeless team. It was for the fun of the school. It was a requirement. Traditional. There had to be a track team every year. Many times over the past twelve years, he had wanted to quit. But how could he? Everyone would blame him for the lack of a team. It didn't matter that no one else would step up; he would be singled out as having destroyed a part of the dream in this part of the country. It would be a betrayal, treason. Once he had started, he was obligated to continue. Trapped.

But every year, after the dust settled on another dismal season, there was a reward. The boys matured. Graduated. They got something out of it. Teamwork. Cooperation. Memories. Their teachers changed every year, but the track coach didn't. They knew him. Confided in him. Trusted him. That was the reward.

In the first few years, there were jokes about his team. He was able to take the losses just fine. But the jokes were incessant. After a particularly tough year and a dismal article in the local paper, the rest of the staff would have a field day. Saunders's Slowpokes, Saunders's Turtles, and Slownder's Snails were a few of the names they gave the team. They called it his team now, not the school's. Davies was one of the worst and most vocal.

One day he had had enough, and in the staff lounge, he had very loudly congratulated Davies on volunteering as the new coach. He then made a formal announcement over the PA. He congratulated him and wished him the best.

He stayed away from the field for a week. Every day, he asked Davies how the team was doing. There hadn't been any practices. They had all been cancelled. Davies had engagements at home and various other excuses. Mrs. Shephard had to sub in and take them to a minor track meet.

Half the team didn't show up for the second practice. Every day in the staff lounge, Saunders would very loudly ask how the team was doing. Every day, silence. Davies wasn't one to admit to any shortcomings and sulked away.

After a week, the principal called Saunders into the office and delicately asked if he would consider taking over again. He feigned ignorance, claiming that he didn't want to step on any toes. He also claimed to be extremely busy catching up on things that he had had to be put aside because of track. Now that he was catching up, he was reluctant to come back. This, of course, was not true.

The following week was worse; only three people showed up for practice.

After the second week, Coach Saunders couldn't take it anymore. He missed the team, and he saw the effect it had on the school's morale. The hallways were glum. Everyone looked at him with pain and longing in their eyes. They needed him back and told him so. He decided not to punish the kids at the expense of proving a point to the staff. At the beginning of the third week, he called the team together. He went into sergeant mode. After the team was assembled, he shouted at them in a military manner.

"Do you mind telling me why none of you were at practice yesterday?" He looked around menacingly. No one dared to answer. He could hear the wheels turning in their minds. He was laughing inside and had to cut it short before exploding in front of them. "Practice tomorrow, 4:00 p.m. Anyone not showing up better tell me now!" He turned and walked out, knowing that no one was going to say anything.

Since then, the staff lounge had become a happier place. Davies avoided him. Mrs. Shephard became the assistant coach.

Then there was this year. From the basement to state team champions. All the golds from Staf. There had also been a silver and a bronze from other team members, but that didn't matter in the result.

He got coach of the year, although he had done nothing more or less than any other year. He finally received an offer to coach a small college team. He declined, of course. But the year troubled him. At first, he couldn't believe his good fortune. Early in the year, he had been giddy with excitement. Hoping for some wins, training, practicing harder. He was ecstatic. The accolades. The cheers.

The state finals were over. Staf had broken five records. Coach Saunders was now a training titan.

He discretely entered the bar, but the bartender recognized him. He introduced him loudly to the whole bar. He didn't have to buy any drinks that night, and he had quite a few. And between idle chit chat, his mind kept wandering to the year. How unsatisfying it was to win. He was worried for Staf. Something had happened, and he feared the worst.

Three-quarters through the year, he called Staf in and discretely asked him if he had taken any drugs. Gangly Staf. He looked nothing like an athlete. He watched him closely and looked for signs of aggression, immediate muscle building, sudden hair growth. Nothing. In fact, it still looked like he hadn't reached puberty. His voice hadn't changed; he had no facial hair. He just plain looked like his usual self. Until he was on the starting line. There was something different in that moment.

And after the meeting, his mind was put at ease. Staf was the same kid he'd always been. Then the regionals, and Staf just barely won all his events. And the bad feeling in him came back. It was ironic. He had always wanted to win the state championship, have his players get gold, set an impossible new record, get coach of the year. He got it all.

Then the calls from the colleges who wanted to scout out his runner. Then a call from a college about a coaching opportunity.

He hated it and immediately turned it down. He was an amateur coach.

He watched Staf closely and asked for a complete drug test before the meet and after the meet.

In the end, he had finally won the impossible state championship, and he was completely miserable.

The deal had lived up to its word, to this point. The real test was yet to come. Staf had just cleaned up at the high school state championships: five gold medals and five new records. There were drug tests to take, but he had already passed the ones at Westside Clinic, so this was not going to be a problem.

He was happily in the center of the attention during the ride home. Happy, but not immune to the reason for his success. The team had forgiven him for his one error; he had dropped the baton in the relay, and the team was disqualified. He managed to put it out of his mind. As the peer accolades died down, he came to realize that Brittany, a cute redhead, shared his seat and was unusually cozy with him. He didn't mind.

They arrived back at the high school, and Coach Saunders opened the door so they could return some of the standard equipment. Brittany escorted him out of the equipment room and down the hall toward the exit. Prior to reaching it, she grabbed his arm, and he suddenly found himself in the girl's change room. They had a short discussion about track stuff. He lost track of the discussion when their lips suddenly met. Shortly thereafter, hands found unfamiliar places, and clothing melted off. Staf didn't know what to do and happily followed along. Brittany took the lead.

They left the school, the doors locking automatically behind them, and after a short embrace, they took different directions home. Staf was suddenly in love.

Staf couldn't concentrate during the walk home. He had done tremendously well at the track meet and had matured with Brittany.

As he sauntered home, a car pulled over. It was Tracy, from the track team. She offered him a ride, and Staf hopped in.

They took an indirect ride home, with a detour to a discreet park. After much discussion of school and track, they spent some time in the back seat. He was still very clumsy and couldn't apply the recent experience with Brittany, but it didn't matter.

After a blur of a drive back to his house, he suddenly found himself in his driveway in love with Tracy.

Staf paused after waving Tracy away. He would have to remember this day as one of the best ever. Some fantastic wins at the track meet. And innocence lost. He was extremely happy about his wins and his losses. Almost equally.

At his high school track meet, Staf had run five individual events. His sixth chosen event, the marathon wasn't included in the meet. During summer break, Staf decided to run the Boston Marathon. He entered and was declined. He was in shock. His investigation revealed that he had to qualify, so he looked up the next qualifying marathon and entered it.

The Boston became his second marathon win.

The race officials found out about his high school state sprint championships and told him it was impossible for a sprinter to win a marathon. They corralled him into a meeting. They talked about red fast-twitch muscles and white slow-twitch muscles. Sprinters are supposed to have more red muscles for anaerobic running. Marathoners are supposed to have more white for aerobic purposes. Therefore, sprinters do not do well at marathons. They called it impossible. The best Staf could do was offer them a chance to look at the color of his muscles. They didn't find it humorous, although it wasn't meant to be. Staf had no idea what the fuss was about.

He submitted to a barrage of on-site tests. They were all negative.

Chapter 8: Staf's Mom

Today was the day Irene was going to watch Staf at a college track and field meet. Apparently, he had received a scholarship for running. But Staf had always been a sort of clumsy boy, so she found it somehow hard to believe unless the college had a particularly bad team. But he said he was good, and his losing high school team thought so too. She was too busy to read the papers, but she did notice one of the articles in the paper that he showed her.

It was tough leaving her favorite TV shows, but after all, it was only one afternoon. It was also the first time Staf had ever asked her to go to a meet. A first-year university final. She was going with her husband, Josh; they were going to make a date of it.

They took the long drive to the college and the stadium and took half a day off work so they could enjoy the drive, taking in a late lunch along the way after a fun, cozy, intimate late morning together. Josh bartered for a romantic later departure to take advantage of the empty house. She almost relented but promised him a long night for when they get back.

They worked hard at their jobs; she worked at the grocery store, and Josh worked in a warehouse. They worked long hours, taking overtime whenever they could and enjoying every minute of their evenings, weekends, and vacations. Strangely, though, when she had asked for the afternoon off because of the track meet, they had understood without further explanation, and she easily got the time off.

They stopped at an anonymous café along the highway and ordered some sort of local specialty. As usual, they each ordered a different plate and sampled one another's food to see what it tasted

59

like. It was standard fare, a specialty hamburger with a strange mixture of spices, and Josh ordered the day's special, liver and onions, which he hadn't had since he was a kid. Somehow, he didn't seem to enjoy eating it as much as ordering it. She didn't enjoy it either and had only the smallest piece of it, which she could barely swallow, chewing for a long time, moving the piece from one side of her mouth to the other, and eventually disguising the taste with some fries and ketchup, which finally made it swallowable. She figured that liver was one of those things that was impossible to make taste good. Like brussels sprouts.

It reminded her of a diet she had tried once that allowed her to eat all the spinach she wanted. She took advantage of this opportunity for three days and lost a little bit of weight. After a week, she broke and gave into a craving for a small piece of donut. A feeding frenzy ensued, and like a shark, she attacked the whole box. She could barely remember eating them, they went so fast and suddenly. "Just one more," she had said twenty-five times. So she fell off the wagon and fell hard, gaining back twice the weight she had lost. Eat all the spinach you want. Might as well eat sand. But memorable meals are not necessarily the tastiest. And liver and onions, after decades without it, will be memorable.

Parking was tough at the stadium, as they had barely arrived in time. She figured it was the farthest possible parking place. But the seats were decent—not quite field level, but only five rows up. The stadium was packed and loud, an environment she was not used to.

Some events started. Which event was Staf doing? Then she saw him. He was on a long track. He started to run. He ran quite fast. Then he jumped—amazingly far. Irene whooped and cheered loudly. Then she realized it wasn't Staf and quietly hid her mistake. She looked around the stadium. It was the busiest place she had ever been. It seemed impossible to put so many people in one place safely. As she looked around, a thunderous roar rose.

"What happened?" she asked Josh.

"Staf just won the two hundred meter sprint, a new state record!" He was standing, so she followed suit. She cheered again, cautiously.

She looked at the infield, which doubled as a football field, and wondered how they made that crisscross pattern with the grass. She wanted Josh to cut the lawn the same way and made a note to ask him on the way home.

She tried to focus on the next event. She generally stood, sat, and clapped when everyone else did. She watched the hammer throw and wondered how someone could aim in the right direction after spinning wildly. She was also impressed at how far the "spears" were thrown and the high, graceful arc of their paths. Another race was about to start, and she finally caught sight of Staf. She watched him line up, watched the referee's call, and heard the starting gun. Staf started well and then slowed down. "Run!" She screamed. Then she asked Josh why he wasn't running. He tried to explain false starts, and as he did so, they missed the race. Another state record by Staf.

It was nearing the end of the meet. She became quite familiar with the personalities of the people around her. They also seemed to become more familiar with her and patient in a way. She caught sight of the college team and Staf. It was the relay. Everyone was cheering loudly. Impossibly, deafeningly more loudly. But Staf was on the field now, and she looked at him closely. He sort of looked the right height. Her heart warmed, and she beamed with pride. Her son was a college athlete. She hoped he was having fun. She was having fun being here. The whole day, and she had missed all his events. But she wasn't going to miss this one. Staf. Clumsy little Staf. As a toddler, he was always stumbling over his own feet, always breaking things—toys, models, dinner plates.

She avoided letting him use her best china. When it was absolutely socially necessary (in order not to hurt his feelings too much), she would let him use it and would sit on pins and needles for the duration. It was also a time she would insist on clearing the table herself, letting everyone think she was doing them a favor. They probably knew anyway and just let her be. They knew better than to mess with her and her fine china.

Clumsy, dopey Staf. But no one knew him better than she did. His favorite colors, foods, clothes. His quirks. And she cared for him immensely and tried her best to make a happy childhood for him.

She had even once been willing to put aside her traditional values for him. As Staf went through high school and other kids went to dances and out with girls, she noticed that Staf's only friend was Jake. One day she had a discussion with her Josh. Was Staf gay? It made sense to her at the time. He didn't hang out with any girls, only Jake. They did everything together.

The discussion with Josh was painful, but they agreed that if he was gay, they would support him. But they didn't know how to broach the subject.

One day, shortly after the discussion with Josh, she decided to clean Staf's room. She cleaned the inside of the drawers, between the mattress and the box springs—a very thorough cleaning. That's when she found a DVD called *Cougars on the Prowl*. She thought nothing of it until one day, when she was bored, she decided to watch a movie and remembered his DVD. It was an eye-opener. She would be embarrassed to admit that she watched more of it than she realized.

She felt a certain relief knowing that her son might not be gay and that maybe the difficult topic might not have to come up. She naturally told Josh, and they both agreed on a wait-and-see approach. They also watched the DVD one night when they were alone.

Then Jake started to go out with Jenny. And a few times, Staf went out with them. When they went out, was there a girl for Staf? She asked him once, and he had told her that he hadn't found a girl he was interested in. She knew him better than he did and knew he was telling the truth. So he was just waiting for the right girl. That made her very proud. In college, and still a virgin. What high moral values. Even she herself had succumbed to desires before marriage.

How did he get good grades in school? They were a simple family. They finished high school and got married, got jobs, got a house, had kids. There was no need to do more. She was happy. Content.

Staf was somehow smart. He didn't read and didn't study. But he learned things quickly. Things made sense to him, somehow. But athletic he wasn't. He couldn't ride a bike until he was ten. Couldn't swim until he was …? She was sure he still couldn't swim. Dog paddle maybe, for a minute or two. But he had a kind heart. That's what she was most proud of. He did things right and properly.

She had to work a lot during her children's early childhood. They were frequently home alone at a young age. Staf had shown responsibility at a young age. He took care of his sister and managed to do just fine on his own. Odd, she thought; he just seemed like a clumsy, lazy, sloppy boy. But he was bright, kind, and responsible. She preferred that, although improving on the sloppiness would have been nice too. She wouldn't change a thing about him and missed him terribly around the house.

So she recognized him immediately on the field and was worried about him.

"I hope he's careful out there."

Someone nearby stifled a laugh.

The race started. They all cheered, and she screamed too. She watched the race intently. It was a virtual tie the whole race. Almost. Their college team was ever so slightly in the lead. Staf was running anchor. It was a guaranteed win. There seemed to be a big jumble of people where they passed on the stick (which, she was corrected later on, was called a baton). Something happened on the handoff. The baton fell. His teammate hadn't handed it off properly (or clumsy Staf had dropped it). She watched him fumble for the stick and shoot off the line. He ran incredibly fast. He made up lost ground. She willed him to win.

But it wasn't enough.

She resisted the initial urge to ask what came next and instead exclaimed how happy she was for his other races. She clapped and watched as the medals were presented.

Their college won the overall team trophy for combined points in all events, and tears gently rolled down her cheeks as she watched

Staf hoist the trophy. She waved at him, and although he couldn't see her, she was sure he knew she was there. Her hands were sore from clapping and her voice hoarse from cheering. They went to the car, and finally exited the parking lot. She had seen and taken in so much and yet only actually watched the last race. They had a happy drive home.

In the end, she had only seen him run one event, the relay, and it didn't go very well. She wouldn't call herself an expert on running, but she was still very surprised that he could get a scholarship with the last-place performance she had witnessed.

Chapter 9: Continuing to Run

Four years later, Staf found himself at his last college track meet. He never sat on the sidelines; he always stood while a friend was running a race. He felt restless during the meet, his legs itching and twitching during the run, as if his movements could help his teammates move. The noise was deafening, and it was difficult to hear. It seemed every meet every year was louder than the last. Surely the Olympics would be louder, and it was hard to imagine. He had run in every sprint event. He would have run the marathon, but the timing overlapped with other events. To date, he had never lost a race.

It was his last year in a four-year bachelor of something. The light course load left enough time to enjoy other endeavors, such as co-eds. But on the track, there was only one thing to do, and he focused on running and the team.

In the women's final hundred-meter sprint, Lynn had a very good start. Staf and the rest of the team cheered loudly. She had steps to go. Suddenly, the runner from LSU passed her in the final few steps. With half a step to go, the runner on her left leaned over the line first. She came in third. Not bad. The cheer was loud, but not as loud as it could have been. It wasn't a gold.

The last event was gearing up. The relay. It was exciting. It was one of his favorites, as far as the team was concerned. But he never ran it. There were two events that Staf never ran: the relay and the hurdles. The relay because he was always too slow on the handoffs, and the hurdles because he always crashed into them. All he could do was run fast. No handing off. No jumping over roadblocks. He was content with his events, his five gold medals, and his three new college records.

It was also the deal he had with the coach. No relays or hurdles. The first semester, he had a partial scholarship to go along with his partial participation. That was okay with Staf as long as he didn't have to jump or use his hands.

The end of the first semester already saw the attention of the national team. His scholarship promptly became a full one. The coach was a tough one, hard on the runners, always wanting more, and Staf always had his back against the wall with him. He liked the team but hated the coach. He sometimes wondered why he stayed at the school at all. Get an education. Everyone said to get an education. And so he was. He promised himself and his parents that he would get one. He was also confident that he would have six successful running years ahead. Surprising prize money and appearance fees were available, and bonuses if he set records. But the biggest money-makers were the endorsements.

As an amateur, he wasn't allowed to take any money, but there were many ways to circumvent the system. For instance, Staf had a car without having to buy one.

He felt like lightning on the track. Everything seemed to go in slow motion just before a race started. He could block out irrelevant noises. He only heard the starting gun and nothing else. Once it went off, everything went on fast forward.

Right now, he was praying for his team, which was huddled in a meeting with the coach. The coach and runners looked over at him and motioned him over. He hesitated.

"Staf, get over here."

He ambled over hesitantly.

"John sprained an ankle in his last race. He can't run. You're in." He tried to focus. Staf didn't understand right away. "Get laced up," the coach bellowed, and Staf snapped out of his short daydream and looked up. The sprinters were looking at him hopefully. It would be the only medal to go with Lynn's third place finish and Staf's five golds.

"But—" started Staf.

"No buts," ordered the coach. "Get the hell out there now." The pressure was immense. Suddenly, his legs wouldn't move, as if they ran on electricity and the plug had been pulled.

As everyone dispersed to do some last-minute stretching, the coach came over, red faced, like a cherry tomato ready to explode. Then it did. Two inches from Staf's face.

"I'm the coach, you little self-centered shit," he screamed, spit flying into Staf's face. "When I say run, you damn well run." Sweat intermingled with spit.

This had happened once before, in the second part of year one. Staf had threatened to quit. And the coach had almost lost his job. Staf didn't know what to say; he was terrified. He slowly tied his shoes.

"But I can't," stammered Staf.

"Get on the goddamn track!" screamed the coach, and he reached out, about ready to grab Staf, until he realized that everyone around (or at least nearby, considering the noise) could hear, and there were also the cameras. The coach's eyes grew wide with rage, and he whispered, "Get on the field, or so help me, I'll kill you."

Staf's heart leaped into his throat. He had never had his life threatened. He fumbled with his laces and had to redo them. The shoes suddenly didn't fit well. His toes were too sweaty and uncomfortable. It felt like his socks weren't on just right. His toes felt claustrophobic in the shoes and itched.

The crowd went crazy when they saw Staf get ready to go on the track. Everyone was well aware that he only ran individual events. If Staf ran the race, it was a foregone conclusion. It was already won.

Staf wasn't sure where to go and asked Dan. All Staf had to do was stand in line, hold a baton, and run. The running part would be easy. He was running anchor, so he only had to receive the baton. He didn't have to hand it off. It cut his risks in half. He could maybe do this just once. Life returned to his legs. He ran out on the track enthusiastically.

He was beside Dan.

"Whatever you do, hand it nice and slow. It will be a poor handoff, but I know I can make up the time. Just make sure the handoff is slow and smooth."

"Not a problem," replied Dan without paying attention.

Staf went into position. His team was lined up. The race started. Staf felt great; he was going to help his team win in a different way. The race was fast, the handoffs smooth. It was any team's race. They were all even. With Staf as anchor, that meant the team was going to win. Dan was coming fast. It was still even. He had run a good race. Staf readied. He wanted to win this for the team. He was ready to go. Dan reached him, and while the other teams had a very smooth running handoff, Staf deliberately ensured his was from a walking speed. The baton was solidly planted into his hand. Staf gripped it and started to run. But he started to run too soon. His grip hadn't tightened enough. It slipped out of his hands and tumbled in front of him. Staf watched it tumble. He could still save the race. He ran over to pick it up. As he reached it, his foot caught the baton and sent it skittering off the track. Staf fumbled after it.

The crowds were screaming—in fear, it seemed. Then they grew quiet. There was some muffled cheering here and there, and a knot formed in his stomach. He knew they had lost. His last college run, for the championship. The last run of his college career. Mr. Untouchable. Stiff Staf. Fan-Staf-tic, they called his running. He didn't know if he should continue. The race was already decided. He didn't want to stumble across the line in distant last place, but really, in sportsmanship, he should. Or were they disqualified because the baton had left the track? He didn't know. He stood there stunned. He didn't know what to do, or where to go He had cost them a medal. The only medal the team could win aside from his five.

The coach called Dan over. Dan was behind Staf, and the coach avoided looking at him. Staf was somewhat relieved about that.

His team assembled twenty yards away. The coach congratulated them, slapped some of them on the back. There was some hand shaking. There had always been camaraderie on the team— "congratulations," "nice try," "next time." And there was now, but not for him. They waited for Dan but excluded Staf. They filed past him as if he were invisible, led by the coach. Dan glared at him as he went by. They always arrived and departed as a team, but today, they left him on the field alone. He felt naked out on the emptying field, while the crowd stared at him in whispers.

In an instant, Staf hated this team. Everyone for himself. That's how it had always been. The final medals were being handed out. While this went on, Staf entered the hallway toward the locker room. He heard his name, followed by laughing. He stood outside the door for a minute, listening to the team humiliate him in his absence. The deep voice of the coach was the loudest. Staf continued down the corridor. He took off his shirt and dumped it in a corner. He ignored security and left through a back door. Closing ceremonies were coming up. All teams were required to participate. He would not be there.

Staf never returned to the college. He finished the courses by correspondence and invigilated exams. No one from the team or college ever talked to him. He only once saw the headline "Staf Stumbles." He didn't show up to the athletic banquet for his All-American award, and no one asked him why. He never forgot the betrayal and rage he felt toward the team and vowed never to let that happen again.

Chapter 10: The Professional Running Career.

Staf's college results, minus the relay, earned an invitation to the US track and field finals. Having marginally set new college records, he was ready to make his mark on the world, and this would be his first chance. He figured it would be good to set new records every time he ran—new records by narrow margins, because he would have to break his own times; he would be running against himself. The fastest against the fastest. It would become boring. He decided he would set one new record out of the six events he ran. For this meet, it was going to be the hundred meters.

He had easily qualified. The stadium was full again. His reputation preceded him. He won all six of his events and qualified for the upcoming Olympics but declined the invitation to the relay team.

On the recommendation of one of the other coaches, Staf was in touch with Devon, an agent. He was quite good and immediately connected Staf with sponsors, the biggest being a sports drink and a small company called Lightning Shoes.

Staf was making a small fortune on sponsorships. They were far more lucrative than award prizes, incentives, and appearance fees. Substantially more. Shoes, shirts, shorts, sunglasses, gum. Underwear too.

His underwear photo shoot was interesting. It sounded like a good idea at first—Staf prancing around in nothing but *gitch,* but once he took his shirt off, the producer decided he needed some help. The makeup crew did miracles to make him look buff. Staf was also impressed with the final result.

He was at the studio again, this time for a sports drink. "Get past the wall" was the slogan. He was supposed to be running, and get tired. It wasn't going very well. The producer came over, frustrated.

"All you have to do is imagine that you're running long distance; you can't run anymore; you don't want to run anymore; you've hit the wall.

Staf interrupted, "What's the wall?"

"Haven't you ever run and felt that you could go no further? You run a little more, and then you have that extra energy to keep you going?"

"Nope," replied Staf truthfully. He had never hit a wall. Or he couldn't remember ever hitting one.

The commercial was difficult to make, and after an eighteen-hour day, a sixty second ad was created. Staf saw it once and was amazed. It showed Staf running through a busy downtown area. He entered a rural area and then a barren landscape. He was breathing heavily, sweat pouring out of him. He had started out running fast, and with no warning, he slowed. Staf stopped at a solid brick wall. It stretched out of sight to his right and left and reached up into the sky. The wall. Hunched over, he took out his sports drink from a pack, stood up, and drank the powerful formula. The words "Don't let the wall stop you" appeared on the screen. The wall crumbled, and Staf continued on his way at an incredible pace.

Staf watched the commercial several times. He didn't get it.

Staf slowly developed an appreciation for the extremes of running. His favorites were the one hundred meters and the marathon. As he won more races, his appearances in marathons became popular too. He had run (and won) the New York and Boston marathons. Those were his first ones. He had kept the races close, narrowly winning over the formerly favored Kenyan. The runner-up promptly challenged him to run the Kilimanjaro marathon in Tanzania. After winning it, he inherited a desire to explore and entered the Saharan marathon, starting in Algeria. And then he went to the South Pole.

Staf now found himself in the Arctic for the Northwest Passage Marathon. They had formerly held it in Arctic Bay, Canada, and called it the Midnight Sun Marathon, the most northern marathon. Then others had sprouted up in Norway and Alaska, and the timing hurt attendance. So they had moved it farther north to Somerset Island and given it a new name.

Staf was up after a horrible sleep in his tent. He woke up and found an afternoon sun shining through the canvas. Startled, he jumped up, knocking over utensils and stumbling around his tent. He grabbed his watch, hoping that there was enough time to catch up in the race. It was 1:00 a.m.; he had slept only two hours. Once he calmed down, he had a hard time telling his brain it was time to sleep.

"The eyes," his brain complained, "they show sunshine. You are mistaken, for surely it is one in the afternoon." Staf looked at his watch.

"Let the eyes tell you this," he told himself. "See, 1:00 a.m.!"

But some part refused to listen. Convinced that the sun was true and the watch false, he opened the tent and looked around. It was quiet.

"It's quiet because they are at the race, because it is afternoon," his brain said.

Staf strained his ears. He could hear some snoring.

"Fine," said his other self, and he took a deep breath and went back to sleep. Then his mind went to work again.

"Maybe it was only one person snoring and everyone else is at the race?" The argument started all over again.

In the morning, that is to say when the clock showed 5:00 a.m., Staf got up and marveled at the sun again. It had merely circled overhead as if suspended on a pendulum. And a few months ago, halfway around the world in Tanzania, he had watched it slowly lumber directly overhead near the equator. The same sun. The same earth. And in Tanzania, it had scorched him with 40° C temperatures. Here, there was more sun and a comfortable 20° C.

As the desert is to sand and the South Pole to snow, the arctic, at this time of year, is to rock. Nothing but rock and a light sprinkle of green. Staf expected to see nothing but snow, indistinguishable from its southern partner, but it was summer now and more fun to think of the contrast. Desert, snow, and rock. Maybe they could make a marathon on water? But that would be called swimming, and Staf could swim just as well as the rocks he was looking at.

Staf numbly had some coffee and breakfast at the lodge and lumbered to the starting line. He didn't feel ready to run a marathon.

It was an informal affair. The race started with a horn. Staf immediately set out to run this race alone and sprinted far into the lead. Then he settled into an average pace. There were no roads on Somerset Island. In fact, it was uninhabited except for one outfitter's lodge. Hundreds of years ago, the Thule had a small village there. They were the precursors to the Inuit.

Much later, the Hudson Bay Company had set up a trading post. It had been abandoned for decades. When the trading post closed, the building was used occasionally by hunters from Taloyoak. Taloyoak had the distinction of being the most northern town on continental North America. There is a community farther north, Resolute, but it is on Cornwallis Island.

Staf followed a rough trail. Stone inukshuks pointed the way. He followed the trail along the rugged rocky coast, dotted with beaches. They looked deceptively inviting in the twenty-four-hour daylight, but this was the Arctic Ocean, and *arctic* implies anything but warm.

Out in the water, he heard narwhals blowing their spouts. There were six. Narwhal, the unicorn of the ocean. Some people thought they were mythical with one large ivory tusk protruding from their head. One of the volunteers proudly walked with a Narwhal tusk cane. They only looked mythical. He heard them and strained to find a protruding tusk. They were probably mischievous, not mythical; they refused to show their tusks.

Somewhere out there were albino beluga whales and monstrous bowhead whales. The bowhead, although not the longest whale, is thick, and therefore only the blue whale is heavier. It feeds on krill and small organisms, filtering them from the water with baleen.

He saw bones scattered on the beach and wondered what whale, seal, or walrus they might have been, and what might have caught it. Possibly a polar bear, according to the race brochure. He wondered if he could outrun one and suddenly needed to look behind him. He was alone.

Somewhere on the island were musk oxen. He had seen one on display in the Cambridge Bay airport. It must have been like a prehistoric ox, who roamed with his extinct wooly mammoth friends. Staf could almost imagine them on the rocks and snow.

Staf kept running, unaware of his pace or time. The scenery of the rock, flora, and fauna floated by.

This was another favorite run, and reflecting on it, he marveled at the hidden life around the world. If there was a cold planet out there somewhere that had the remotest chance of having life, it would probably resemble something from the arctic or maybe the antarctic. Or if it was a hot planet, it must be like the Sahara. He wondered if polar bears could survive in the antarctic and penguins in the arctic.

The run was finished. It was over too soon for Staf.

Year one was finished. Today was the first day of year two. Staf wanted to start this one off right, and his old Lightning shoes were in the garbage. Out came his trusty old Asics. Unfortunately, they were not his sponsor. But his feet liked them, so he would have to do without the million dollars that Lightning paid him to wear their shoes. No problem. His feet were worth more than a million.

The changing room was uncharacteristically new and clean. It was full of track athletes preparing for the finals. Staf found a lonely corner and changed while listening to his MP3 player. It was playing "An Honest Mistake" by the Bravery, his favorite running tune.

He saw his agent, Devon, enter and waved him over. His agent was an energetic fellow, always on the phone, always excited about the latest contract. He enjoyed arguing and haggling and then would come out as your best friend. He was fairly short and stout, slightly bald with messy dark brown hair. He also wore neat, black-framed glasses that fit him well and gave him an air of professionalism. He always wore a suit.

He made his usual big smile and ran over to Staf and gave him his customary firm handshake.

"Staf, my friend," he said warmly. *He really isn't a friend*, thought Staf; it always sounded like it presumed too much, like it forced Staf to be his friend.

"We have a great opportunity today."

Sure we do, thought Staf.

"Do you think we can break another record today?" He paused and smiled ever bigger. Whenever Staf thought that the false smile was as big as possible, Devon proved him wrong. "But of course we can. We need to have a big meeting after the race. The endorsements are beating down our door. We are talking big time. I've been holding off. I've been holding off because if we set a new record today, we will almost certainly double our money. We are talking millions, Staf."

Staf never had the heart to correct him about the *we* part. He thought it would offend him too much. Then their relationship, whatever it was, would never be the same. He thought it was decent enough, secure enough. Devon had been recommended by one of the few coaches from college that Staf liked and at a time when he really started to need an agent.

"Sounds exciting," said Staf. "Consider a new record already set."

"I know we can do it." He gave Staf a hefty slap on the back and smiled incredibly wide.

Any wider, thought Staf, *and that smile will break his face.*

"But wait, what's this? You can't wear those shoes; they are not a sponsor. They're not paying you to wear those shoes. Lightning are. You have to wear them. They are nicer shoes."

"I used to have to wear them," corrected Staf. "One-year contracts only, remember? Today is the first day of year two. They were my first endorsement, and the shoes are, well, they are shitty. I'm going back to my old pair."

The smile vanished instantly. The agent actually had quite a small mouth.

"You can't, Staf," said Devon instantly. "They exercised their option to renew for another year. It was in the small print. I thought I told you. I'm sure you forgot, busy with all your running." Suddenly the *we* had turned into *you*.

Staf couldn't believe what he heard, but he restrained himself. "I was very specific. One-year contracts only. Even if it means less money. One year only, so that means I will not wear these shoes."

The smile had now turned into a frown. "I am afraid you will have to. It would open your up to a huge lawsuit. You could lose everything." The *we* was still notably absent in his statement. "I will talk to you about it after the race. After you wear those nice shoes. Then it will be sorted out. Just get ready for the race. Get ready to set a new record." Half of the smile came back. He turned and walked out.

Staf fumed. He was not going to wear the shoes, but he couldn't start destroying what he had already started. One hour to the race. He was at a dead end. He didn't want Devon to be negotiating these contracts anymore. He decided he wasn't going to set a record today. But he had to run. And when he ran, he had to win. He just couldn't lose.

He sat in silence. *Legal mumbo jumbo*, he thought. It was foreign to him. And then he grasped at a straw. He would call Jake. Jake was a lawyer, albeit a new lawyer. He had a small office in downtown L.A. on the fifth floor of some building. He had refused offers from firms connected with his father. It caused a lot of friction.

"Hey Staf, ready for the race?" Jake had a knack of knowing who was calling even without call display. Staf usually ignored this irritating habit.

"Jake, it's Staf. I need some advice."

"Best advice I can give is run fast. Everyone expects you to set a record today. There isn't a TV in the country that isn't focused on your race today. So that's my advice: run fast. I'll send you the bill for that tomorrow."

Staf groaned, and then he related his problem.

"Well, I can't help you from here. I would have to see this contract," said Jake thoughtfully. "I think you are in a bit of a pickle".

Staf was deflated. And then he had a new idea. "Jake, I'm flying out tomorrow. I'm bringing all my contracts for you to review before I sign them." Staf thought about it more. "Hey, maybe you can take care of all that sort of shit from now on?" He sounded more excited as it came out of his mouth.

"I don't know," replied Jake hesitantly. "I am sort of busy." He looked at his calendar. It was wide open. "Maybe I can squeeze you in at two. How's that?"

"Piss off," replied Staf happily. "I'll be at your house at seven with beer and steaks for the barbecue. And make them good this time." Jake always made good steaks; Staf just wouldn't admit it. He was about to hang up.

"Oh, and Staf, if you really don't want to run in those shoes, be sure that you are fit to run. Don't hurt yourself before the run starts."

"I never do," replied Staf confidently.

"Good," said Jake, but he wasn't sure his friend really got it, so he added, "It would be a shame for you to have to withdraw from the race for injury, but we will all understand."

"Ohhhhhhh," said Staf, thinking now.

"Good, now go out there and break a leg," threw in Jake.

"I got it already," groaned Staf as he rolled his eyes and hung up.

He was deep in thought, and then he had an idea. He drew out some toenail clippers. He cut his toenails to the skin. Then more. It hurt. But it didn't look that bad. That wouldn't be enough. He took out some scissors. Without putting too much thought into it, he quickly sliced the tip of his big toe. The pain was not too bad. At first.

At seven, Staf met Jake in his downtown condo, with his contract, a case of beer, Crown Royal, and some tip sirloin. He had already read it and knew it now word for word.

"Jake, you know the story here. What can I do about it?"

"Whoa there, first things first." He opened a beer and slowly, deliberately took a long swig. Staf contemplated throwing Jake's steak out the window. Instead, he took his beer out to the balcony and put the steaks on the barbecue. Jake joined him, and after most of the beer and steak were done, they attacked the Crown Royal. In the meantime, there was light discussion on the contract.

"Nothing," said Jake. "It spells it out here in black and white. You're screwed, dude." He said it as he quickly leafed through the contract. Staf slumped back.

"It was the only stipulation I wanted in the contract. For how long?"

"Two. Two years, and then the terms are renegotiated. I suspect that after two years, the renegotiations will not go well? The limits are as much for their benefit as yours. You might not have been a good sprinter."

"Fair enough. But I can't keep Devon as an agent. He screwed up the one thing I really wanted. How about you? You know some of this stuff. Why don't you take care of it? Or let your firm take care of it?"

"I don't want to," replied Jake. "Besides, you can't afford me." Jake worked in a small office. It had a noisy air conditioner and water stains on the ceiling. A secretary worked part-time in the late morning.

"Well, what does an agent normally make?"

"A percentage. Four or five is typical. Although there is a trend to an hourly rate too."

"I'll offer you 10 percent. Just get me the one-year term. And lots of money. Oh yeah, and let me wear what I want, particularly the shoes."

"I suppose I could clear up a few minutes on my schedule." Jake recalled the empty calendar. Ten percent was a little high, but he didn't know what he was getting into with Staf; it might not be enough.

They finished the rest of the Crown Royal, looking out into the streets of Los Angeles.

Chapter 11: The Last Run

Five years later, Staf found himself in the locker room again. He had already won gold medals in the two hundred meters, the four hundred meters, the fifteen hundred meters, and the marathon. It was one hour to race time. The Olympic hundred-meter sprint final. Everyone was predicting that this would be his first loss. He had only barely beaten the Canadian in the last meet, and the Canadian was rumored to have broken the record in practice.

The locker room reminded him of the Pan Am games six years ago when he had sliced his big toe to avoid running. Today was the culmination of his career. Six years at the top. He had never lost a race from the hundred-meter sprint to the marathon. What made it even more astounding was that he didn't have a coach or trainer. His training regimen was secret. They tried to pry Staf's secret out of him with sly, indirect questions, but he couldn't come up with anything. There was no secret. The secret was he didn't train at all. That was the hardest secret to keep.

Born to run, they called him. When he sprinted, they called him "the bullet." When he ran the marathon, they called him "perpetual".

Staf liked to find a quiet corner in the changing room to collect his thoughts. It was usually in the back corner, hidden from the other athletes. Sometimes, he used a boiler room, janitor's office, or manager's office if he found it unlocked. Today it was the corner of the locker room again.

He was very happy with the results of his running career. He was going to set another record today and cement his untoppable career. It would be impossible for anyone to touch his accomplishments even in one event, never mind six. It was amazing how many records there were—event records, state records, national records, international records, indoor and outdoor records, personal bests, records for the most medals in an event and the most medals in a meet. Most medals in history. Most consecutive medals. Longest standing record. The list was endless, and so was his money. He could barely keep track.

Jake had become his official agent in year two. Not Jake personally, but his firm. This vaulted the firm into prominence not only in the state but also nationally and, to a certain extent, internationally. Because of Staf, Jake had outdone his father. And better yet, he had outdone his father alone—that is, without his father's help and influence.

It was rumored that Jake's dad avoided the exclusive country club. Everyone would ask him how Jake was doing or comment on how successful Jake was, and it would burn him to know it had all been done without the slightest help from him. He had absolutely nothing to do with it. That was not Jake's intention, but the accomplishments that come naturally are sometimes the easiest. Unlike Staf's.

Jake didn't deal with all the endorsements personally. There was an assistant hired to deal with Staf's monstrous account. But any final contracts and endorsements went through Jake's desk. Sometimes Staf looked at them but not often.

Devon still ran Staf's Lightning Shoes account. Staf didn't have the heart to fire him from that one deal, but he didn't have to wear the shoes anymore; that was part of the renegotiated deal.

Staf had become the richest man in sports. That was another record. It was hard to say how much money he had. At any moment in the day, it could change by millions.

Staf focused on his pre-race meditation. He was trying to relax, collect his thoughts, and then put them out of his mind. He needed to visualize. He needed to find an inside source of energy. Running fast was not merely a matter of commanding his legs to move fast. The legs already knew how to do that. The visualization was the medium. Thinking too hard would interfere with his legs' intuition. It would screw things up.

His favorite in the short sprints was to visualize being a bullet fired out of a gun, or sometimes a slingshot. When he ran the thousand meters, he imagined being chased by a pack of wolves. For the marathon, he was just a wheel constantly rolling downhill. Today, he was going to be lightning. When the gun went off, he was going to be faster than light.

His time was up. Thirty minutes till the final sprint. It was time to go out and warm up in public. The other racers would bend and contort, jump, and do little pretend sprints. They would scout the competition, maybe stare them down, intimidate them.

As he left the locker room, it was as though he hit a wall of pure noise. The stadium was the largest he had ever seen and packed to the sky. Not an empty seat. Everyone was standing and screaming and clapping and blowing horns. He had probably just broken another record for stadium noise.

Staf didn't need to stretch. He did sometimes, just for show. Today, he would touch his toes and maybe do some light jumping jacks. His legs crackled with energy. This was going to be the biggest race in history.

Staf focused on being a ray of light. The noise faded from his mind, and so did the people. He didn't hear anything or see anyone. The other runners faded too. The runner from Canada glared at him. Staf didn't notice. That pissed the runner off.

Staf only saw the track. Then he only saw the end. The energy in his legs couldn't be contained. It crept up into his arms, all the way to his hair. He was just one big ball of energy. His heart beat fast. His breathing was deep and restrained. He could feel the blood running through his body, also full of energy. His body was relaxed, but pure energy was in his blood, in his heart, lungs, and muscles. He felt like a vicious dog straining on a leash.

He lined up. Time slowed down. He visualized the electricity escaping his body. It was all around. He crouched. He waited for the switch to be thrown. Bang. He became light. He instantly hit his target at the end of the track. He was still light. Light doesn't care if it wins a race. He needed to convert back and find out what had happened.

Chapter 12: Joey's Perspective

Joey was an average child. He knew exactly when his favorite TV shows were on, and between them, he had his favorite video games. He liked sports too; he played hockey in the winter and baseball and soccer in the summer. He was an average player in all of them. He had developed a mild interest in this year's Olympics. It sort of grew on him. In particular, he was fascinated by the successes of Staf Nurren.

His parents were always trying to inspire him into some activity. One afternoon, his dad asked him what he might like to see—a hockey game, basketball, football, baseball. Playoffs or finals, of course.

Joey replied with the only sports thing he had heard about. He thought it would be cool to watch Staf run in an Olympic final since Brazil was not too far away.

His dad had the resources and connections in the government to arrange just about anything, but this request seemed to catch him off guard; he looked concerned.

"I'll try, but that's a really tall order there. I can't promise anything." Joey was somewhat relieved. He was hoping to try out the new Badge of Honor game. He could watch the Olympics on TV.

His dad came through. Joey tried to be enthusiastic, but the news came while he was close to getting to another level.

The excitement slowly built on the day of the race. Staf had won five gold medals. He was going for his sixth to tie his previous two Olympic outings.

They arrived at the stadium; it was packed and noisy. They had amazing seats for the hundred-meter final. They were five rows up, just down from the starting line. He could feel the excitement, unlike anything he had ever felt before.

He had researched the final sprint lineup, and sure enough, Staf was going to be there. Joey was going to cheer for him.

There was quite a mix in the final race. Russian, Jamaican. The Canadian was supposedly favored to win this race. There was also another American from the same college as Staf. Apparently they didn't like each other.

As Joey got used to the noise, it went up several decibels.

"What happened?" he screamed at his dad beside him.

"The runners just came onto the track. Look, there's Staf in the black and red pants."

Joey searched the field and immediately spotted him. Staf looked intense. He already had sweat beading on his face. He was looking down the track at something. His eyes were wide. His legs bulged. He looked ready to run. He looked like he needed to run. It looked like he couldn't hear the crowd. He didn't notice them or anything else. Joey decided to start cheering. This was the most exciting thing he had ever seen.

He watched them line up and was nervous for them. He wondered about all their effort and training, all put into this one moment. Was it worth it if you didn't win?

The gun went off. The crowd roared. Staf shot off the starting blocks, already in the lead. Joey cheered louder.

He watched Staf explode off the line and zip by like lightning. Amazing, he thought, that someone could run that fast. In such a short distance, he had left everyone else far behind. Joey was proud of Staf and wanted to be just like him.

His dad pointed him to the scoreboard. It was a new record. *That's nice*, thought Joey. But wait, it was a new world record. The old one was shattered; Staf had completed the race in 7.98 seconds. So that's what the crowd was crazy about.

Joey watched Staf again. He didn't seem to know about it. He watched him catch his breath, acknowledge the other runners, and then he took a quick look at the clock, the time, and the happiest look appeared on his face that Joey had ever seen. And the crowd loved him.

Something happened to Joey. He was inspired. This event changed him. He wanted to be just like Staf. He wanted to be a hero. Was it something he could do? He might have to put away the video games, might have to skip his favorite shows, but this sort of stuff looked great. He thought about it.

What was he good at? Well, he liked to play soccer. He wasn't that fast, but he could work on that. Maybe even Staf could give him some advice? He was an average kicker, but that could be worked on too. The main thing was he really liked to play it. Playing lots of soccer would be fun. And who knows, even if he played it for years and got nowhere, maybe it would still be worth it.

His dad was all too happy to buy him a soccer ball and register him for other related sports, such as running. Joey packed away his games. All he could think about was soccer, thanks to Staf.

Chapter 13: Staf Visits Jake's House

It was a Sunday, two days after the Olympic triumph, and things had just started to settle down for Staf. He was in bed, alone by choice in his glass Malibu house. The windows were all closed and everything was quiet. As he woke, he looked at the clock. It was 7:00 a.m.—too early. He rolled over, dozed for what seemed like just a moment, rolled back, and checked the clock again. 9:00 a.m. Time to wake up. He didn't like to sleep in much later than nine. He closed his eyes for a second. Another moment's snooze, and he looked at the clock again. It was eleven. He shot out of bed. Half the day was gone. He hated that. And true to form, the extra sleep made him feel more tired. He lazily had a coffee. He sat on one of the corner decks of his house, and although he was enjoying the peace, he wanted to go somewhere. He called Jake.

"Hey, Jake," he said when his friend answered. Jake had probably been up at seven or earlier with his kids. "I was thinking of coming by early this afternoon. Are you busy?"

"Sure," responded Jake quickly, indicating that nothing was planned for this lazy day. "Plan to stay for dinner. I'll tell Jen."

Staf hung up. He lazily climbed up to the bathroom, brushed his teeth, and had a shower. Everything was in slow motion today. He glanced at his clock. 1:00 p.m. It was early afternoon already, and he had done nothing more than have a coffee. He decided to get more done today and quickly got dressed and shot downstairs to his car.

Mrs. Wilson was outside doing some gardening in a wide-brimmed, pinkly flowered sunhat. He shouted a quick hello, and as she raised her head, he gave a quick wave and turned away to his car. He wanted to avoid striking up another endless conversation that might be difficult to escape. He would probably have to explain some running things to her as she asked the same questions she always did. Then it would move on to one of her stories. The same ones, over and over. He could almost complete them for her. But she was a nice old lady and a good neighbor.

She had brought him an apple pie when he moved in. It was a legitimate gesture, as she had no idea who he was. It was also very delicious, and he secretly wanted another one and frequently dropped hints about his birthday and other occasions, hoping that another would find its way to a short existence in his kitchen. He had regrettably shared his first pie. He wouldn't make that mistake again.

He hopped into his car and carefully drove out of his driveway. It was a nice day, Sunday and so not busy, and this was the ideal day to take out the Ferrari, which he rarely did.

There were three things that Staf treasured most in his life right now: his glass house, his Olympic gold medals, and his 1961 Ferrari 250 GT Spyder. And he treated them all with incredible care.

It had been a Sunday not unlike this one a few years back when Staf had been sitting in a café by the ocean with Amber, a girlfriend, and had seen the black convertible drive by. It had mildly pissed off Amber how quickly Staf could fall in love with a car.

He immediately set out to find the owner, a wealthy, eccentric retired developer. Staf phoned him but had to make an appointment through a secretary to call back. Staf called back at the appointed time. When Earl found out who Staf was, he refused to talk to him on the phone and insisted he come over. Staf immediately drove over and felt embarrassed in his average, practical car.

Earl was in his seventies and lived in a specially designed home on the hills. He received Staf in his study. He was smartly dressed and had a full head of white hair, which was neatly combed. He projected a smart and sophisticated, if eccentric, image. He was quite formal with Staf, and Staf figured he applied this formality to strangers as well as his closest relatives. His granddaughter Lenore was visiting too. They had tea in a nice secluded courtyard. A stable in the back housed Lenore's horse, which she apparently took frequently to the trails in the back. As Staf looked around, he started to like Malibu and could picture himself building a house here. He was beginning to wonder how much more he had in common with this old fellow.

After a short discussion on track, the Olympics, and marathon races, Staf was finding it difficult to bring the topic around to the car. So finally he cut into the conversation.

"Earl, the reason I'm here is that I want your car."

It was suddenly silent. Earl looked confused for a moment. He probably had many cars, many nice cars. Then there was a sudden look of understanding; he had figured out which car Staf was talking about. Earl's icy blue eyes became penetrating. He stopped sipping his tea. He was motionless. Then he chuckled, which Staf figured must have been a big deal for him.

"Young boy, that car is not for sale. I know you probably could afford one if you could find one for sale. The problem is there aren't any for sale, including that one out back. And don't insult me with money. I paid ten million dollars for "Chelsea". Apparently the car had a name. But Earl was a very shrewd man. It didn't take him long to come up with another offer. He was at an age when he was usually driven around; he rarely drove himself anymore, and he was having a hard time figuring out what to do with his car. Whoever got the car in his family would likely sell it at an auction. There was a sudden change in Earl. He became a businessman again. Staf sensed he was out of his league.

"But maybe we can work something out."

Staf was scared.

"I'm sure you hold your Olympic medals dear to yourself. How about I trade the car for your six Olympic medals?"

Staf felt like a hammer had hit his ears. His Olympic medals? His most prized possessions. It was impossible. That's when Staf realized how much this car probably meant to its present owner. He couldn't part with his medals. His medals meant everything to him, even though he could win more in the next two Olympics. His mind raced. He felt stressed. Earl chuckled again.

They continued to make small talk and went around to the garage to look at the car. Earl allowed Staf to sit in it. Staf didn't have the nerve to ask if he could drive it, and since the offer wasn't given, he knew the answer.

Staf visited twice afterward for some dinner parties. The guests were generally older, all well established, successful. Rich. They were particularly interested in Staf's stories. He tried to relate them freshly each time.

A month after the last dinner party, he received a call from Lenore. Earl had passed away and left her that car. She offered it to him for fifteen million dollars. He drove it home an hour later.

Staf was driving that same car now to Jake's house, which was just about an hour away, south of Los Angeles in Oceanside, which is also on the coast as the name implies.

As had become customary, Staf picked up some prime steak, some nice wine for Jen, and some beer for himself and Jake.

Jake's house was also a custom home, a bungalow with a brick exterior. It was shaped like a U and surrounded the pool in the backyard, with access to each room through a patio door. As Staf came around the final corner to the house, he put the car in neutral and revved the engine a bit. This was part of his announcement that he was there, and true to form, as he pulled into the driveway, two young kids bounded around the corner. He feigned fear and put the car into reverse as if to get away. The two screamed at him. He stopped and got out.

"Hi, Uncle Staf!" came the chorus, and they hugged him tightly around the thighs. Simone was six, and her brother was four.

"We saw your run!" shouted Simone as she smiled up at him.

"Oh really," he replied. "Who won?" She punched him. "Well, let me bring some things inside, and I will tell you about it." He reached into the back and brought out the steaks. "Bring these inside, okay?" And he held them out to the kids. They just looked at him.

"What?" He said, feigning innocence. Simone just looked at him with a scowl, and young Peter, after glancing at his sister, tried to mimic her pose, with poor effect.

"Ohhhhhhh," said Staf with a look of understanding, "you want your Olympic presents. Gee, I almost forgot. Here you go."

Simone and Peter beamed, and exploded with excitement as he reached into the back and pulled out another package of steaks. They resumed the original pose.

"Well, I'm sorry you don't like them," he said, and he picked up the bag of steaks and the wine and beer and delicately grabbed another bag that clearly held some shirts, banners, posters, and other souvenirs.

The two simultaneously screamed. Staf wasn't finished.

"After you bring the stuff in?" he demanded as a question.

"No," said Simone, and she grabbed his leg tightly so he couldn't move. Peter did the same to the other leg.

"Have it your way then," he said, and he proceeded to walk toward the house with each child riding a leg. He casually entered the house and went to the kitchen and said hi to Jenn. Simone and Peter clung furiously to his legs. Staf dropped the packages on the counter and sauntered out the door into the back.

He greeted Jake as he carefully plodded to the patio. He ambled to the pool and loudly declared, "Time to go for a dip, feet first, of course," and crouched as though he were about to jump in. Simone and Peter ran off.

As Staf sat in Jake's backyard, it occurred to him again, as it had many times over the years, how opposite they were. Jake never had a childhood. Staf never grew up. But Jake had a family and all the rewards that came with it. He looked happy. Staf had no one and would always be alone. Side by side, it was difficult to tell who had the better deal.

Chapter 14: Staf and Amber

Staf was preparing for his traditional party. He held one after every major event. There would be members of various Olympic teams and some other celebrities. His marathon friend from Kenya had come last time.

He also took the unusual step of specifically inviting Amber, which he did on certain occasions. Amber was the closest thing he had to a girlfriend. There were girls through high school and college, and Staf had never really gotten attached to any of them. There were some that wanted more, and some that Staf had wanted more of, but nothing had ever really worked out for more than a few months. He had known Amber for most of the past six years, but then, he didn't really know her at all. He learned little bits every time they were together. She was the only girl for whom he could remember details, maybe because they came in small amounts.

Staf had just ordered the catering for his party, and it was a typical L.A. day—sunny with a slight breeze. There were a few puffy clouds in the air, and it was one of those days when you notice it if a cloud blocks out the sun for a moment; everything gets shaded, and the temperature seems to cool down. Staf noticed a quick shadow race across his lawn as he returned from Mrs. Wilson's house. Of course he would invite his closest neighbor. She usually came in the late afternoon and left when it got too noisy, which merely meant that music had been turned on. But it was also one of the rare moments when he didn't avoid her.

His mind came back to Amber. He hadn't seen her for two months and sort of missed her. She had a dolphin tattoo on her left shoulder. He found that the first day. They had met at a bar. Staf had had way too much to drink, and when he stumbled into the bar with his friends for one last round, they had all squeezed in to where she was perched talking to someone else. Otherwise, the bar was empty. They had some sort of light bar chit-chat. Clearly she didn't know anything about running and had no idea who he was, and the topic never came up.

Five minutes of light drunk talk later, Staf's friends decided to go outside for cigarettes, and she joined them. Staf didn't smoke but wasn't about to sit in the now-empty bar by himself. Another five minutes later, they were making out on the bench, and a few minutes after that, he uncovered the dolphin in his room.

In the morning, they had some hotel room coffee, he copied her phone number into his blackberry, and they said a quick good-bye.

Almost as an afterthought, he called her two weeks later when he was downtown again. She was late getting off work, and so there was no need for wining and dining, and they promptly shared a room again underneath the soft down duvet.

This time, he found the other tattoo. It was her late mother's name written in Chinese letters. She had committed suicide several years ago. Amber was just getting her life together after years of therapy. Staf didn't know what to say. It was a tragedy. Was therapy working? He was temporarily on the lookout for some signs of instability and started to work on an excuse to go to sleep. He was very tired, of course. Then she asked what he thought of threesomes.

So every few weeks, they got together and learned a little about each other. The threesome had never happened. And she would matter-of-factly tell him about the men she met. Staf elected to keep his sex life to himself.

It was getting late in the afternoon, and he was a bit surprised that he had managed to keep his white attire clean. Some folks would be arriving soon, and he had already hit the sauce, numbing his mind a little. Clouds were constantly floating in front of the sun, and Staf briefly recalled how much he disliked dancing shadows.

Chapter 15: Amber's Perspective

Amber's cell phone rang. It was one of her friends. She answered while driving down the Santa Monica Freeway in her small convertible. Her friend was distraught. Amber almost had to pull over.

"What's the matter?"

She listened patiently as her friend sobbed that her boyfriend of three months had just broken up with her. She was devastated. This was her soul mate, the one she was going to spend the rest of her life with. Again. Amber wondered how many soul mates were out there. But she did seem to be terribly upset. Amber couldn't remember her friend being that upset last time, but then every time seemed worse.

She told her to calm down and come over right away. It was late morning. Amber decided to hold off on going to the mall and went home and thought that maybe she would take her friend with her for some shopping therapy. She pulled into the underground parking stall and entered the twenty-five-story condominium complex.

Her sniffling friend intercepted her in the foyer. Amber's heart went out to her.

"Come on, dear, let's get you upstairs and clean you up."

Amber had a small, one-bedroom condo that she kept very neat and orderly. She was very proud of her independence and accomplishments. Although she was not very successful in the entertainment industry, she did make a little bit with the small roles she picked up here and there and had become accustomed to and somewhat satisfied with her job at the bar. Her friend sat on the couch sobbing, already into her second box of tissues.

"Well, Tammy, I don't know what to say. But how about we go shopping? I have to buy a new outfit for Staf's party tonight." And then she had an idea. She knew her friend well and what she needed. "Hey, why don't you come with me?" Her friend looked up with red-rimmed eyes, a red nose, and red lipstick. At the thought of shopping, red returned to her cheeks too.

"I don't know," Tammy replied, "I'm in no shape to go out tonight."

"Nonsense. I know Staf very well. He is having a big Olympic party today, and there will be lots of cute guys out there. And if we don't find a cute guy, well, there's always Staf." A sly smile came across her face. "We could share him too; that might even be the best idea." She tried not to let the idea run away. She and Tammy had done this before. The red vanished from Tammy's eyes and nose. Amber also got a little flushed.

She grabbed her friend, ran out the door, and headed for the mall. During the drive, she filled her friend in on Staf. He was a regular guy, someone you would never take for an athlete. She prided herself on knowing him intimately, perhaps better than anyone else, even his mom, who probably thought he was still an innocent little boy. He liked to ham that innocent boy thing up, and she played along.

He was rich too, filthy rich, stinking filthy rich, and although he didn't flaunt his money, he got whatever he wanted and treated his friends very well. He had very few friends, and she considered herself to be among the closest. She explained to Tammy that he was mildly eccentric. He spent a small fortune making a huge four-story glass house in Malibu and another buying a dumb car. It was hard to describe and imagine the house; everything was glass and set in a concrete frame. Glass floors, walls, ceilings—even the roof was glass. All the walls were like large sliding patio doors. And then, for privacy, he hung curtains on the all walls and put rugs on all the floors. She explained that the master suite had opaque glass, for obvious reasons.

He would be celebrating his Olympic success, and so he would probably be wearing all white. Spotless, brand new white. Since he lived there alone, the whole package was somewhat exotic and erotic.

Her friend quietly hid her growing enthusiasm. They spent several hours at the mall, trying on various blouses. Tammy was well endowed, and had more to spare than Amber's small perkiness. They carefully selected some nice blouses with low-cut lines. They also bought new brassieres, Amber opted for black to sport above the cut of her blouse, and Tammy bought a white one with delicate lace to peek out and catch attention.

At the condo, they got ready. Skirt or dress? Amber couldn't decide. Tammy had her mind made up right away. A dress. But she had bought a blouse today, not a dress. She immediately produced one from Amber's closet. It stretched over her nicely. She then waited patiently for Amber.

"How is this one?" asked Amber. The skirt was impossibly short. Tammy thought it looked okay. Amber changed anyway.

"How's this?" she asked, sporting hot pants. She looked almost like a cheerleader. It was nice, but she changed again.

Two hours later, she came out with her new blouse and a short-but-not-too-short miniskirt. They looked at each other in the mirror. They looked too different. Now Tammy had to change into something similar but not too much the same. The final assessment in the mirror proved satisfactory. They then proceeded to do hair and makeup.

It was a cool sunny day in L.A.; Amber and Tammy enjoyed the drive to Staf's house. It was in Malibu, built in the hills with a fantastic view of the ocean and Los Angeles. There was little traffic, and Tammy was impressed with her friend's connections. In fact, she was a little jealous of her—a nice condo, nice convertible, nice friends. She had none of that.

They pulled into a swank neighborhood. All the houses were unique. Some were built into the hillsides to blend in nicely. Some looked like they were forced into the hillside. Others looked like they belonged in colonial Washington, and still others would have looked at home in a trendy Staten Island neighborhood. Staf's house, therefore, both belonged and didn't belong at all.

Tammy gasped at the large glass structure as they passed a row of tall, dense cedar hedges and an open iron gate. There was a fancy black car tucked to the side of the driveway.

"That's Staf's Ferrari," remarked Amber with a hint of jealousy, recalling the afternoon when Staf had first seen it. "Love at first sight." She sighed.

They parked in the long driveway among many fancy cars and entered the large wooden door. In fact, it was the only part of the house that wasn't glass, but it was an ornate, solid wood door with a large animal bust carved into it with a nose ring as a knocker. It was open, and they went in.

Amber immediately spotted Staf, squealed, and ran over to him, wrapping her arms around his neck tightly and making sure her breasts squished against his chest, and kissed him on the cheek.

"Congratulations!" she poured out.

Staf smiled, his usual self, trying to remain calm and look cool. She knew she had an effect on him, as all women did. But she also came by more than most. She grabbed his hand and brought him over to Tammy and introduced her. She watched him as he formally shook her hand.

Doofus, she thought. *Give her a big hug; that's what we're here for.* But she saw the slight twitch in his left eye. He knew. She would keep an eye on him a few minutes later. If he looked casually over at them again, they were in, and they would both stay over.

This happened later, in the back, while he was standing with one of his agents by the pool. She casually smiled at him and carried on with another friend. Then she discreetly found Tammy and told her the good news.

The afternoon wore on, and Amber suddenly noticed how extremely hot she was beginning to feel. The sun was still out, but was it not as bright as it usually was? She noticed the black birds circling just beyond the backyard, slowly circling closer. Why should she notice this? She shivered, an odd thing for such a hot day.

Her stomach started to lurch, and knots formed. She was sweating profusely.

She found Tammy. She did not look good either. Her hair looked flat, her boobs saggy, and the outfit suddenly looked out of place, as if it didn't fit anymore. She looked at her own and felt embarrassed. Tammy looked at her pleadingly. Suddenly, she just wanted to leave.

Chapter 16: The End of Six Years

It was another nice evening at his spacious L.A home. It was his summer home and consisted of four offset square levels, looking like a pile of children's blocks that were not exactly on top of one another. The exposed corners made balconies. The inside was an open concept; in the middle, you could look right up to the top. Aside from the frames, the outside walls had plenty of moveable glass; Staf had wanted to let the summer breezes through. The balcony railings where chrome to avoid conflicting with the glass.

The house usually seemed white during the day because of the sunlight, and Staf enjoyed wearing white when at home to feel like he blended in.

On certain days, he would specifically wear all black just to stand out. He almost never wore anything else—no red, green, or blue, although his closets held those colors in ample quantities. There were blinds and curtains on all the windows to keep the sun out on the hottest days, but they were mostly left open during the day to admit the sea breeze from the Pacific. Today, he was wearing white.

He was having one of his Olympic parties, a large get together. Amber was here with her girlfriend (he couldn't remember her name), but he casually intermingled, trying to determine why Amber had brought her. Possibly to join them later on? Staf was trying to read the signs.

People came and went. Jake came by for a moment and made the usual promise to try to come back later with the emphasis on *try*, which Staf usually took with a grain of salt. He didn't want to keep his friend from his family anyway. In fact, sometimes he wished he would bring them over, and it hurt him that he never did.

Staf kept his home neat, unlike he had when he was younger, and few would have looked at it and accepted that he didn't have a housekeeper. He was proud of this. His kitchen and living room were stylish, modern, neat, clean, and smartly decorated.

It wasn't money that bought the style; most of his things were unique and really quite inexpensive. He liked to marvel at the small details instead of the price tag and flashiness.

Staf had also practiced for this party.

At his first Olympic party, he had invited his old high school friend, Chester, who happened to own his first Super Bowl ring. In the spacious backyard patio, someone asked Chester to repeat his touchdown dance and threw him a football. Chester performed an elaborate dance. Then he threw the football to Staf's Kenyan marathon friend, who improvised a different dance. The ball made its rounds, each pass resulting in a new dance. The ball came to Staf. He hobbled, jumped, and contorted. His attempt was not deemed adequate. They threw him into his pool.

The next year, to his horror, the parlor game recurred, and Staf was second in the dance sequence. Staf tried to create a coordinated routine. He looked at his guests. They were not impressed, so he threw the ball to Amber and voluntarily jumped into the pool.

Amber was a very good dancer and performed well. She threw the ball to another guest but jumped into the pool anyway. By the end of the game, most of the guests had made a jump in.

If the game continued this year, he was prepared. He had devoted several hours to his touchdown dance and was determined to earn a dry evening.

As the afternoon wore on, the normal sea breeze seemed to stifle, and the air became quite hot. As Staf walked down the driveway with Devon, something caught his sight under one of the hedges that lined the way. He thought it seemed to move, and it reminded him of something. As he talked to Devon, he casually leaned on a car. The heat started to make his sweat noticeable. Still, the talk was light, but shadows seemed to catch his attention throughout his yard, always moving suddenly and then stopping or turning into normal shadows when he looked at them directly. It was an odd thing, and Staf started to wonder if he had had too much to drink already. He decided that he was not going to finish the drink in his hand.

"Odd, it seems that as the afternoon is going on, it's getting hotter; do you notice it?" asked Staf, as he wiped his damp forehead.

"Not really," replied Devon. "Seems like a nice evening to me." He paused. "Maybe you're coming down with something." He said it with barely a concern, obviously not really caring about Staf's state. His real concern was only that he himself was in good shape. Staf was sort of an asset. Devon was here just to do some PR and keep on his good side; by keeping the sponsorship, he could keep his salary, car, house, and boat. Keep the Staf contract, and you can keep everything else. The person really didn't matter, just the paper that he signed every once in a while.

"Take care of yourself; get some rest, maybe. Let me know how you are tomorrow."

Staf acknowledged him absently as he caught sight of more flickering shadows wavering around the corners of his house, shadows from unseen sources. He really had no patience for Devon and wondered why he had bothered to invite him over.

Devon would probably ask him about his health every day for the next five years just to have something to talk about and pretend concern. But this happened often.

I'll just stop inviting him over, he would say to himself. False friend. The one he hated most was the ambiguous "How is your family?" Devon still knew nothing of them.

Last year, Devon had specifically asked how his parents were, although he had never met them. Staf had lied and said that they had passed away in a car accident the year before. Staf was not surprised when, a month later, Devon asked again how they were. Staf had dryly replied, "Still dead" and immediately regretted being intentionally mean to someone who was trying to care. But Devon had never asked again, and Staf was both relieved and sad for it.

A month later, his father had a stroke while driving and had been in a car accident. Although he survived, Staf felt incredibly guilty about the coincidence.

As Staf stood on his driveway about to enter his house, noticing the shadows creeping around it, he decided to evaluate his life. Mainly, his friends. He never worried about money. Jake took care of that quite well. He wondered who his friends were—besides Jake, of course. He really couldn't think of anyone else. Not any other runners, coaches, reporters, agents, sponsors. He had known Amber on and off for six years. She would be his next closest friend. There were others that he cavorted with, Candace and MJ, but he did not see anyone on a regular basis. In the end, he really only had one friend. He wondered if Amber and Tammy were going to be his new friends tonight, and he lost his other thoughts.

Just as he entered the house, he had another strange feeling and turned to see a limousine coming up the road. There was something he didn't want to think about, and he quickly put any foreboding thoughts out of his mind and decided to find Amber and Tammy.

As he looked up the loft into the glass square of the floor above, a few more guests said their regards and quietly departed. He went out back to the pool and noticed that everyone had left. *Odd*, he thought as he went to the stereo to turn it off. He vaguely recalled them saying bye, but there were many more hours to go into the evening. He wondered if Amber and Tammy had anything to do with this and chided himself for assuming too much of Amber.

"There you are, honey," came a familiar voice from the side of the pool. "I just remembered that I have to get something done. I'm sorry to have to go. Maybe we can come over tomorrow night if you're not too busy." She always looked most beautiful when she was leaving. She wore a tight-fitting red blouse, low cut, revealing something black underneath that he imagined removing. Just the right combination to contrast with everything about her—the light complexion, the black hair, and the red dress. He did note that she said *we* when she talked about the next evening, meaning her and ... what was her name again? But he knew the answer, and his slight smile belied it. She caught this too and blew a kiss and ran down the side of the house to the gate and quickly drove off.

Odd, thought Staf again. Usually there was some kind of snuggly hug and kiss with her on departure, especially when there was apparently no one else there. How very odd. He hated the snuggly good-byes but missed them now. He preferred to hate them than miss them.

There was very little left to do but go inside, and no sooner had he passed the patio doors than he heard a loud knock at his wooden front door. A loud, deliberate knock, repeated three times. There was something in his mind that he wanted to suppress about this. As Amber and Tammy had driven away, he hadn't noticed anyone else arriving; no other cars were in his driveway. He was going to send whoever it was away; the party was over. But then again, his guests didn't usually knock. He went to the door. It was a tall, fine, neatly dressed, professional man. It was Rial.

The implications hit Staf like a brick wall, as if the image of Rial alone could punch him squarely in the face and flatten it. His thirteen years were up. He had to think about it for a moment, a quick moment. Had it really been six years since college? Shit. How time flies. It's not that he hadn't thought about the time, thought about what he would do, about his future as an agent. Or as a carpet.

"Hello, Rial," said Staf in a somewhat cheerful way, as if he had been expecting him. "Please come in."

Rial hadn't aged a year, had not changed at all. Staf wondered if it was even the same perfect suit that he still wore. "You have done quite well for yourself," he said. "Your career and home. You have used the talents well." He paused. Staf almost wondered if he was supposed to say something, acknowledge what was well known. Rial promptly continued, "You won't be needing these things anymore. Come with me. It is time to get you a suit and start your new service." He emphasized the word *service.* "You are required to deliver a package to New York by tomorrow morning."

It wasn't that Staf hadn't known this day would come. In fact, he had prepared himself for it for quite some time, but not recently. He hadn't thought about it since the Olympics. In the two months since then, he had sort of hoped they might have forgotten about it.

Staf again sensed shadows moving about the walls of his house, in the corners, and up the stairs—parts where the light couldn't quite reach. As he noticed them, he focused on Rial. He was sure Rial was going to speak again. He recalled that Rial was very precise and meticulous. At length, Staf mustered some courage and tried to speak in a loud, commanding, deliberate voice. Instead he squeaked.

"I'll go later." He tried to stand taller and more confidently, realizing that his stupid mousey voice gave away his fear. His shirt was quite damp now from the heat and stuck to him in places. A bead of sweat rolled down the side of his face. It was extremely hot, and he resisted the temptation to let the heat make him feel weak.

Rial's expression did not change. However, in response, his voice was icy, curt, and deliberate.

"You are in his employment now, and are required," he commanded and said nothing else.

Staf had gotten the worst out of the way; he felt that he could continue down this path now that it was started. He became confident.

"No problem. I'll go later."

"It is required now."

"I don't feel like it."

"That doesn't matter."

"Look, I'm not going to say I'm a great employee or anything. In fact, I'll offer that I am a very shitty employee. One that doesn't always do his job well. But that wasn't spelled out in my contract very clearly, was it? I'm just an employee. I'll deliver the package later. Just drop it off."

"That will not be possible. I am to see you on your way immediately."

"Well, give it to your next guy. I will try for employee of the month next month."

Rial looked at him with a steely stare. The response did not seem to perturb Rial. Staf figured nothing could.

"Has there been any shortcoming in our part of the contract during the last thirteen years?"

Staf thought about it and after a moment said, "No."

"Do you feel you are keeping up your end of the contract by not completing this simple task?"

Staf remembered the red carpet, and a great fear went down his spine. He tried to hide his shiver. "I will get the delivery done. When I get to it. I don't see how that is not keeping up my part of the contract. Also, I am in his employment, not yours. Perhaps we can set up an appointment, and I can drop by and see him."

Rial still held the package. The steely stare remained. Then he abruptly turned and left.

"See ya!" hollered Staf.

When the door was closed, Staf cursed to himself. He let out a big sigh and could feel his nerves coming up, tension. He ran to the window and looked for the limousine. It wasn't in the driveway, but he could see some dust blowing around down by the road either from a departing vehicle or merely from wind.

Staf was drenched in sweat and needed to get changed. The phone rang, which startled him. He looked at it. He was suddenly afraid to answer. He wondered how long he was going to be afraid to do a lot of things. On the fourth ring, he ran to it and snatched it up. He paused, listening for something in the earpiece. At length, he answered. It was Jake.

"Hey, Staf. Fantastic news—you wouldn't believe the offer we've just got from a new sponsor. It's a new clothing line and cologne. And then, because of the new records, when we renew the existing contracts, I think we could double the endorsements. Do you realize how much we are talking about? Are you ready? Are you sitting down?"

There was a moment of silence. Staf didn't know what to say to this.

"Staf, did you hear me? Double it, for one season. Keep this in mind. I'm going back to all the sponsors tomorrow. Staf, another record! You are going to double last year's salary record!"

The voice was excited, genuine. Staf's hands were still trembling. He was shaking. Sweaty. The phone almost slipped out of his hands. His heart was racing after what had happened. He let out a big sigh.

"Staf, what's up? Are you okay?"

Staf looked up. He took a deep breath. Another impossibly hard task, although this one was slightly easier than the last.

"I'm retiring," whispered Staf.

Now it was Jake's turn to pause. A long pause. Then Jake continued, "What's going on?"

"Jake, you remember what I told you thirteen years ago after the trip to the fair? The deal I signed? Well, my time is up. Rial was just at my door. I have to start paying the piper. I have to retire from running races and start running errands, starting with a delivery tomorrow." Jake knew the story. Staf continued. "For thirteen years, I've been trying to figure a way out of this. I signed it under duress., but I don't think legal help will get me out of this one." It was a slight joke, but no one was laughing. "I turned down the job. Well, not directly. You see, I've accepted that I am in his employment; I'm just determined not to be a good employee. I figure that's the only way to get back at them." There was still no response from the other end. "Look, Jake, I'm tired of running. I need to retire and take some time to think things over." The words made his chest hurt.

Jake laughed.

"You're tired of running? You? Tired of running?" Staf realize how ridiculous this must sound to his friend, who had had to endure years of nonstop races. It sounded absolutely ridiculous to Staf too, and he didn't mean it.

"I have to do this," continued Staf. "I have to retire. I need to do some other things. And my retirement starts right now. As in this very minute. Since I only have one-year contracts, I don't have any obligations. Hold a press conference whenever you want. I won't run again. I have to go."

He hung up the phone as he heard his friend start to protest. He then lifted it off the receiver, and laid it on the table. He took out his cell phone and turned it off too. Staf went upstairs, had a quick shower, changed, and came downstairs.

The afternoon had turned to evening, and it was dark now. The phone was still beeping from being off the hook, and it suddenly stopped, as expected. Then another noise stopped. The clock on the kitchen wall always made a small ticking sound, and it was silent now too. The silence was stark. A crow cawed like a shout in the sudden quiet. A breeze shook the light that hung in his kitchen, and it sent strange shadows dancing around the walls. He went to the window and shut it and noted his distance from his neighbor. They would be just out of range if anything should happen at his house.

The light stopped shaking, but the shadows kept moving about his kitchen walls. The movement seemed deliberate. Staf had a bad feeling.

There was a popping sound. The room became darker. Another pop. The room became darker still. Pop. The room plunged into complete darkness. The lightbulbs had exploded. Something was happening, and he was on alert. He felt like he was being hunted. He couldn't control his breathing anymore and started panting in the hot, heavy air. He was in the kitchen. He fumbled for the drawer and found the flashlight. It didn't work.

This didn't surprise Staf. But he also had matches and a candle in the same drawer for the same emergency. He was able to light it and felt slightly relieved. But it had an eerie red glow.

As he walked out of the kitchen, he went to a shelf where he knew another candle stood (a dumb gift from someone a while back). As he neared it, his candle cast more shadows about the room. They were moving along all the walls as if they were alive. As he neared the shelf and was about to light the other candle with his shaking hand, he noticed the plant beside it move. He looked closer at it. It wilted, withered, and dried before his eyes. It was a brown, dead stalk in seconds. The candle before him suddenly flamed with a dim red glow, but he hadn't lit it.

The air grew even hotter, and his shirt was soaked in sweat again. His candle fought with the shadows, and its glow about the room seemed to diminish. He could only see two feet in front of him now, where before it had lit up the whole room.

The shadows stretched from the kitchen to the living room. Staf slowly followed them and had to pick his way carefully with the limited light. The candle was becoming slippery in his sweaty hands. The silence was pierced by another caw from outside. He could hear the slight hiss of the candle in his hand. It was working hard to create a little light.

The shadows led him into the living room. He knew what he would find there, and his heart was pounding in his chest. Where it had ached earlier from having to retire from running, it was pounding in his throat now. Although his hand was shaking, the shadows did not waver. He took a step into the living room. He had two candles in his living room, and they had already been lit by someone or something, and he knew what it was. Out of reach of the light, there was a larger shadow. Something large, hot, dark, and angry. The shadows fluttered briefly as the figure turned around, and two red eyes, boiling with anger like bubbling volcanoes, were fixed on him. The boss was here. Staf dropped the candle, and darkness engulfed him.

Staf could only see red eyes. Everything else was dark. The other candles let out only enough red light to show that they existed; they revealed nothing else. A quiet voice seemed to thunder in the room. The drapes and shades fluttered. He could hear them but not see them.

"Why?" was all it asked. Staf knew that it felt words were wasted on him. Staf wanted to play dumb and ask 'why not?', but he changed his mind just in time. He thought he had practiced this conversation, but he couldn't think of it now. The conversation with Rial had been hard enough, but it was a walk in the park compared to this one, and only one word had been said so far. But he decided to stick with it. His voice squeaked, barely audible.

"But I am honoring the contract. I am in your employment."

The eyes grew impossibly redder and larger as the figure grew. It loomed over him. Its height reached the ceiling.

Staf's voice got quieter, barely audible. "I'm just not a very good employee." He looked away at this. There was more silence, but energy grew in the air, and a hot wind moved. When Staf looked up, the monstrous volcanic eyes looked down, revealing a hideous sneer as its mouth opened and its heavy breathing burned Staf's face.

As he watched it in fear, he was glued in place. He gave his legs the command to run, but they didn't seem to work. His heart was beyond beating, it seemed either to have broken through his chest or throat or stopped altogether. As he watched, the thing seemed to slowly shrink back, and the red, bubbly volcanic eyes paled and grew smaller. Staf eased a bit and was able to get a quick breath in. His heart, if it had stopped for a moment, started pounding impossibly hard in his throat again. His head hurt. Was this thing moving on? Retreating? Maybe something more important to deal with had just come up. Staf was grasping for hope.

As the boss shrank, the two candles seemed to be allowed to light up the room a little more, and Staf discovered that he was standing on the red carpet again. The red carpet was in his house. He didn't look down at it. A quick look behind him confirmed that the door was not impossibly as far away, as he had feared. But he remembered last time. He wouldn't be able to run.

The boss's face—or at least its vague outline and the red eyes— shrunk into the hooded cloak. The figure stood there, partially shrouded in darkness, holding an odd wooden pole or stick.

The pole swirled into a blur, and it shimmered and expanded. It grew longer, and on the side, halfway down, two twigs sprouted and grew. The bottom was capped in metal, which also cracked with a clinking sound and divided into two. The top then expanded like a balloon, stopping short of bursting the wood. As Staf's attention drew to the transformation, he adjusted his perception, and it became clear this thing was like a wooden mannequin with no eyes or mouth, just basically a wooden frame with seeming arms and legs. He wondered what kind of trick this was. He worried about his soul and wondered what sort of technicality he hadn't counted on. He was ready to run, and he knew he could. His legs would listen if they had to; they wanted to keep living too.

The voice thundered in his ear as if it were right beside him although the boss was at the other end of the large living room. It was still like a loud whisper, but with malice, not anger as before. A whisper hissed in his ear: "Unstoppable."

Staf realized that the boss meant the wooden mannequin. He was relieved to see that it was not moving, so its being unstoppable was not an issue for the moment.

Staf noted a crystal ball gently and slowly roll on the red carpet toward him. He knew this was not a trick and did not fear any kind of hidden trap. As deceptive as this thing was, Staf knew very well that contract or no contract, if some kind of rules weren't governing the situation, he would already have met his fate. Something was in store for him. The crystal ball gently stopped just short of his feet. There were no further instructions, and none were needed.

Staf knew what to do. He slowly bent down and put his palm on the crystal ball. There was an immediate, painfully blinding light, and something wrapped around his chest and started squeezing. He heard his ribs crack and could see them pierce his clothing as blood seeped out. It felt like he had been stabbed. Something came toward him, a blade so sharp that it was almost invisible. It descended toward his head. Staf struggled but couldn't move; he was in the iron grip of whatever was crunching his ribs. The blade sliced into his skull. The pain was blinding. Blood oozed down his face. He had to blink rapidly to keep it out and had to breathe slowly to avoid sucking it in. He could barely keep his eyes open. He hoped for a quick death.

His head dropped, and he saw beetles and spiders appear out of the red carpet. The beetles pinched his toes. Staf kicked them despite the pain in his chest and head. One would not let go. He kicked more desperately. It ripped open his toe and burrowed in. More followed. Staf tried to kick them off and cracked two more ribs, each one shooting impossibly more pain into his compressed spine. There was nowhere else for the pain to go, so it went to parts he never knew could hurt. The beetles scuttled into his toes and pushed out his toenails. He could feel them crawling up under his skin. Spiders joined the beetles climbing up his legs, their legs tugging his skin as they held on, ascending his body. They reached his chest and entered through the holes made by the broken ribs. He squirmed as much as he could, but the vice on his chest got tighter, and at the same time, moving his head caused blood to spill out of what he could sense was his exposed skull.

He was horrified and helpless as the spiders and beetles enlarged the holes in his ribs, ignored the blood, and entered his body. He could feel the sticky legs cling to flesh. They filled his chest and scurried around inside his lungs. They forced air out, and Staf couldn't breathe. Beetles nibbled at his beating heart, what was left of his lungs were being filled with spiderwebs. Others piled into his stomach, and each organ produced a different type of sharp pain. They crawled up the inside of his neck and into his nose, and worst and most painful of all was when he realized that they had reached his eye. His right eye fluttered a bit as he sensed a beetle eating the back of it, and then could feel its prickly, hairy, sticky legs enter the eyeball. He screamed. A spider hopped into his open mouth and immediately started to build a web. He tried to chew it, attack it with his tongue, but it was too quick and elusive.

He bent and twisted in the grip and heard his back break. He managed to turn his head and look back. The last thing he saw with his remaining eye was the thing that gripped him, something wooden.

Staf had no energy left; he waited for the end. The end didn't seem to be coming fast enough. The pain lingered and grew, sprouting again where he thought he could feel no more. Spiders crawled into his skull to lay new webs in new spaces created by beetles. Staf felt his mind go. In a last, desperate effort, he bent an arm at an impossible angle, and reaching behind his leg, stretching to the limit with white grubs emerging from new cracks in his arm, he gripped something wooden, and with every possible ounce of energy, he pulled. He didn't care about anything else; he just pulled with everything he had left. It was impossible to move. A beetle entered his remaining eye. He shook his head to force it out or prevent it from burrowing farther, but he could feel the hairy leg enter the orb, and its shadow blurred his vision. He could feel the beetle in his other eye clamp the side to avoid falling when he shook his head.

The grip released, and he crumpled to the ground on his hands and knees. He opened his eyes and took a deep breath into the void that moments ago had been filled with webs. The pain was gone. His back was normal, his ribs intact. He was looking at the red carpet and could see his twisted form being squeezed in the grip of a wooden mannequin with beetles and spiders scuttling all over his body. And inside too. He didn't need a full brain to realize it was him in the image being eaten from the inside out.

The crystal ball gently rolled up the carpet and disappeared in the dark shadow under the boss. It emerged again and rolled up the side of the wooden mannequin to the top, where it melted into the head.

Staf's breathing was impossibly heavy, harder than it had been in any run he had ever done. He needed to get away. There was no way he was going to get into this trap. He looked at his hands on the red carpet and saw red dye starting to creep up on his hands. In the carpet, he could see other images, the ones he knew were already there.

Staf looked up again. The boss was gone. He was cautiously relieved. The candles flickered and went out, and he could just make out the image of the wooden mannequin left behind. *Damn. It's still there*, he thought. He was transfixed by it. Somehow, this wooden thing had the ability to cause untold pain. He peered closely at it. It didn't move, and Staf decided it was best not to touch it, ever, not even to come close to it. He could use fire to burn it away; he just couldn't touch it. He didn't want to take his eyes off it, just in case it did something unexpected. But it was difficult to see without the candlelight. He squinted, and the mannequin sort of got lost in the shadows, some of which annoyingly started to dance again. Or was it the shadows? Did a finger twitch? He squinted more to try to focus on it with what little light came in through the glass walls of his house. The other arm moved. Damn! But it was slow. *What's going to happen now?* he thought. He saw a leg move, more deliberately this time. He heard a clip as the metal on the end of the foot hit his glass floor. The thing was coming alive. He already knew what would happen if it caught him. His eyes widened, and the horror of what was coming went up his spine again. The second foot came down. Clop. A slightly different sound than the first. His head hurt again at the mere thought of the impending pain.

He got up slowly to sneak away; he didn't want this thing to see him. The next clip came sooner, and then another clop. Then clip–clop, clip-clop. It was coming. Staf lost it in the darkness of the living room. There just wasn't enough light coming through the windows. He heard the clip-clop coming rapidly closer. His heart was pounding again. There was no time.

It lurched forward amazingly quickly. It was wooden, but it was fast. Unnaturally fast. Staf had a large living room, and the thing was at the other end in the corner, almost fifty feet away. Staf was frozen in shock. Five steps, and it was racing toward him. Clip–clop, clip-clop. *Run!* He desperately commanded his legs to run. He heard a swish and knew it was right in front of him reaching down. Staf rolled backward as a wooden limb brushed his hair. Some spiders appeared on his hair, and started running to his face. He rolled back and rose to his feet, and with a slight turn, he ran out of the room, shaking his head and swatting spiders out of his hair and face. The thing immediately lurched forward again. Staf bounded out of the living room into the kitchen. He didn't know where to run; his house suddenly felt like a prison, keeping him in. He needed to get out. It exited the living room right behind him, just one step behind. Staf didn't dare to stop and turn and ran around the island in the kitchen. He could hear the clip-clop keeping pace right behind him. The front door—he had to run to it, get out. Staf reached the door with the thing right behind. There wasn't enough time; it would take too long to actually open the door, and he didn't want to get caught. He made a quick right turn to run around the couch. He heard the mannequin slip on the tiled floor and bump into the door. This gave him an extra foot of leeway. Was the patio door open? He couldn't tell and couldn't remember if he had closed it but decided it was the best way to go. Around the couch, around the table, back toward the kitchen to the patio door. The mannequin took a shortcut at the table, and the glass shattered. It gained a foot on Staf's run to the kitchen. It reached out again. Staf dove for the floor and slid on glass toward the patio door. He felt the wind again from the arm that just missed him, but it missed his hair too, so he was spider free.

The slide gave him an advantage, and Staf regained some distance. He stopped his slide and got up at the door. It was open. He looked back as he went outside. Stray light from outside entered the kitchen patio and windows and made a brief outline of the featureless mannequin. It stood up from the crouch it had adopted while trying to catch the sliding Nurren and lurched forward again. Staf continued his run outside and heard the crash as the mannequin took a shortcut through the kitchen wall, shattering more glass. The backyard was fenced. Staf's only option was to run around the side of the house. The clip-clops were a few feet behind him.

He knew his front door would be unlocked. He opened the large heavy oak door quickly, stepped in, snapped it shut, and locked it. The clip-clops rang off his steps, and it hit the door with a thud.

The door was going to hold, thought Staf, and he decided to hide upstairs. Halfway up the stairs, there was a larger slam into the door. He was upstairs when a third slam splintered the door. *Shit*, he thought. It was inside before he had a chance to hide. Staf walked quietly down the hall, past the first bedroom (too obvious to hide there), and went into the bathroom. He gently closed the door and locked it. He immediately heard the new click clack as it started to climb the stairs. How did it know he was upstairs? It didn't pause at all on the second floor, came to the third, and came straight for his door. Staf was stunned. It seemed to be able seek him out. Staf stood back from the door. There was a loud thump. Staf looked behind. The bathroom door to the second bedroom was open. He was in the door frame when he saw the first bathroom door disintegrate. The mannequin lurched toward him. He slammed the second door shut, which he already knew would only briefly halt this thing.

He needed to get away. Out of the house. He needed to get far away fast. His car. The Ferrari would do fine. He was out of the bedroom, down the hall, and at the stairs when the second bathroom door exploded. Doors were getting easier for it.

Staf didn't bother with the stairs. He jumped from the third floor to the second floor landing. The thing came out of the bedroom. He jumped from the second floor to the first. The thing was at the stairs, running down them. But Staf had created some distance now.

The front door wasn't there, so it was a quick run outside to the car as he reached for his keys. His pant pockets were empty. The keys were inside. His wallet too. He heard the somewhat fainter clip-clop in the house. It was on the second floor coming down. Risk getting the wallet and keys? He needed time to think, to get away. He ran out the driveway to the road. It was clear there, and the streetlights would give him a better view. It would be better to be outside instead of in the close, cramped quarters of his house. His house used to seem roomy and airy. Now it felt constricted.

He ran down the sloping and winding roads toward the Pacific Highway. He turned frequently. He heard the clip-clop as it reached his steps, and then the sound disappeared. The fence and hedges blocked his view of it. Another few steps, and he heard a loud rustle in the hedges. The fence splintered. The thing was heading straight for him. Fear mounted in Staf. This thing was going to run straight to him no matter where he was or what obstacles were in the way.

Blood rushed from his face, his legs felt weak again, and he thought of giving up to see what happened. The wind blew his hair and reminded him of the spiders, beetles, knife, and cracked ribs. He heard the clip-clop again as it reached the road. His legs obeyed quickly, and he sprinted down the road. The clip-clops seemed to fade, and a quick look behind him confirmed that his all-out sprint would outpace this thing. He ran another two blocks and thought about turning straight for the highway. He quickly changed his mind and continued straight, already remembering that this thing made a straight line for him and didn't necessarily follow the road. The distance between them was growing. *This is easy*, thought Staf. He knew he could run all day, and he just needed to outpace this thing. He lost respect for the Boss. He had outsmarted him again.

A curve in the road and it was out of sight, just a faint clip-clop. Then the sound stopped again. *Maybe I am not so smart*, realized Staf. He felt uncomfortable when it was out of sight and running on grass instead of road, rock, or tile so he couldn't hear it.

Staf kept his pace up and decided to keep running away from his home. Thankfully, his home was on the Malibu hillside, and his run was downwards, but he kept a direction basically away from his house, as much of a straight line as he could keep. He reached the ocean highway and proceeded north with the Pacific off to the left. After a moment, he risked a quick look behind. Nothing.

He was now half a mile down the highway from his neighborhood. The slower running had allowed him to keep a pace with easy breathing. He still felt like he could keep this up forever. He stopped and continued to look into the darkness. A shadow came to the road. His heart skipped a little. It was just the headlights of a car creating shadows. Another shadow across the road. It was just a pedestrian. A rustle behind him. He turned but couldn't see anything in the darkness. There was darkness and shadow all around. He had never noticed that much before. Twigs snapped here and there. The sound of the ocean. Cars. People. He scanned around, uncertain which way to go. He looked down the road again, and suddenly it emerged. It was unmistakable. Yes, it was like a shadow when there wasn't much light, but an unmistakable shadow. Staf felt oddly relieved to know where it was and how far away it was. He continued running north on the highway, uncertain what to do or where to go.

He passed the gas station and convenience store.

"Hello, Staf," came a friendly voice. Someone shouted and waved. It was his neighbor, Mrs. Wilson. He waved back and smiled. He was good at faking a nice smile. He continued to run. Mrs. Wilson frowned a bit. Staf just continued to run and smile. He thought he looked perfectly normal, just out for a jog.

He continued down the road. A car beeped at him, and Mrs. Wilson was at his side. Sweet Mrs. Wilson, elderly, good natured, the type of old lady that would always make cookies on Sunday morning and had the best treats for kids at Halloween.

"Good evening, Mr. Nurren. Would you like a ride?" she offered. Staf wondered why she would offer him a ride if he was out for a jog. He was a sprinter, after all. He looked down at his white pants and loafers. Ridiculous running attire. He was sweating profusely again.

In reality, he never jogged. Ever. Certainly never in a white shirt, pants, and loafers. Staf took a quick look behind. He couldn't make out anything. He accepted the offer.

"Oh my," she continued kindly. "I just assumed that you were going home. Is that where you are going?" He had clearly been running in a direction away from home. Sweet old Mrs. Wilson. Sweet, slow, deliberate, patient Mrs. Wilson.

Staf usually avoided her. When he had first built the glass house, they had slowly become friends. This had lead to a terrible afternoon when she felt compelled to talk endlessly about nothing— stuff involving her gardening, and possibly every plant in existence. Somewhere it had diverged into her relatives and friends. Staf had to tune it out just like he used to do in school, and tried not to be rude. After several gentle attempts, he escaped when she waved to another passerby on the road. Staf avoided her at all costs but always said hi, making sure not to stop and be held hostage again.

So while he was in the car, patiently waiting for Mrs. Wilson to start driving, he discreetly looked behind. Nothing. The thing was out of sight again. He squinted to look past some oncoming car lights. There was also some light from the gas station and strip mall.

"Is something the matter, Mr. Nurren?" she asked with concern.

"Oh no, not at all, Mrs. Wilson. Thanks for your concern. It seems that I overextended myself during my jog, and I am keen to get back, change some clothes, and have a nice shower. In fact, it is very fortunate for me that you came along. Thank you."

Mrs. Wilson nodded at him with understanding fidgeted in her seat to get comfortable. She apparently needed to adjust her rearview mirror and gently looked over her shoulder for traffic. She seemed to move in slow motion. Staf felt trapped in the car. They were going nowhere fast. Was this better than being outside? He wasn't so sure. She waited for a car to pass before entering the road. Understandable. It passed quickly, but she didn't make any move. Staf looked behind. There was a car some distance off. Surely she wasn't waiting for that car? She kept looking back. Yes, apparently she was.

Staf resisted the urge to say something. The other car was taking forever to come up the highway. Was it moving at all? It might have been going to the gas station, but there was no turn signal.

Sure enough, the car turned into the gas station. *Shit,* thought Staf. More time went by. He took another look, and there were still no wooden mannequins in sight. But then he caught a shadowy movement from the corner of his eye. Staf stared, and to his horror, he saw that the mannequin was at the gas station, not nearly as far away as he had expected. He instinctively reached for the door handle, ready to move it if there was any more delay. The mannequin held a steady jogging pace, but with molasses Mrs. Wilson beside him, there was not much time left. Slowly, patiently, Mrs. Wilson pulled onto the road. The mannequin reached the trunk of the car, and Staf pulled the door handle slightly. But then the distance increased. It continued running, but the distance increased quickly. They continued to the next entrance to the neighborhood. Staf was relieved. This would give him time at his house to get some things.

"I haven't seen you in a long time," remarked Mrs. Wilson. "What is it that you do again?" she asked kindly.

"I run sprints and marathons. I just finished the Olympics last week," replied Staf with respectful patience.

"Oh yes," she remarked. "Now I remember. Can you actually make money on that? In my day, running was just a pastime. We all had real jobs the rest of the time. How do you like it? Did you have a good year?"

Staf wished he was outside. They had had this conversation before, and this time, he was content to leave his running career unexplained.

"Yes, I did well in a few runs," he said, waiting to see if this registered with her at all.

"Oh, that's nice, as long as you have fun." Clearly, she was focused on driving. Staf decided to keep it safe and talk about the weather. He didn't want to hear about her grandchildren again, or else he might just throw himself at the wooden mannequin. The thought of that horror made him regret the idea as quick as it came.

Mrs. Wilson came to a stop sign. She started to slow down much farther back than Staf thought possible. He thought about getting out and walking to the stop sign to wait for her there. She stopped and slowly looked down one road, then the other, and then back to the first again. It took forever. Staf looked behind again and then reminded himself that this thing took shortcuts; it could be anywhere.

There were three more endless stop sign rituals and the climb up to the hills. She slowed and turned into his driveway.

"That's okay, Mrs. Wilson. Don't trouble yourself; just drop me off at the end of the driveway," Staf quickly said. Too late. She pulled up to his house, and of course noticed the broken front door. People never miss what you don't want them to see.

"Oh dear, Mr. Nurren! Look at your door!" she said. "Is everything okay? Shall I call the police?"

"Oh, it's nothing. I'm just in the middle of some renovations," he said. He could barely get it out, knowing how ridiculous it must seem for him to have been running down the road away from his renovations project in the dark in casual pants and loafers.

He quickly got out, trying to look normal, and with a quick thank you, he ran into the house, leaving Mrs. Wilson stunned in the driveway with a mild frown on her face. She sat there for two minutes and then slowly backed out and drove next door to her house.

Staf ran past the living room, ignoring the shattered glass table. He also ignored the big hole in his kitchen wall. The lights were on again, and the kitchen clock was making its familiar noise. He sprang upstairs and got a suitcase. He threw some things into it. He remembered not to leave his keys this time and ran downstairs and put them in his pocket. He ran up again and put another shirt in the suitcase. He then realized that he could just get his wallet and buy everything as needed and ran downstairs again and picked up his wallet. He lost track of time, and as he went back upstairs, he tried to remember how long he had been there. How much time until the mannequin arrived? He wasn't sure. He stopped for a second and tried to calm himself down.

Okay, think, he said to himself, *You have some time. Instead of running up and down the stairs, just get what you need. Keys, wallet— that's all you need. Hmmm, anything else?* He went to the bathroom, still thinking, and then remembered that his phone was down on the living room table. He ran down for the third time and searched among the broken glass for his phone. He had wasted enough time now running stairs and really not accomplishing much. He couldn't find his phone. Finally, as a last resort, he looked under the sofa and caught sight of it. He stretched, but it was out of reach, so he ran to the other side, and then he heard it. A faint clip-clop. It was just down the road. Staf's heart raced. He grabbed the phone. Clip-clop. It was very clear, almost at his driveway. He had to run. Wait. He needed to get his Olympic medals. At least one. He wasn't going to abandon his house without them. Clip-clop. Maybe it wasn't that close. Clip-clop. He ran to the stairs. Clip-clop. It sounded impossibly close. He was right; it came running through the door. Staf ran up the stairs, turned left, and entered his room. The mannequin came through the door, blindly went straight up the stairs, and made the same immediate left turn. Staf ran into the room, passed the night stand, and grabbed his most recent Olympic medal. He hoped that the patio door was open. It wasn't. He crashed through it at full speed and stumbled onto the balcony. Something hurt, but he didn't dare stop; he knew the mannequin was right behind him. He ran along the balcony to the stairs but jumped to the ground instead of taking them. The mannequin crashed through more glass above. Staf paused for a moment too long. Should he go to the car or run down the street? The mannequin was at the stairs. Staf ran toward the car. The mannequin was just coming around the corner after him. Staf had his key out before he reached the car and tried to put it in the door. It took a second too long, because his hand was shaking, and he tried to turn the key too soon. His impatience cost him. The mannequin was jogging around the car and reaching out to him. Staf left the half-entered keys and ran down the driveway to the street. He ran a block. He had a plan. He couldn't be caught unless he let it. He could easily outrun it.

He could hear the distance growing again, the clip-clop getting fainter. He turned and ran straight toward the sound. He was looking at it, studying it as he ran toward it. It was featureless, smooth—no face, no eyes, no mouth. It seemed to have a perfect running form. Staf sped up toward it. They were closing fast. Two quick steps to go, and it reached out. Staf leaped into the air, did a somersault, landed behind the mannequin, and continued running. He heard the clip-clop behind him slow to a stop and start again, indicating that it had turned. A quick look behind told him he had enough time to get his car going. He entered the driveway and reached the car. He calmly slid the key in and opened the door. He quickly but calmly closed the door and started the car. He slammed it into reverse and gunned it. It squealed tremendously in his driveway, and accelerated backward. He sped out of the driveway just as the mannequin approached. It slammed into the rear of car. Staf was looking back and saw it happen, but the result took him by surprise. The mannequin didn't break stride. The car slammed into it, stopping instantly. The rear crumpled. The front of the car flew up on impact, and at the same time, it arced sideways in a circle from the off-center impact. The 1961 Ferrari Spyder slammed into the road with the left wheels first but remained upright and was clear of the driveway. Staf looked left to see the mannequin a few feet away, starting the run toward him. He slammed the car into gear and sped away as the mannequin's hand reached the door. It scraped along the side of the car as it drove away. Staf sped down a few blocks, turning as he had done earlier when he was running. He passed several cars. One was a police car. Just before reaching the highway, the police car appeared in his rearview mirror with the lights flashing. Staf weighed his immediate options. He was obviously speeding, and he didn't know how much damage had been done to his car. He was sure this was going to take too long. He figured he had five minutes. The officer remained in the car for a moment. He wondered why the police were even in this area and then realized that Mrs. Wilson must have called them after seeing his front door.

A minute had passed. There was no sign of the mannequin yet. Staf looked in the rearview mirror. He turned and looked back just to be sure he hadn't missed anything.

The rear of the Ferrari was a wreck. Staf wasn't as bothered by that as he should have been; he had something else to worry about, but he knew he was going to be upset about it later.

The door of the police car opened, and the officer stepped out. He slowly ambled to the Ferrari. Staf couldn't believe how slow he was going, Mrs. Wilson could embarrass him. What to say about the speed, the damage, and the door to his house. As he neared the Ferrari, a flashlight came on, aimed at Staf's face.

"Good evening, Mr. Nurren," said the officer artificially kindly, and then he added sarcastically, "In a hurry this evening?"

"No, sir," said Staf patiently. "Just some excitement left over from the Olympics." He gave the officer a large, innocent smile.

"Have you been drinking?" Staf knew he was in a corner now. There would be a speeding ticket, a breathalyzer, more questions. This was going to take too much time. Time that he couldn't afford.

"No sir, not at all," he replied. "I was just going to … get some gas."

The officer looked at the gas gauge. It was full.

"Please step out of the car," he ordered firmly. Staf promptly obeyed.

"Follow me," the officer commanded sternly, and he walked to his car while speaking into a microphone attached to his shoulder. At the cruiser, he turned and said, "Mr. Nurren, I am going to have to ask you to …" Staf was nowhere in sight.

As the officer stood, scanning the area, shaking his head, a brief wind passed behind him. He turned for a quick look and found nothing again.

Staf was running. He took the same route north on the Pacific Coast Highway. For the second time, he ran past the gas station, and then he continued. He passed the second intersection into his neighborhood but kept running. He didn't want to go back to his house. The police were going to hunt him.

He looked back every few minutes for assurance, but he never stopped running. He settled into a comfortable pace and collected his thoughts. He relaxed for a moment, knowing that this thing could never catch up to him. But he wondered what he was going to do about this. He felt confident that he could always outrun this thing. But he felt some gnawing dread. What was it the boss said to him? Unstoppable? Did that mean it wouldn't stop? No end? The realization hit him like the crash in the Ferrari. He would have to keep running. That's what he did best. But that was the last thing he wanted to do right now as he ran north to nowhere in the lonely night.

Jake stood at the kitchen counter, pouring a strong morning coffee. He was frustrated, as usual, with Staf. Always hanging up, always on the run, no time for anyone or anything. He briefly thought about quitting again. But it had been a good few years and had allowed him to escape his father's influence. He would stick around. But what was this about quitting? What had happened? He figured Staf had had too much to drink.

Jake decided he was going to wait before calling sponsors back. Staf always changed his mind; you never knew what he was going to do next. That's why last night's phone call hadn't caused Jake to lose any sleep. Besides, he had enough money anyway; it wasn't the job he was worried about. He was a perfectionist and always did the best he could. It had been easy enough the last few years. The contracts and endorsements came from all directions and were easy enough to sign. Hiring help for reviewing the contracts was straightforward. And the amounts just kept going up. Always short-term contracts, no more than a year, and so there were always new endorsements to sign.

As he stood at the counter, sorting his thoughts, the phone rang. Jake had a special knack for knowing which friend was calling before answering the phone. This was a stranger.

He took a casual sip of his coffee. He was still in his pajamas, and somehow, he found it tough to talk business in this attire, even at home.

Jake listened carefully and could only repeat no several times, and he ended with an "of course." It was the L.A. police. Staf had gotten into some trouble, his home was a wreck, and he had badly damaged his prized Ferrari. A warrant was out for his arrest on possible impaired driving charges, and he had run from the police. This seemed a little more serious than the usual antics. Staf kept his house immaculate, his car was one of his prized possessions next to his Olympic medals, and he absolutely never drove impaired. Jake ran up the stairs, changed, and went out the door. He needed to go to Staf's house and see for himself.

Jake was around the corner from Staf's house when it struck him to call Staf's cell. He was, after all, just one of the few to have Staf's number. He dialed it, and it went straight to voicemail. *Odd*, thought Jake, *Staf is always available on his cell*. He turned up the gentle hill into the Malibu neighborhood, and after some stops and turns came into Staf's driveway. Then he saw what the police were talking about. The front door was in ruins, with splintered wood strewn about the step. A pair of long tire tracks marked the spot where a car had rushed out of the driveway. Some black debris and glass indicated where the familiar black car had struck something. But what? And judging by the amount of debris, it had hit something hard and fast.

The police were at the hedges talking to Mrs. Wilson. She was a nice lady, Jake thought, sort of always watching out for Staf and the neighborhood in general. He started to walk over to the hedge, but the officer motioned him to wait, presumably while he finished the interview. Jake decided to look around the yard a bit more, conscious of the officer's occasional glance; he no doubt wanted to make sure that nothing was disturbed. Jake decided not to wander too far and went near the front door to have a brief look. It was completely shattered, as if from an explosion. The hinges, with a little wood, were still in place. The rest of the door was in tiny shards, just a few inches long. But there was no sign of an explosion, and it would have been too much effort to chop it all up.

He peered inside and saw glass everywhere, which he should have expected considering the state of the front door and the fact it was basically a glass house. He could make out the shattered glass coffee table and two holes in the kitchen wall. This seemed like more serious trouble than what Staf usually got into. It was very odd.

"And you are?" came a stern voice from behind. Jake whirled around to find the officer behind him.

"Jake Johnson," he said quickly, and then seeing that this meant nothing, he added, "Staf's lawyer and agent."

The officer registered mild recognition and remained very serious as he wrote something on a notepad. Jake noted that Mrs. Wilson watched intently from the hedge, mildly pulling at the hedges as if she were doing some normal gardening. Her intense, frequent looks gave her away, as did the immaculate condition of the hedges, which did not require any attention.

"Do you know where Mr. Nurren is?" asked the officer. The officer's badge gave his name as Johnston.

"No, not at all," promptly replied Jake. "What happened here?"

The officer ignored his question. "And you don't know where he might be heading?"

"No, not at all," replied Jake again and decided he'd better change his answers a bit to at least sound like there might be some thought. But he was worried about Staf and what might have happened to him.

"Where were you last night? Did you come by here at all during the evening?"

Jake related how he had come by in the late afternoon for the traditional Olympics party and how everything seemed normal. He gave a quick list of some of the people he knew were there. This seemed to satisfy the officer, as he had probably determined from the way the answers were delivered that Jake was not privy to what had happened and had answered honestly. Jake didn't bother to ask again what had happened. He realized he was not going to get any answers. The officer did ask if Staf had been drinking.

"I think so," said Jake quickly. Usually Staf did have some drinks at his parties, and most of the guests did too. Jake tried to recall his short visit the previous afternoon, but he couldn't particularly remember if Staf had a drink. It was such a normal thing, one didn't pay attention to that detail. Jake quickly added, "Come to think of it, I don't recall at all." The officer looked at him suspiciously. Jake hated talking to cops. He always felt that his answers sounded incriminating, even as a lawyer.

"Well, if you remember anything—anything at all—you can contact me at the precinct. I assume that you will direct Staf to us *when* he gets in touch with you?" directed the officer, not really asking a question.

"Of course," answered Jake, and he gave a friendly smile to show sincerity, although he wasn't sure why; the situation did not require any friendliness, and he didn't need to make a friend out of this cop. He did catch the emphasis on *when*, indicating that the cop knew he was going to be in touch with Staf sometime.

Jake took another look into the house.

"That will be all," indicated the officer, implying that Jake should move away from the door. He took the hint and went over to the hedge to Mrs. Wilson. She saw him come and quickly tried to look busy on the perfect hedges. She didn't smile her usual friendly smile. Instead, she just looked like someone with lips curved up on the ends.

"What the …" Jake paused to keep his language respectful. "Um, what on earth happened here last night? I came by at about three, and everything seemed all right. It looks like a disaster."

"Well," replied Mrs. Wilson, and Jake knew he was in for a story, "I don't know what time you left at"—Jake knew this was a lie; she knew what time everybody came and left—"but into the evening, things really got out of control. The music was loud, and there was lots of shouting and screaming, you know the way Staf's parties usually go." Jake nodded in understanding. This was the old, excitable Mrs. Wilson talking. Jake knew very well that these get-togethers were relatively mild—lots of people, some music. But Staf had particularly chosen this location for his house because of the privacy he could have and give his neighbors. Jake had helped him pick out the place. There could be very little that would disturb neighbors as far away as Mrs. Wilson's house. Then again, there was quite some damage to Nurren's house. But he needed to hear the rest and figure out what happened between the lines.

"I had to go to the store just to get away from all that racket," continued Mrs. Wilson. Jake recalled his short phone call of last night. It had seemed pretty quiet to him at the time.

"While I was at the store, I saw Mr. Nurren going for a jog down the Pacific Highway." Now this caught Jake's attention. Staf never went jogging. He was too lazy.

"Yes," nodded Jake in understanding, showing Mrs. Wilson that he was listening very closely and trying not to show his shock that Staf would be out for a jog. He wondered what part of this story might be an exaggeration.

Mrs. Wilson continued. "But he just wasn't himself. He was dressed up in those nice clothes that he wears, and he was always looking around suspiciously, like he was being followed. I was very worried for him. Now, Mr. Johnson—oh, did you know that the officer there has almost the same last name as you?" She was going off topic. This was going to be a long talk. Jake started to tune out some of the excess and tried to piece together in his mind what might have happened. Someone had been chasing Staf, he had run away, and then he had come back to get some things and taken off again.

"… and that's when I got worried and called the police," said Mrs. Wilson. Somehow, this was connected with Staf wanting to quit running. Quit running, and then go for a jog? Trash the rare Ferrari? Something very serious was going on. He wondered how it was related to their trip to the flea market almost exactly thirteen years ago.

"And then I heard the car start, a big squeal, and then a big crash. I saw his fancy car fly through the air and parts go flying everywhere.

And then he just drove off. Funny thing though, it didn't look like he hit anything. There was nothing there," said Mrs. Wilson.

Jake was at a loss. He slowly walked to his car. Halfway down on the other side of the driveway, the hedge looked ruffled, beat up. Something had torn through there. An intruder, speculated Jake. He was fairly certain someone or *something* was chasing Staf. He got in his car and turned out of the driveway, and his phone rang.

"Hello, Staf," he said, not needing to see the number.

Staf had run blindly up the road all night. His thoughts were a jumbled mess. After an hour of running with wild thoughts and frequent looks behind him, he settled down and tried to figure out what had happened and what to do. By his estimate, he had put about a mile between him and the mannequin. That should give him some time. This thing was going to chase him. For how long? Forever, Staf figured. This was an evil creation. He would never be able to stop for long. He could never run competitively again. And that was ironic, considering he would not be able to stop running. He thought about it again. He would never be able to run again. It had hurt him to say it to Jake last night, and he stumbled a bit at the thought now and then regained his composure and continued running. He would have to stop for a bite somewhere and make a call. *A call. That's it!*

He took out his phone and waited for the screen to pop up. It didn't. *Shit.* Did the phone work? He pressed the red button to turn it on. It came on, told him his battery was low, and before he could make the call, it was off again. He would have to charge it or use a pay phone. He ran for two more hours and created some plans. He might be able to rent a car to get some distance. Taking a flight would put some long and quick distance between them, but there was probably a warrant out for an arrest. Would airport security be on the lookout for passengers with traffic violations? Maybe not. If he took a boat ride, could it follow him in the water? He needed to put all this to some tests.

There was no sign of the mannequin behind him. The red sky suggested the start of a new day. It reminded Staf of the red carpet.

The sun peeked over the horizon like a volcanic red eye of rage. It was already starting to get hot. Staf hated the color red right now. It was early morning. He hadn't slept. The thought suddenly made him tired. Cars started to show up on the highway with increased frequency. Someone pulled over and gave him a ride to Ventura, where he found a greasy spoon. It was quiet, with a few morning customers trying to jumpstart their morning with coffee and breakfast.

Staf found a stool at the counter and quickly placed an order with the bored middle-aged waitress. Average height, average weight, average looks. Just a typical, anonymous waitress. He looked at his phone as if to verify that it didn't have a charge and then spotted a pay phone. He took out his wallet. No change. In fact, his wallet was empty. He never used money, only credit and debit cards. He went to the waitress.

"Can I use the phone?" he asked.

"The pay phone is over there." She pointed impatiently while loudly chewing her gum.

"I see that," he said. "I don't have any change. Can I—"

"We don't make change for phone calls."

"Fine," said Staf. "Can I use your company phone? It's an emergency."

"Sure it is," she replied dryly, squishing the gum in her mouth loudly while talking. "The company phone is not for public use." She had probably recited it innumerable times. Staf was agitated.

"Look, I'll give you twenty bucks if you let me use your phone for a minute." She studied him patiently, still chewing her gum loudly, which was starting to really irritate Staf.

"Sure," she said and stood there. Staf looked at her for a moment. Then it hit him. He reached into his wallet. No money, of course. He looked up sheepishly, then slowly drew out his credit card and presented it to her like a bouquet of flowers. She looked at him blankly. He wasn't going to get the phone.

Staf groaned.

"Where is the nearest bank machine?" He didn't bother to offer an IOU.

"Go right at the lights." She pointed out the window. "It's five minutes down the road." She dumped his breakfast on the counter in front of him and walked away. Staf thought for a moment, developed a plan, and wolfed down the breakfast. Then another thought occurred. He could just use the credit card for an operator-assisted call. He raced over and made the call to Jake, who picked it up in half a ring.

"Hello, Staf."

"How the hell do you know it's me all the time?" But there were more important things to talk about.

Staf was finished at the diner and took advantage of the free refills of coffee. He was hoping to annoy the gum-chewing waitress, but maybe she sensed this, and she kept his mug full before he could call her over. He had already paid for breakfast.

He was going to meet Jake in Ventura at a little park by the sea in one hour. Lots of time, thought Staf. He ordered a taxi and kept a constant watch out the back of the car. He was beginning to wonder if the mannequin had already expired.

He took the cab to the park and waited at the appointed place. Jake arrived a short while later and came up from behind him with more coffee and some pastries.

"Staf, you look like shit," he said and sat on the bench beside him, looking out at the Pacific. "What have you got yourself into this time?"

Staf sighed. He had tried to tell him things as they occurred over the years but had never been able to show anything concrete except his ability to run phenomenally fast.

He related the events of the previous night and how they tied in to the events from the flea market years ago. Jake listened patiently, like a therapist, nodding every once in a while.

"Hmm," said Jake. "Demons, magic, potions, thirteen years of running, and unstoppable wooden mannequins out to send you to hell? And you are not running right now, I mean at this precise moment, so I take it we are going to wait here until it arrives."

There was a short silence. The Pacific beat therapeutically against the shore. Birds hovered peacefully in the sun and light wind. A few people walked casually down by the shore.

"Sounds like a golem."

"A who?"

"A golem. An inanimate object that is brought to life by an incantation, inscription, magic spell, or whatever else you want to call it. One story has it that Adam, from Genesis, was made by God from mud or clay and given life. He would be sort of golemlike. That changed when he ate from the tree of knowledge. I think there was a story of an old rabbi in Prague who put a word on the forehead of a mud man. The golem obeyed his orders in defending the ghettos. You might say that voodoo spells that possess the dead are the same. Are they called zombies? Dracula and his minions, because they are supposed to be dead. Or undead. You might even go so far as to say robots are golem-like. And androids too, until they become sentient if their AI develops far enough. If you say this stick is chasing you, well, golem might be one way to define it. They have really come along too, with various adaptations in games like *Dungeons and Dragons* and *Heroes of Might and Magic*. Frankenstein—"

"I get it," groaned Staf.

They sipped their coffees. Then Jake broke the silence.

"You could even say that Pinocchio was a type of golem. An inanimate thing, running around hoping to become a real boy. Pinocchio was made of wood too. You are sort of being chased around by Pinocchio." Jake laughed. Staf did not.

They sipped coffee again.

A few minutes later, Staf broke the silence.

"Let's head out to your car."

Jake took the hint. It was getting close. He was sort of interested in seeing this thing and didn't know whether to hope it was really there, or to hope it wasn't so that he could continue with the sponsors. Either one would be interesting, though the latter would be better, of course.

They stood beside Jake's Porsche. Staf admired it and missed his Ferrari.

"Look, if I don't get a chance to get in the car, I'll head northbound ... no wait, I'll go south toward L.A. along the Ventura Freeway. Come pick me up; it will only be after me."

"Where do you want to go then? And remember, I'm a lawyer; I am supposed to advise you to turn yourself in. I could get disbarred for helping you."

"I think I'll head to the airport and fly out somewhere, anywhere. Maybe New York, maybe overseas, Europe, somewhere far from here. And can I borrow your phone? Mine's out of charge." Jake hesitantly tossed it to him.

Staf looked down the road. He saw a faint glimmer approaching in the distance, fading in and out among the cars. It was getting larger.

"And there he is," said Staf, "right on time."

Jake looked down the road, shielding his eyes from the sun with his hand. "I've got nothing," said Jake expectantly.

Staf kept his eyes on the horizon and watched the figure slowly get larger. He thought he could almost start hearing the clip-clop, but that was just in his mind. The thought of it started to make him nervous. He studied it in silence, watching the constant pace. It was an ugly thing. Plain. A featureless wooden head. No eyes, nose, or mouth. *It could look so much better with even just a little hair*, thought Staf. Constant stride. There was a break in traffic, and he could just faintly hear the clip-clop.

"There! Just beside that driveway a mile down the road." Jake followed Staf's outstretched arm but saw nothing.

There was no doubt to Staf that if it did have eyes, they were looking at him. Its movements were very smooth, deliberate, constant. It was about thirty seconds away.

"Is you car unlocked?" asked Staf, anxiety in his voice.

The thin silence was broken by a faint click from Jake's keyless entry. Jake was wondering about his friend, but the timing and the pausing seemed so deliberate, his friend must be seeing something. He wanted to see it too.

"Twenty seconds to go," Staf said to Jake. "It should be plain to see, one driveway away, right side of the road, next to the blue Ford right now."

Jake still saw nothing. He was straining hard to find something, like blowing dust. Then Staf got an idea and he reached down and stood up.

"Watch this," he said and threw a rock. The rock held a smooth arc and abruptly stopped midair and bounced to the side.

"I saw that," said Jake. "It almost looked like it might have hit something." Staf was annoyed. Almost? He bent down again. His heart was pounding now, his breathing already heavy, sweat starting to form.

"Can you hear it now?" Clip-clop. It was dangerously close. He thought about last night. Staf was ready to run.

"Five seconds!" He hollered. Jake still saw nothing. Suddenly, in a surprise to Jake, Staf threw up a handful of sand and bolted. Jake saw the spray of sand go into the air, and then a gust of wind scatter it, some of which went into Jakes eyes. Jake turned his head, eyes stinging from sand. But had there been a split-second outline of something in the sand? For a second, it had made a brief outline of something looking like what Staf had described as a wooden stick with arms and legs. Skinny. Small head. A person's height. Just for a second. If he had looked at it any other time, it would have just been some sand blowing around. Jake had seen something and felt a rush of wind go by on a calm day. Or was he just looking too hard? He cleared his eyes after a moment and looked around. Staf was gone. The air was still. He got into his car and headed south.

He found Staf a mile up the road. He didn't pass anything else. He pulled over, and Staf jumped in immediately.

"Did you see it?" He said expectantly.

"I don't know," said Jake honestly. "I might have seen something in the sand that you threw up. I just don't know, but there was an odd wind." It was too hard to ignore what he saw, and Jake was generally open to abnormal possibilities.

"Man oh man Staf, what have you gotten into now?"

They drove toward L.A. in silence for several minutes.

"Where is it now?"

"It should be about ten minutes behind us. I wonder if I can get to the airport and catch a flight out. Hey! How about we just charter a plane?"

"*We* don't need to charter anything, but maybe *you* do." Staf made some quick arrangements with the local FBO, and a small jet would be ready in an hour. This would take a lot of variables out of the way—checking in, boarding delays. And he could get to New York and have a few days of peace while figuring out what to do.

They were a few minutes from the airport. He gave them a quick call and absently returned the phone to Jake. Everything was ready to go. Jake stopped at the front of the hangar office, and Staf shot out of the car.

"Thanks, Jake," he said quickly and paused. Without turning, he quietly said, "Can you look into fixing up my car and house? That accident last night was a shame. It hurts just to think about it."

Jake made the promise as he leaned on his Porsche. He watched Staf run into the office, show some identification, and hurry out the front to a waiting jet. One engine was already running.

The door closed, the second engine was quickly started, and the small jet taxied away. Jake watched it line up, take off, and climb out of sight. He sighed and took a moment to figure out what to do. He reached for his phone, and made some calls while driving home.

He was busy in his den for several hours making various phone calls, and then he went about his home life. He was now waiting for a call. It came three hours later, an unknown number.

"Hello, Staf," answered Jake. Someone shouted "Piss off" and then "thanks" in the earpiece. Jake laughed.

Staf arrived in Teterboro in the late afternoon. He had a good sound sleep on the plane and felt refreshed. But it was equally good to get out of the plane. He suddenly felt claustrophobic in small, sealed spaces. *Two days*, he thought, *two days before it arrives, unless it flies too.* But he doubted that.

He got off the plane, and there was a limousine waiting for him. A ramp attendant handed him a package as he got into the car. The door was closed, and they left the airport.

The limo driver was used to picking up important people and had very little patience for their arrogance. He expected the worst from Staf and wasn't disappointed. The driver picked him up right at the plane on time with packages waiting, and the first thing this guy did was call the guy who arranged all this and tell him to piss off. He rolled his eyes, raised the divider between sections, and drove him to the Waldorf Astoria in silence. When Staf arrived, he was escorted to his suite by the porter, who handed him the keys. The papers had already been taken care of, of course. He searched the phone book and made a call. An hour later, there was a knock at the door. It was not a lonely night.

Staf woke up the second day. He was alone. His escort had slipped out during the night, which was how he preferred it. Better than having some sort of awkward good-bye and stupid small talk. He made a mental note of her name so that he could request her specifically.

This was the day that Staf expected the wooden golem to arrive sometime in the evening. He hadn't bothered to calculate the time.

The phone rang. He predicted it was Jake.

"Hello, Jake," answered Staf confidently. He was lucky it was. But it was an empty guess; only Jake and the front counter knew he was here.

"Yo Staf," was the response. "I think you are going to have company later today? Your car is downstairs, coffee is waiting, plane is at Teterboro. Gulfstream IV. Let me know where you want to go. I told them Switzerland for now. Change it if you like."

Staf was embarrassed. He himself should have been proactive in this challenge. Although he paid him well, he knew that Jake's firm did a lot more for a lot less than they had to. He felt guilty. He would be penniless already if it weren't for Jake's smart handling.

"Ah, Switzerland. Shit, Jake, why don't you come meet me there? Bring the family." He regretted the words as soon as he said them. They sounded lonely and empty.

"I don't think so, Staf. We are a little busy here. You just keep your phone and charger handy, pal. Give me a yodel from the Alps."

Staf groaned. A trip to the Alps. Jake's firm was like a travel agency now. Staf knew he had a lot of money, but he had no clue exactly how much. Only Jake did. But Staf trusted him. This next little while was going to cost him a lot of money. At least Switzerland sounded like fun.

Jake was sitting in his den again. The kids were asleep. He had told Jenn everything. She laughed at Staf's antics. He had promised to come up to bed when he got the phone call. He sat back and reflected on how things had turned out for him. He had the most beautiful wife and lovely kids. His firm was unbelievably successful; with Staf's reputation, his was one of the most sought-after agencies in the country. They were set for life based on his friend's endorsements, contracts, and reputation. And his escape from his father's influence had been easier than he had expected, because of Staf's contracts.

When he had first graduated from law school, his father had attempted to influence his career. Jake received sudden offers from the most prominent firms in the state. He declined them all and created his own practice in an anonymous office downtown. He knew his father wanted him to succeed with his help. His father had developed a tremendous reputation. The only thing his father needed to cap his career was a successful son. With a successful son, he could ascend to the next level, like in a video game. Jake wanted no part of it, even though his practice struggled as a result.

The deal with Staf had allowed him to squeeze out from under his father's thumb.

Oddly, he had stuck to their original handshake, a fee rate that was slightly higher than average. Nothing was signed on paper.

Other athletes, complete strangers, only paid half of what he charged Staf.

He didn't need to worry about anything. And Jenn gave him lots of leeway in dealing with Staf.

Things had turned out very well for Jake. He considered himself to be helping a friend with this problem, not a client.

It was easy to deal with marketers, endorsements (for which he was authorized to sign), and any contracts. It struck him how ridiculous the money was around him, and he laughed out loud, because he knew Staf had no idea how much money he had. Good thing he was considered family. Jake felt haunted by that image in the sand, and the wind it had created as it passed. What Jake had ignored was the shot of evil he had also sensed, which had made his hair stand up and made one breath of air taste foul.

Chapter 17: Shattering Invisible Barriers: Jake's Story II

As Jake sat in his den alone, he felt that a new direction was developing in his life. Things were not going to return to the way they had been. He recalled another event, long ago, that had changed his direction. If his life could be represented by diverging rows of dominos, it was as if one row had fallen and he had started a new path.

It had happened a long time ago, when he was ten and delivering newspapers on a typical summer afternoon. The weather was hot, dry, and clear, and he went about his daily task in the usual fashion, glad to have a diversion. He was very responsible, which showed in his dedication, consistency, and determination to deliver newspapers to perfection. He was never late and never missed a house. His motto was like the post office's—rain or shine. But he was also very shy and preferred not to get noticed. He was like his dog when he did something bad; he became quiet and looked away; if he didn't see them, then they couldn't see him.

So on a routine day delivering routine papers at the routine time in routine weather, he turned the corner on his way to the first house and saw a peculiar scene. A bus was pulled over to the side with a car parked awkwardly behind it. This was unusual, because buses never stopped for long in that neighborhood, and cars never parked on the side of this street. He started to imagine the possibilities, and it seemed exciting for a Tuesday afternoon; anything would be a nice diversion.

His first thought, of course, was that the bus had broken down and people were going to be late for work and important appointments. He had a good imagination, and his mind began to wander ridiculously, culminating in the end of the world.

Or the bus and car might have had a little fender bender (boring). He tried to make it sound exciting; there might be a cut, some bruises, and maybe an argument. But the world would remain intact.

He was getting closer and could make out a small crowd of adults in front of the bus. But it was very quiet for such a large group, and that was odd and very interesting. He walked up slowly, hoping to hear something useful, maybe even catch some shouting and swearing. Everyone was eerily quiet. The silence hung so thick it seemed to sort of shade out the sun. A pall was over the group. He couldn't help but stop.

Someone noiselessly whisked past him carrying something (was it a blanket?) and melted into the quiet circle. Jake was on the outside of the circle, unable to find space to sneak through. He tried to look into the narrow gaps between arms and legs, under bodies, and over heads (he was tall for his age) but could not see through them. Another new bystander must have asked his question, and an explanation came from an elderly lady with a somber expression who turned slightly to face them and talked in a whisper.

As the bus stopped to drop someone off, a young girl had seized the opportunity to run across the road and was hit by a car coming the other way. He scanned the faces to see if there was anyone he knew. Somewhere in the small mass, he caught sight of a uniform and recognized the distressed bus driver. He was drawn a little closer to the crowd.

An old, heavy man stood up breathing heavily with a serious look on his face. Another man spoke, almost a whisper, but it rang like an urgent and desperate shout among the somber group.

"She lives at 112 Fallbrook! Someone has to go there quickly and get her parents!"

Everyone looked around. *The key word was quickly. Jake looked around the adult crowd. One young man looked fast, but his suit and loafers would hold him up. There was a woman who could probably do it except for the obvious high heels, hair, and the effect running would have on her make-up (it could cause the end of the world). Everyone was dressed for work or too old or just plain too clean. He searched harder.*

Others did too. More than a few eyes fell his way. Gradually, all eyes turned to him.

Silence.

It was obvious—he was the best, maybe the only candidate. He decided to volunteer. It was an easy decision to make, and simple too. He was ready to speak up; he was obligated to. Everyone expected him to. He just needed to say it.

But he was scared for some reason. Kids don't speak out among adults. Kids are dumb; they don't take on responsibility. But this was an obvious exception.

Suddenly, he heard an inner voice: *Wait a minute. This could be risky and embarrassing. Think about it. What if you forget the house number? What if it's the wrong house? What will you say when the door opens? Probably something stupid and embarrassing like, "Excuse me, sir, I think it might be your daughter who is about to die down the road over there," or "Hello, ma'am, do you have a daughter who just got hit by that car?" How would you deal with a furious dad or hysterical mom? What if they blame you? People like to blame the person who brings bad news. That's why they usually have adults take on this sort of task. They might tell everyone, "There's the boy who delivers bad news. Don't let him deliver to your house." Screw this up, and you could screw up the paper route and your whole future. Keep your mouth shut and don't embarrass yourself!*

He was in turmoil from wanting to do the right thing and being afraid to do it. He knew exactly where the house was and could run there in a minute even with all his papers. He always delivered his papers as early as possible in the summer. It allowed for contingencies just like this. He had lots of time. There was no reason not to go.

His inner voice continued. Don't you dare! Don't be naïve and don't be stupid. This is a job for a smart adult, not a dumb boy. Besides, the girl has to be okay. She was able to give her address, so she's just fine. The traffic around here is so slow, no one could possibly get hurt. Adults are always overly cautious where little girls are concerned. Keep your mouth shut and don't embarrass yourself!

He could see the house in his mind. He didn't know the occupants, but he knew the area very well, as any responsible paperboy would. One small minute of his time would be nothing. He wanted to help. The crowd was waiting for him to step forward. His heart raced, and he took a deep breath. His heart was pushing the words up his chest and throat. Everyone continued to stare at him and sensed his words coming.

The heat accentuated the agonizing silence. The group's silence seemed to block out the sun somehow, but he felt like there was a spotlight on him. He was beginning to feel like a small, cornered animal with no options left. He didn't know anymore if he was going to volunteer or be appointed. It was so obvious that he had to go, it seemed like there was no need to say anything.

The quiet hung, teetering like a large, delicately thin pane of glass; a small pebble could easily have shattered it. Everyone held their breath. Even the birds and crickets stopped chirping and looked at him.

His tongue felt thick and disobedient. His jaw opened while the lips somehow stayed shut. Time stopped. His knees felt weak, and he started to feel like he couldn't stand anymore.

Suddenly, without his permission, his eyes looked away.

A reluctant saint immediately cast the pebble, shattering the moment.

"I'll go," said the old, large, heavily breathing man, and off he went. His slow pace was noble.

The same words were sitting on Jake's lips and hung there like spittle, ready but still hanging on. *Why didn't that old man wait a moment and let you volunteer? If only he had waited another second so you could have volunteered instead. He might never make it either if he hurts himself on the way.*

But Jake had taken too long. He probably would never have said anything no matter how much time there had been. *Well, too bad no one had the courage to suggest you do it.*

He wanted to agree. They should be blamed. They were old enough, experienced enough, and mature enough to speak up in a group. They should have said something. He tried to feel better.

But something felt wrong. He was mad at his tongue and lips. His heart did not feel well, and sank away in the corner of his chest; it would have left him if it could.

He wanted to wait, to see the ambulance and see the parents arrive, but he had to get away from here. His papers needed to be delivered on time or early, preferably the latter.

He left the scene as slowly and deliberately as he had come. Maybe a little faster to make up time, escape the eyes, or put the scene behind him. He couldn't remember which. As he left, the crescendo wail of the approaching ambulance echoed his bottled feelings inside. Everything else was still and silent.

He was with Staf and his neighborhood friends the next day. Chris told them about the accident and that a little girl from their neighborhood had died. He pretended not to know about it. Chris was usually wrong anyway.

His parents broke the silence during dinner to talk about it. No one knew he was there.

Did her parents make it in time? He didn't want to know and never found out.

He gave up the paper route the next day.

He quickly forgot the day and absolved himself, but occasionally something brought it back.

Years later, he came across a poem by Robert Frost, and wondered if the road less traveled would have made a difference. What is the value of the last seconds of life between a parent and dying child? *Certainly more than on-time newspapers.* Perhaps a frightened young girl looking up at a mob of giants would then have been able to depart with parental love, comfort, and security. He suppressed that thought.

Thus a domino fell and started a different path for Jake, and the last domino fell for someone else.

It had changed his life forever. He would always step forward when someone needed his help. That's when he had chosen to become a lawyer, despite his father.

It was another of many reasons he felt obligated to help Staf.

Staf jumped in and out of the shower, grabbed his few things, and left the hotel room. He was about to enter the elevator but stopped as he put a foot in and decided to take the stairs instead. Something about small spaces didn't sit well with him.

There were no bags, to the disappointment of the porter, who was hoping for a generous tip, and as Staf strolled through the atrium, someone recognized him. He wasn't used to this. In his neighborhood, most people left him alone, and he kept a low profile among other celebrities. It was a young boy, and he ran over with big, wonderful eyes.

"Aren't you Staf Nurren?" he asked innocently.

"Why yes, I am," said Staf, and he knelt down. Somehow, it reminded him of his earlier years with hopeless dreams of gold medals. This was an anonymous young kid that enjoyed sports.

"Are you going to win some more medals?" asked the young fellow.

"Maybe." He patted the young kid on the head. "Are you going to run track?"

"No," he replied. "I'm way too slow. I think I'll do something else, maybe be a doctor or lawyer or something like that." Staf felt humbled. He had risked everything for this dream, cheating reality, and here was a young child facing it logically. The young child gave him a hug. This was always an awkward thing for Staf. He did not particularly like little kids, but he always felt obliged to accommodate them. He studied the young boy and brought out his Olympic gold medal. He took it off. He placed it on this anonymous young child.

"Oh man!" shouted the young boy, and he ran to his patient, proud dad. "Look, it's Staf's Olympic gold medal, and he gave it to me!"

Staf looked awkwardly at them and their happy faces, and he wanted it to be like that, but that wasn't it at all, and he didn't like it.

Like hell I did, he said to himself and went over to them.

"He misunderstood," explained Staf with a meek smile, "I was just showing it to him." He held out his hand and maintained the

141

smile. The father reluctantly lifted the medal from his son, and put it in Staf's palm. The young boy started to cry. The father scowled at Staf.

Staf stuffed the medal in a pocket and promptly left. *Last time I'm going to do that,* he thought, and he muttered "stupid little shit" as he went out the door into the waiting limousine.

It was the same driver as the other night. Staf wondered what he could do to make the divider come up again. He manufactured a loud fart noise. The divider came up.

Chapter 18: On the Way to the Airport

They pulled up to the terminal, and Staf noted that he was being dropped off at the front door instead of at the plane as was customary. He thought about making the request, but other things were on his mind right now. He sensed that the mannequin was getting near. It struck him as he neared the FBO how he could sense it. His heart rate went up, he perspired, his skin started feeling tight and itchy, his hair stood up. Maybe it had something to do with touching that crystal ball, creating a sort of connection.

He was therefore too distracted to be bothered with the details of where he was dropped off. He got out of the limo without saying thank you or good-bye. The driver hadn't bothered to open the door anyway, which was also something Staf expected.

He entered the FBO, which was nicely tiled and decorated and had a glass viewing area that reminded Staf of his house. He approached the wooden counter, which he assumed was the reception. A very attractive, buxom brunette sat behind the counter. He could guess why she got this job. Standing behind her, apparently reviewing something on her roster, was a ramp agent. This ruined the effect that she was supposed to have.

Staf was greeted with a lovely, toothy, perfectly white smile.

"Can I help you?" She had big blue eyes, heavily outlined with the black mascara. A hint of mystery. Almost enough to make Staf forget why he was here. Back to reality.

"I'm—"

"You look a lot like Staf Nurren," interrupted the ramp agent, disrupting the atmosphere again.

"Why yes, I am," responded Staf normally for once. Usually he had some sort of smart ass comment for this sort of thing. Ramp agents usually come across lots of famous people at FBOs.

"Fantastic run two weeks ago. Congratulations on the medal and the records." Staf was tempted to show his medal again, but the earlier problem with the little boy lingered.

"Your plane is ready to board. It's up front. The pilots have completed their checks. One is on board, and the other is still filing the flight plan. You can board now or wait until the plan is filed." Staf liked this FBO. A little recognition and right to business. No wasting time.

"I will board now," he said, although he wished he had another moment to bother the receptionist. Then he promptly changed his mind, knowing that she came across asses like him every day.

The ramp agent disappeared around the corner to advise the other pilot, and the receptionist smiled again,

"Would you like a coffee?" she offered.

"Sure," said Staf, not knowing why; he really didn't feel like having one right now with all the stress building inside of him. He noticed that his breathing was increasing, and there was the hint of perspiration starting. He figured he still had some time.

"It's just over there," she replied and pointed to a table with a coffeemaker.

Maybe this wasn't such a great FBO. Staf could be a bit rude and rusty sometimes, but he had his quirks. If you offer a coffee, you should complete the process. If you merely want to point out self-serve conveniences, then do so without a question-and-answer game show. He decided he didn't like her anymore. He went out to the plane, and as he exited, the other pilot came out too.

"Hello, Staf," he greeted him warmly, which was unusual for pilots, because they generally thought they were better than everyone else.

"Off to Switzerland today," he remarked or asked; Staf wasn't sure which, but it had better be Switzerland if they were going somewhere with fuel calculations in mind. Staf wanted to say something smart about going to Australia or China but wasn't in the mood. He just wanted to get on the plane and leave the fear and tension behind for a while.

As he entered the Gulfstream, he was conscious that he didn't look back at what he was going to leave behind and didn't know when he was coming back. It was a sad feeling.

He passed the bar, went down the wide aisle, and sank into the comfortable leather couch.

"Here is your coffee, Mr. Nurren," came a familiar voice. He was puzzled and looked up to see the receptionist there holding out a tray with a cup on it.

Whoa, thought Staf, and his perception of the place changed again. He must have stared at her a little too much, and she laughed. Then he caught on. A typical man mistake. He looked at her chest, and noticed that it was just a little more revealing, and she had a nice light blue scarf smartly wrapped around her neck. He smiled.

"Ah, do you sometimes trade places with your sister?"

"You're quick," she replied mischievously.

There was some kind of play on words with the term *quick* that he thought about building on, but he couldn't come up with it fast enough and decided to leave it alone. He liked this place again, but he now wished her twin sister was on board too.

He sat back and daydreamed while she went about the safety briefing—exits, seatbelts, etc.—when a pang hit his stomach like a punch. It was getting close. Maybe about a mile away. That would be about five minutes. He looked around the cabin. The noise, although faint in this nice plane, indicated that both engines were running.

She had finished her briefing and asked if he had any questions.

"Can we hurry up? It would be good to get into the air in four minutes." He tried to hide the anxiety in his voice, but it was surely there. She smiled, but it was a slightly more irritated smile, practiced from countless impatient passengers.

"We will be in the air very shortly," she replied, still in a nice voice. "Typically, from here, it is no more than a few minutes."

A few minutes, thought Staf. What did that mean? Six minutes (that would be too late) or two minutes (that would be acceptable)?

Staf looked out the left window. It was coming from that direction, from the south. The FBO building was in the way.

The plane taxied forward, and he strained for a view down the road as they passed the building. Nothing but cars. It was too busy out there for him to make out anything, but it was close and getting closer fast. Faster than they were taxiing. This plane was suddenly incredibly slow. His neighbor, Mrs. Wilson, must be the other pilot, he figured.

The small oval windows obstructed his view as they went down the taxiway, and he felt claustrophobic again. He absently took a sip of his coffee and burned his tongue. The captain came on the PA.

"Looks like a fairly smooth morning here in New York. We should have you in the air momentarily." Staf let out a sigh of relief. "We are only number three for departure, and the tower advises us there will not be any delays."

Shit, thought Staf. Three planes before them. What was normal for no delays around here? He had about three minutes left to go. Staf was fidgeting. He was breathing heavily, and sweat dripped from his forehead. He looked out the windows uneasily. The flight attendant sensed this and asked him to relax, figuring he was a nervous flyer. The smile did nothing for him.

"Can't we sort of just sneak into line and take off? I really need to get out of here," he said sort of quietly, hoping that everyone, particularly the pilots, could hear it.

His heart was pounding now, and he could hear it in his head. Almost deafening. He wondered if he would be able to hear the clip-clop with the beating in his ears. The plane moved forward. Number two, Staf figured. Maybe two minutes to go. It was going to be tight. Staf was jittery and craned his neck out the left side. The edges of the windows distorted the image, almost making it foggy. He thought he saw something approaching from behind. He squeezed his sweaty face against the window to look back. He was sure he saw something. His heart was beating as if it wanted to break through his chest. He needed to let his instincts take over. They needed to get into the air now.

He looked at the front door, then the emergency window exit? How did it operate again? Pull the lever and then lift the window in or throw it out—which was it? He looked out the left window, and there it was, right in front of the side window. It lurched at the plane. Staf leaped across the seat and fumbled for the emergency exit lever.

"Mr. Nurren!" shouted the Flight attendant as she undid her seatbelt. There was a sudden jolt in the plane, and a loud clang. The left side window exploded inside as Staf lifted the lever and heaved the door in. Right choice. The flight attendant was right beside him, reaching out as another jolt moved the plane several feet sideways. The left side of the plane cracked and adjacent windows shattered.

Staf leapt out and ran away from the plane. The path took him onto the runway. As he reached the runway, he turned and saw the mannequin jump out of the emergency exit. He crossed the runway right in front of the plane that was just starting to take off.

After crossing the runway, he crossed some grass and reached a fence. He scaled it easily with only minor rips from the razor wire at the top. His heart was no longer racing as it had when the mannequin was at the plane, although it was still beating very fast. It was more comfortable knowing where the mannequin was and knowing he could keep distance from it.

He blindly ran toward the nearest road and randomly took a right turn to go with traffic.

Chapter 19: Take the Boat

Staf was still breathing heavily as he approached the busy highway, and a quick look behind him showed that he had gone about half a mile; the distance was increasing again. His tension indicated the same.

He watched for taxis on the road and tried to hail one, but none would stop. He continued to run eastbound with the traffic. To run westbound would have meant crossing the highway, which would have been tricky with the traffic. Besides, eastbound would take him toward the Big Apple. A sign on the road indicated that he was on Highway 46.

Five more taxis passed without picking him up. Then it hit him; a guy running on the side of a road was not an ideal fare. He had some distance, and so he decided to make it look like he was out for a leisurely walk, although this was still suspicious along the highway. The next cab stopped for him. He quickly hopped into the back, and the cab continued.

"Where to?" asked the driver.

Staf had no idea where to go, so he said the first thing that came to his mind, "Waldorf Astoria," and immediately realized that it was a useless place to go. He needed another airport, or boat, or ... and then it hit him: the train station. He immediately advised the driver to take him to Grand Central. He would take the next train to anywhere.

He sat back, relieved with the new plan. He decided to call Jake and realized that his phone was still on the plane.

"Do you have a phone?" The driver looked at him and shook his head. Staf still had his wallet and took out a hundred dollars and handed it to the driver.

"Now do you have a phone?"

The driver tried to hide his smirk as he handed Staf a Nokia.

"Just so you know, it will be a long distance call to L.A."

Jake answered the phone quickly.

"Hello, Staf. What happened to the other phone?" Staf ignored Jake's intuition and introduce himself anyway.

"Hey Jake, it's Staf. The flight failed. Pinocchio reached the plane before we took off." He related the story of Teterboro.

"I had to leave everything on the plane, including my phone. I think you will get a call soon; the plane is a wreck. I am on my way to Grand Central Station right now. What do you think?"

"Whoa, Staf," replied Jake, alarmed. "Are you trying to make this more difficult? You're going to be in a bit of a pickle now. I'll have to get back to you, but this airport thing, unlike the municipal driving problem, is a federal offence. You won't be able to get anywhere out of the country soon. Can I reach you on this phone?" Staf looked at the driver. He threw out another hundred dollars.

"Can I keep the phone?" The driver muttered, shook his head, and held out his hand for the phone back. Staf gave him another five hundred dollars. He muttered some more, but quickly put the money in his coat pocket pretending inconvenience.

"Sure Jake, get me on this phone, but I am on my way to the train station. Where do you think I can go?"

"Let me get back to you," answered Jake. "Give me an hour or so. I'll put the Supreme Court case on hold," and he hung up.

Supreme Court my ass, thought Staf. He knew very well there were nothing but athletes tied to Jake's firm, and some charity work, but his services as a lawyer and as a friend were invaluable, especially now.

Staf sat back as the car wove its way to Highway 9 and crossed the Interstate 95 bridge. It was nice to have the time to sit back and think after the events on the plane.

After twenty minutes, the phone rang.

"Hey Jake, what have you got?" answered Staf smartly. Something was said on the other end. A different language, spoken very rapidly. It wasn't Jake. Staf hastily and rudely replied, "Call back in an hour." He noticed the driver glance at him in the rearview mirror. Staf didn't want this phone anymore; he would ask Jake to arrange another.

The phone rang after another ten minutes, and it was Jake.

"You have a few options. How about Newark and another flight? Maybe you can beat out the national warrant for your arrest. Or the port for a cruise leaving in an hour."

"Cruise, eh?"

"I thought so. It's really your only option. The flight was a red herring. Get to the Manhattan Yacht Club and look for Captain Harold. And Staf, I pulled a lot of strings for this. Get your ass there, but don't be an ass."

Staf gave the driver the new destination, which he accepted with feigned reluctance.

At the club, Staf handed the phone back to him.

"$123.55," demanded the driver. Staf looked at him. He had already given him seven hundred dollars and returned his phone. Staf stared at him, and the driver shrugged. He gave him a credit card number, and asked for the phone back.

He signed the slip for exactly $123.55 and made sure the driver watched him throw the phone into the river.

He entered the Yacht Club, introduced himself to reception, and asked for the captain. He was treated rudely until a phone call. If aviation thought they were the best, sailors believed they were better. Once it was established who he was, he was gently escorted to a waiting limousine, and he found himself at the dock. There were several large boats there and a liner. He was escorted to the liner. Apparently it was a Trinity superyacht—larger than a yacht, and larger in price. It reeked of luxury and excess, but that was right up Staf's alley. This was going to be a relaxing trip.

An hour later, which was a little longer than he would have liked but still adequate, the yacht started to move and slowly left the dock.

Staf had only just started to feel a little tense. The mannequin was probably a mile away.

They slowly left the pier and chugged along the river toward the bay, parallel to the city, without putting much distance between them and the shore. Staf stayed aft and kept a watch on the pier. It wouldn't be there for another five minutes, he figured. They entered the bay and slowly picked up speed. Just as they reached the bay, Staf could make out the wooden figure as it reached the seaside. Without stopping, it dove into the water. Staf's question was answered. It would follow him through water too. The boat sped to its full 22 kmph and headed for the Azores.

Chapter 20: The Azores

Staf spent his time uneasily on the yacht. He couldn't gauge how fast they were going, and he didn't like the feeling of not knowing where the mannequin was. There were times when his nerves were more on edge than others. It also seemed to him as he had watched it enter the water in New York that it was moving faster than before. He was also aware that he felt more tense when it was near.

The boat ride was fast, with mixed weather. Staf usually sat in the upper deck enjoying the sun and the peace or leaned against the aft railing looking out at the sea. There was too much time for reflection; he wondered how he could have done things differently. He had not yet reached the point where he would regret it all.

They sailed for five days, and he spoke to Jake once via the satellite phone. There was also some TV to watch during the evening.

He also spoke to his mom. Things were tough for her at home since Josh's stroke. He was not doing well. Staf wished he could go home.

As they arrived in the Azores, Staf was torn as to whether to stay in Ponta Delgada and enjoy some night life or go to another island for some more peace. He decided that he had had enough peace on the boat, and despite his slowly growing tension, they anchored in Ponta Delgada and took a Zodiac to the docks. There was a cell phone available on the superyacht for Staf to take ashore.

He wandered around the quaint town with its old churches and city gates hidden behind modern hotels. He found a few empty restaurants and bars to spend some time in. He occasionally managed to forget about the mannequin during the afternoon, and then, when he remembered it, he felt the tension again, each time a little more than before. The drinks seemed to ease this, and later, the thoughts of his pursuer rarely came to mind.

As the afternoon wore on, it became busier, and despite his usual habits and the nice atmosphere, he decided to make it an early evening. He checked into the Hotel Talisman near the docks.

He had a restless sleep and the same recurring dream: the faceless wooden golem always within an arm's reach or just around the corner, always the clip-clop sound nearby, echoing in his ears, growing louder, incredibly louder. The sound enveloped him. He felt small and tiny in the sound, with a huge shadow encompassing him on a featureless plain. He felt like an ant fleeing a hand.

He woke with a start, sweating, with a clicking noise in his ear. It was loud, incredibly loud. Staf bolted up and looked around. Nothing changed. After a frantic look around, he allowed his nerves to settle and took a slower look around. The clicking was coming from the clock beside the bed. It wasn't digital. He unplugged it, and the sound went away. He immediately relaxed and took a deep breath. It was 2:00 a.m. He leaned back and tried to let sleep come again. In the quiet, there was another noise. A rumble, but rhythmic. Could it be a distant clip-clop? He sat up again and had another look around, and it didn't take long to notice the ceiling fan whirring; there was a slight click as it wobbled. He promptly turned it off, strained his ears, heard nothing, and lay down again. It was almost quiet. His heart beat loudly—a low, rhythmic thump. This also caused him some jitters. Sleep came slowly.

It was a deep sleep. More clocks and ceiling fans. Clip-clops, tick-tocks, clicks and clacks everywhere from everything. He felt small again, and while he couldn't see the objects making the noises, he sensed they were huge.

The clip-clop became louder, pounding again, drowning out the other sounds. He didn't want to sleep anymore. He knew he was dreaming and wanted to wake up. For some reason, he couldn't. The noise became louder. He shrank from it. More noise. He tried to run. His legs moved but slowly. He commanded them to run fast, but they wouldn't or couldn't. He was desperate to wake up. The shadows grew. There was something reaching out behind him. He sensed it; it was closing in on him, and he couldn't run fast enough. The shadow was almost touching him. He couldn't even risk turning around to look at it, because that might slow him down for a fraction of a second. Then, somehow, he fell, and he reached out, and the floor shattered below him.

He woke to a shattering sound, heart racing, the clip-clop still in his ears. It didn't stop. It was loud. It came from the door. The door disintegrated, and the grotesque golem charged into the room and went straight for the bed, reaching out with gnarled, knotted fingers. On instinct, Staf rolled out of bed. There was nowhere to go. The bathroom looked like a quick door to go through, but there was no way out of it. Beside the bed, there was a window. Was there a balcony, ledge, or fire escape? He didn't know and took a chance, diving at the window. The golem immediately changed directions to follow him. Staf closed his eyes and crashed through the glass. He immediately opened them, flailing his arms hoping to catch hold of something. There was a black metal pole that he held on to, and he felt the muscles in his shoulders strain. The golem promptly came through the window and, missing the pole, continued to fall the five floors to the street below. In midair, it stopped running. Staf held on to the pole, which was part of a narrow ladder that served as a fire escape, and watched the golem fall. This was the most he had seen of it without being in an all-out run. It was smooth, with an almost polished grain running lengthwise. It was completely featureless. Arms and fingers, but no fingernails. No hair.

It landed on the ground with both feet. It didn't move. Staf looked down, and he had a moment to examine it further. It was the middle of the night, but there seemed to be enough light from the street and buildings to reflect off it. It cocked its head up as if to regard him five floors up on the fire escape. Its smooth face was awkward, needing attachments like an empty Mr. Potatohead. There weren't even recesses or protrusions for eyes, nose, mouth, or ears. It was completely featureless except for the general shape of a face.

Staf sensed it was looking at him but wondered with what or how. It really didn't matter, because sticks aren't expected to have features anyway. But then again, if this stick could run, it could probably look at him without eyes. They regarded each other for a few seconds. Then the golem ran back into the building. Staf hated that. It was better to see it and know where it was. Was it taking a run through the building? Or was it waiting behind a corner? Could it plan like that? Should he climb down or wait? It was a bit precarious on the escape ladder; he was very lucky to have caught it.

There was silence except for the light purr of a moped somewhere. Staf climbed down a few rungs on the ladder. His tension told him the golem was still nearby.

There was a light thump from the bricks behind. Staf started down the ladder. There was another loud thump a floor above, and a few bricks became dislodged. Staf was halfway down to the ground, taking three steps at a time. It was painfully slow compared to sprinting. At twenty feet above the ground, he jumped.

The wall exploded above him, showering bricks down. A quick look above showed the golem flying out the side of the building, descending on him. Staf bolted down the street. The golem followed. It was faster this time. Staf was in an all-out sprint and only slowly increasing the distance. It followed him around one corner and then another. Staf would need to find a way to get distance—a car, a bike, something. He was breathing heavily; he had only just woken from a deep sleep a moment ago, and the rest of his body was not quite awake yet.

The golem was quick. There was no need to turn corners or try to lose it in the dark; it would easily be on his trail. The clip-clop on the pavement behind him indicated that he had opened the distance. A quick look showed him that it was now twenty meters behind. Staf was sweating again despite the cool dawn. He needed to get to the yacht, but it was off shore, so he would have swim to it. The crew had taken the Zodiac back to the yacht, waiting for his call. His phone? It was in the hotel in his pants. He suddenly realized that he was shirtless, running around the Azores in his pajama pants, a lightly colored plaid pattern. The flap in the front ensured that this attire would not pass as colored pants. But that was a minor problem now. He also had his Olympic gold medal around his neck, flopping against his chest. He was also glad that he never took the medal off, even at night.

He had lost another phone and wouldn't be able to arrange the yacht. The distance between him and the golem did not seem to increase appreciably, and he had to look back frequently to ease his nerves about the distance. Staf was trying hard to think of something to do. He decided to keep running around a few blocks to keep in an area he knew and to keep the golem in a place where he could keep an eye on it until he could come up with a plan. Back to the hotel to get the phone and some proper pants? Possible. But people might be up now; it might be cordoned off, and the police might be there by now. *Shit*, he thought, *the police*. They might get involved here too. Could they have access to his growing US record?

He would have to leave quickly. Then another plan occurred to him. He made another circuit around the block, the clip-clop ever present behind him. Surprisingly, the streets were relatively quiet, given how long establishments stayed open here. But he was careful to avoid the busy main streets and generally stuck to small lanes and alleys. He did pass a few people in his circuit. They looked quizzical at his second pass, and some were still there on his third pass and stared at him. Some looked scared, probably because of his pajamas. On the third pass, breathing heavily now and with legs starting to complain, he saw a small truck on the road.

Staf sprinted as hard as he could, and just as the truck was about to speed up, he lunged and was able to get a light hold on the back and get himself onto the ledge. The speed of the truck was enough to increase the distance from the golem more rapidly. The golem was turning smaller in his vision. As he looked back at it, there was nothing more to learn about its features or lack of them. In fact, the initial excitement about studying it from the fire escape earlier in the night was gone. He just didn't want to see it anymore.

The truck took him to the edge of town, and spotting a phone booth, Staf jumped off. He knew he had a bit of time and hurried to the phone. As the sun was just starting to peek over the horizon, he made a collect call to Jake. He updated him on his whereabouts and asked for the superyacht to be ready.

156

As Staf got off the phone, his heart slowed down, and his breathing returned to normal. But in the corner of his gut, a tension grew. He looked up, and sure enough, the familiar shape was coming to him. Was it faster yet? He could hear the faint clip-clop, and it did seem to be a bit faster. It made his calming heart beat faster too.

Staf wrenched the phone booth door. It was stuck. Staf wrenched harder. It wouldn't budge. The golem neared, quickly. Staf looked down at the door briefly, took a deep breath, and slowly tried the door again. The door opened easily. *Dumb door, one of those stupid things that work easily as long as you don't try too hard.*

He stepped out and ran in the direction of the coast. The early dawn made for a quieter city than the late night. He tried not to get distracted about his pajamas. The golem was directly behind him, about twenty meters away again. The timing was going to be close. He wondered if he should stick to the plan. It was getting very hard to stay ahead of this thing. He wondered if the golem was going to be faster tomorrow, if he was going to constantly have to be in a car, boat, plane, or something rather than just outrunning it. It was going to be a ten-minute run to the dock. A long ten minutes. A constant picture of him running just ahead of the golem.

The scenery seemed to fly past him. It flew past him like his present life. He was missing everything, unable to enjoy it, unable to stop and smell the roses. He wondered if he had done that with his life up to this moment. Had he appreciated the peaceful time when he had it? He competed, had some parties, but that was it. None of that had prepared him for this.

Jake, on the other hand, went to school, became a lawyer, had a family, and had his charitable projects. He was always working on something and always had something new to do. After running professionally, which he had known would end, what did he have to look forward to? What did it lead to? As it turned out, more running.

It struck him that he had never made plans for after his running career. It had to end sometime, and he hadn't prepared for it. It had passed by like the Azores streets and really led nowhere in particular. There was no one waiting for him either. It wasn't going to change anytime soon. Staf needed to do something to change this; he needed to find a way to stop this. Nothing came to mind. He would have time to think about it on the next boat ride, if he got there.

The distance was not increasing. He was getting tired of running. He couldn't live the rest of his life like this. *Take charge*, he told himself. *Don't just let things play themselves out; do something.* He ran faster.

The piers were a few blocks ahead, and the clip-clops where diminishing. He scanned the water for the superyacht. So many, and they all looked alike. This was not part of the plan. He needed to get to it quickly. It was supposed to be out in the water again, ready to go, engines on. Everything looked the same. His lungs hurt. His heart was starting to feel weary. His legs were starting to feel like rubber.

The thought came up again. Should he quit? Give up? Surrender instead of living this hell? Like a recurring theme, he recalled touching the crystal in his house. The pain. Thoughts of quitting vanished from his mind, and his legs, heart, and lungs found new energy.

He reached the dock but still didn't know where his yacht was. Among the many boats and yachts, everything seemed very quiet. He might have to abandon this plan. An elderly man was on the dock climbing into a small aluminum boat. He had just started the light fifteen-horsepower engine as Staf entered the dock and ran up. He looked up curiously at this man running up the dock in his pajamas. He looked down quickly in order to ignore the strange stranger. Staf jumped into the boat. The man stood up angrily.

"Please," pleaded Staf, "take me to the superyacht over there." The man put up his arms in protest. Staf pushed him overboard.

He gunned the engine, which put the front of the boat at a high angle. The golem reached the dock and promptly jumped into the water. Staf steered blindly in the crowded harbor. He tried to follow his instincts. He gently turned to the left. Then, realizing the exit from the causeway was to the right, he cranked the boat and sped to it. The yacht deck was quiet. Staf quietly muttered under his breath.

He looked behind. The waves disguised any semblance of the golem swimming to him. He was seconds from the yacht.

Someone on the yacht must have heard the screaming engine from the boat and appeared. He waved. They waved back and directed him to the side. The deck hand looked a little concerned at Staf's speed, but Staf was determined not to mess this up. And just as the deck hand was going to shout, Staf released the throttle. The boat instantly slowed. He steered it to a slow stop beside the yacht, quickly grabbed a ladder, and kicked the small aluminum boat away. The deck hand looked at him and the aluminum boat. Staf just calmly walked toward the cabin.

"Let's go!"

The deck hand shrugged and followed Staf to the cabin. He noticed Staf's pajamas, shook his head in disgust, and told the captain they were ready to depart. Outside, the golem had just swum past the aluminum boat and was reaching for the yacht stairs as the boat sped away and out of reach. It promptly continued after the yacht.

Chapter 20: On the Run in Europe

Safely back aboard the superyacht, Staf settled in for a two-day journey to Europe. It had been another close call in Ponta Delgada, but as the distance between him and his pursuer grew and the tension eased, he had a moment to enjoy the journey. But what was it he had promised to do? Stop and smell the roses? Make long term plans about retirement? He would start tomorrow.

But right now, he used the moment to think of the places he could travel to. Maybe run through Africa. He pictured himself running through the Sahara again. He could run down south from Egypt through Sudan and watch the desert become sub-Saharan. He could stop in Meroe and take in the smaller pyramids there. Follow the Nile to Khartoum for the union of the Blue and White Niles. Follow the White Nile to South Sudan and into Uganda, or the Blue Nile to Ethiopia. Or take both. Drop into Kenya, visit his marathon friend. What a journey that would be, and only partly done. He could go visit mountain Gorillas along the borders of Uganda, Rwanda, and the Congo. Maybe the gorillas could stop the golem for him.

Or he could go to the coast, follow the Indian Ocean down from Kenya to Tanzania, and then take a ferry to Zanzibar. Ferry? Nah, the superyacht would do just fine. The journey would only be half done there. It sounded fun. And the only reason he was doing it was to avoid death.

He went aft and looked out at the endless ocean. It was out there somewhere, continually on the move toward him. He was going to end his boat trip in Portugal. That was where his land trip was going to start. Where else could he go to make it difficult for the golem to follow? Air travel would be the fastest, and maybe he could fly in Europe regardless of his US warrants. Then again, maybe not. He wasn't sure of the nuances and politics between the United States and Europe where warrants were concerned. He could take the train.

Staf landed just outside Portugal. He took the Zodiac to a small port to the north of Lisbon and feigned a call to customs. He spent a day there, planning to spend four.

Jake had hired an assistant to handle all of Staf's 'bullshit'. He received his passport and the phone that he had left in the Azores. And then he got another phone so that he could return the borrowed one to the yacht. It arrived after one day. Staf decided his passport and phone were safer in his pockets instead of the knapsack.

After one day, Staf's tension began to rise. The mannequin had arrived in Portugal. He decided not to tempt fate, so he went to the station and took the next train east. It didn't matter where. He didn't speak Portuguese, but heading east meant Spain, regardless of what the ticket man said. From there, probably France.

In Madrid, Staf took a break from the train and wandered the city. He was in a different sort of mood and took a tour of the Musio del Prado. One painting that caught his attention was an El Greco, *Annunciation*. In it, the angel Gabriel visits Mary with a message. Staf took particular note of the angel. It reminded him of someone. It hit him on his next train ride to Paris. There was a similarity between the image, and the person he had noticed at the fair, the androgynous one. He decided to research this more, combining his research with visits to more museums and art galleries throughout Europe. He bought a laptop and did some research on his train rides. This brought him to Berlin.

He noticed a drawing in the Berlin Museum. It was a rough sketch and didn't really help him out. Florence, Italy was on his list; the San Marco Museum had a Fra Angelico, also of the annunciation, and the Uffizi had a Leonardo da Vinci. After he viewed them, his research was still inconclusive. He figured Rome would be an ideal spot to get more information.

The happiest man in the world was the curator of the Vatican Museum. He was a Christian scholar with a penchant for the arts—sculpture and painting, mostly. He was an amateur himself and quietly worked away in his small apartment with independent zeal. He had almost a reverence for the Sistine Chapel. His enthusiasm made him an ideal candidate for curator at the Vatican. He had a very close relationship with the church there and knew the art intimately. He often walked the halls, was involved in new acquisitions, and participated in some of the tours. He had a medium build, thinning dark hair, and was clean shaven, but he also had big, black, bushy eyebrows that needed trimming. His biggest assets were his patience, friendliness, and enthusiasm.

It was a regular Tuesday, and as he walked the corridor, there was another tourist admiring the Gentile de Fabriano. He knew it well, as he did everything in his museum, and he approached the young man.

"A nice interpretation of the annunciation, no?"

"Slightly different than the Leonardo in Uffizi, the El Greco in Madrid, the two in Florence, and the Rembrandt sketch in Berlin. Why so many interpretations?"

John wondered if this was a real enthusiast with expertise and knowledge that they could share and debate. Or this might just be another wannabe with half the knowledge trying to pass off as an expert.

"Did you think that they would all be the exact same interpretation? It would be quite a miracle if they were all identical. At the same time, they may have influenced each other, no? Which one do you prefer? Although the others are depictions of Gabriel visiting Mary, the Rembrandt in Berlin is not specific as to which one appears to Joseph in a dream. You are assuming it is Gabriel too, no?"

He was very conscious of ending his sentences with a questioning 'no', but when he got into a conversation, he usually forgot himself, and it came out more frequently.

"Is Gabriel male or female?"

This clearly indicated to John that this was an amateur. He felt a little disappointed. No one had asked him about Gabriel for quite some time. This could be a nice review. He might even come up with a new question that he could research.

He launched into an oratorio.

"The study of angels is quite wide, and interpretations vary. They are preceded in a way in Persian and Egyptian ideas of beings with wings. The ones we see here and are generally familiar with are from Judaic, Islamic, and Christian interpretations. Some argue there are different types and different levels of angels. Of course, the ones we are most familiar with are the archangels Michael, Gabriel, Raphael, and Uriel. The earliest references also include Raguel, Ramiel, and Zerachiel. All seven have different names too, because, as I said, there are many interpretations and variations. We should also include Lucifer. You might be familiar with other names for him, such as Satan, the Devil, and maybe Beelzebub. And to demonstrate the inconsistencies, one might argue that Lucifer and Satan are different angels and of different orders. Is Beelzebub Lucifer or another angel that followed him when he was cast out of heaven? And the reasons are also varied. He may have been banished because he refused to bow to man; he felt he should only bow to God. Or he may have wanted to replace man. Who could tell which version is true, no? But you are referring to paintings that generally depict Gabriel.

"One of the first references to angels is in the book of Enoch as Gabriel is delivering a message to Daniel. But we are looking at this Gentile de Fabriano depicting Gabriel and Mary in the annunciation. Gabriel may have been the angel in Joseph's dream. She also appeared to the shepherds. It is also possible she was the messenger to Moses. It is also interesting that archangels are generally regarded as male, with Gabriel being the only one sometimes depicted as a female, although a more androgynous interpretation is common, no? What do you think?"

This was an opening for the stranger to tell him something, to reveal his interest and knowledge and possibly teach him something, although that was unlikely.

"I think Gabriel came to me with a message thirteen years ago at my county fair."

John was deflated. Last week, someone had come in claiming to have seen the Virgin Mary in a piece of cheese. The other month, it had been a potato chip that looked like the Shroud of Turin. It had been quite a while since anyone claimed a visit from Gabriel. He gently excused himself and went for lunch.

For the next several months, Staf wandered from city to city in Europe with only one day's rest between journeys. The rests were becoming shorter and shorter, and Staf tried not to think about his fate as he realized that the golem was constantly getting faster. He had less time to take it all in. It was becoming very tiring, and so to buy time, he took a long train ride from Germany to Hungary. He wandered around Budapest and stumbled on another fair. As he wandered, he found an area devoted to fortune tellers, palm readers, and tarot. He spotted a crystal ball here and there. There was one booth to read bumps on your head and something about your feet. As he wandered, he approached a few stalls. They seemed to be keen to recruit passersby for readings. As he approached, they all became quiet or looked away or seemed busy.

Odd, he thought. They seemed to recruit most other pedestrians.

Staf continued on his way and occasionally found one who did not ignore his appearance. He had the courage to stop at one of these and dropped a lot of money. It was the stall of a well-dressed middle aged man, who seemed to have all the craft tools with him.

"It is not good to pay before a reading, in case it is not a good one," advised the gentleman, who noticed the tidy sum without actually looking at it.

"Okay," replied Staf, "but it's here." He folded it and put it in his coat pocket.

"What reading would you like to have?"

"Give me the gamut," replied Staf.

"Well, today I feel that you could benefit from a tarot and palm reading."

"Fine," replied Staf, feeling at ease. The gentleman nodded mysteriously.

"Tell me what you would like to know or what questions you have to ask."

Staf related his story for the next five minutes. The gentleman listened patiently. Finally, Staf said, "I need to find out how to get rid of this thing chasing me."

The man thought about it for a moment and looked at the deck of cards. He asked to see Staf's palm. Apparently he didn't see much, and he gave nothing away. Then he casually asked Staf skeptically, "Well, although it is a very durable wood, considering the damage to your vehicle, have you tried fire? Fire is a logical ..."

Staf didn't pay attention to the rest. This was far beyond this fellow, but he had a good idea. Fire. He hadn't thought of that. Fire burns wood. He needed to find a way to explore that.

The palm reader finished his presentation, and Staf numbly dropped some money on the table.

The reader watched Staf leave. He had met all sorts of people during his time. Admittedly, he was decent, but he was not that good. The gift was in him in a rough way; he only saw the very strong signs. Some things stuck out more than others. But he was generally on the mark.

When this man had arrived, there was a cloud, a veil. When he told his story, fire seemed to stick out to the reader, although a small nagging in his mind had told him not to say anything.

He watched Staf run away after leaving a hefty fee. He heard a bird crow and started to notice the smallest insects buzzing around or walking in the laneway, even the spider that glared at him from its web in the junction of an awning across the way. He hesitantly shrugged and noticed the torches playing with shadows on the awnings too. At the same time, the crow's loud caw demanded his attention. The sound crept into his bones. He read the signs. A fear enveloped him, and he felt a shadow pass. He immediately regretted talking to this stranger. He hurriedly packed his belongings and fled.

Staf was impatient with his new idea. He wondered how to burn this thing before it got to him. He thought about digging a big hole for the thing to crash into so he could burn it with blowtorches or flamethrowers. He even thought of a Crematorium. He couldn't figure out how to get one or how to buy himself enough time to use it.

As he walked down a lonely street, he came upon a construction site. The concrete founding was set, and they were getting ready to erect the rest soon—maybe tomorrow. And the idea came to Staf immediately. If he could get it into the concrete foundation, maybe it could remain trapped there long enough for him to try some fire. The golem would scrabble in the basement. With enough time, it would come out, but not before Staf could experiment with fire. He bought some jerricans and hauled them to the site full of petrol, as they called it here. He bought a lighter and matches.

Then he set about preparing the site. The mannequin would come from the north. Staf would act as bait in the basement. He set up a ladder on the south side. He put rags at the base of the ladder and soaked them in gas. He surveyed the scene. Then he waited. Sleep should have come, but he was too excited about this new plan.

It was getting into the early morning. The wait was excruciating, like the slow ascent of a roller coaster ride. He was waiting for the next part, the exciting part.

At first, the hair on Staf's arm stood up, and then it was joined by the hair on his neck. Shortly after, his heart started to race, and he started to feel numb. Then the faint, familiar clip-clop. He hated that sound the most. It was always the loudest, most prominent sound.

He crawled to the middle of the basement and surveyed the ladder. He had a mental picture of the equipment above. The clip-clops got louder and rang in his ears. His heart leaped into his throat. He started to sweat profusely. He inched back from the middle of the room, just a little closer to the ladder. It was dark. He was worried that he wouldn't see it in time. He was worried that he might slip. The ladder would fall. Too late. The clip-clops arrived.

A shadow jumped into the pit. Staf had no time to think. He turned and slipped on the smooth concrete. Things were starting to go wrong. He stumbled to the ladder and hobbled up. It felt like the golem was breathing down his throat. He had never been this close to it since the Azores in his hotel room. It felt worse every time. He wondered if it had reached the ladder too. Then his plan would be a waste of time. He got to the top, turned, and heaved the ladder up. It was light enough, and with relief, the thing was not on it. He looked down, and it was running against the twelve-foot-high wall. It was not going to make it up the wall anytime too soon.

Staf got out the lighter and dropped it into the pit. The fire fluttered out before it reached the bottom. More bad luck. Forces were working against him. He got out the matches. He struck one. He struck it too hard. It broke. The thing continued to claw at the concrete wall. Staf fumbled for another match and struck it. It didn't light. He was sweating. Maybe it hadn't lit because of that. He took another match and, folding the cover, dragged the match quickly between the flint and the cover. There was a spark but no light. He took another and tried again. The thing scraped at the wall furiously. Staf looked at the blank face briefly but tore himself away, not wanting to waste the opportunity. He tore another match and repeated the procedure. A spark. And a light. He threw it into the pit.

He watched it descend in slow motion and extinguish in the wind again. Nothing happened. He should have kept a gasoline rag at the top to light. It was a dead end. Staf's heart was beaten again. Nothing worked. He fought the urge to run and decided to try again. Another match and another spark. The match lit. At the last moment, he decided to use it to light the whole pack. As it flared, he threw it into the pit. Nothing.

That was it. Staf needed a head start and turned to start getting away. Then there was a sudden burst of flame behind him. For a moment, he was worried that the boss was behind him again, but the heat was different. It wasn't evil. He turned, and at the edge of the pit, he peered in. The thing was still scraping at the wall among the flaming rags. Staf grabbed a jerrican and poured petrol onto the mannequin. Fire shot up towards the can, so he threw it in. The mannequin burst into flames but continued to scrape the wall. A foot had found a hole, and it was working its way up. Staf poured and threw a second can. It continued to burn. The smoke blurred his vision. Another can. The fire was having no effect. Or was the mannequin slightly turning black? Staf doubled his efforts and carefully poured another can on it. The flames continued to burn. The golem didn't seem to notice. The arm lunged for the top. It missed and slipped down the wall. It was a charred twig. The fire was working. Staf poured another can on it. He only had two left. He wished he had more. It lunged at the wall again, and the arm broke off. It was burning through! Staf poured another can on and decided to wait with the last one, to keep the fire burning. He was ecstatic. He was defeating it. He was winning the war.

The mannequin's leg snapped, and it fell sideways. It crawled to the wall and continued to scrape. Staf watched as the fire continued to eat it. Fingers broke off. The other arm dissolved. The body shrunk from the limbs in red embers. There was twitching, but nothing moved more than an inch. As the last fire burned, Staf dragged the ladder to another side and climbed down with the jerrican. He was worried about being careless, about letting his guard down. He came to the small, smoldering sticks and embers, and was careful to stand back as some sticks tried to twitch toward him. He poured the last can of gas on it and watched it burn to ashes. As it burned, relief took him. His heart rate returned to normal and sagged into his chest with relief. No goose bumps. His ears recorded the silence.

It was over. Staf was numb. He didn't know what to do. He just looked at the pile of ashes. He needed to get away, but he wanted to savor the moment. He was free again. Thoughts rushed into his mind so quickly, he didn't know what to do. It surprised him so much that he couldn't think clearly. Return to the United States? Check into the nearest hotel? Run away again?

Staf inspected the pile of ashes. There was nothing solid left. He was too tired, too happy to show it. He numbly walked up the ladderandwenttothetrainstation

ladder and went to the train station. One of his happiest times since the chase began had been on the superyacht. He was going to take the train to Greece and charter the nearest superyacht. He formed this plan as he climbed the ladder. He smiled and started to run for the station. He entered the train station stifling his laughs and glee. Unstoppable *my ass*, thought Staf over and over.

In the pit, the wind swirled. A fly buzzed near the pile of ashes, thought better of it, and zipped away. The wind spread some dust around the pit, but there were some ashes that fought back. They trickled against the wind and started to make a small pile. It was a small pile of ashes, and it was imperceptibly growing, but growing nonetheless.

Chapter 21: A Break

Staf emerged from the station in Athens, still in shock and unable to think of what to do. It felt unnatural not to think about running, to evaluate, to find a way out, an escape. There was no need for that anymore. He stood there noticing the peaceful breeze that brushed his face and gently tousled his hair. He looked up to the sky and noticed the sun. It felt warm and peaceful on his face, like a warm pair of oven mitts on his cheeks. He stood there, appreciating the contrast of the warm sun and the cool breeze. He was finally smelling the roses. The contrasts of the constant struggle in life. The sun and the breeze were like fire and water, land and ocean. He delved into this philosophical thought for a moment, and after what seemed like hours of meditation but was really only a few minutes, he looked down again into the street. A woman. He must get a woman, one that he could spend a long, worry-free night with or maybe even a couple of days. He made a quick search of his pockets. They were mostly empty: a few scraps of paper, a used Kleenex (he absently put it back in his pocket). Then he found some change, some money, and in his jacket pocket, he found his phone. It had only a little charge left in it. Full bars though—his luck was changing, he felt. He called Amber. It was the first person he thought of. He started to smile mischievously; the playboy in him was coming back. The phone rang. He got a little excited thinking about a night with her. After a ring and half, it answered. His heart leaped. Then there was a voice—a familiar one, but the wrong one. It was the standard monotone female voice; the line was no longer in use.

Shit, he said to himself. He would miss her. But wait, there was always directory assistance. He dialed and waited for the voice prompt. After saying Amber, he suddenly felt a little foolish. The robotic assistant paused for a moment and then requested something more specific. *Damn.* Her last name would have been handy. He searched his mind. What the hell was her last name? Did he ever know it? *Shit.* He had spent almost six years with her, on and off, mostly off, and he didn't know her last name? He hung up as a human voice came on the line requesting a last name. He had spent quite a bit of time with her; in fact, he didn't want to admit it, but he really liked her. He remembered the dinners, the shopping, the games. They had shared some special times together. Then he snapped back to reality. He would try to find her tomorrow.

He dialed Candace's number. He had a knack of remembering phone numbers. Not last names though. Candace … she was hot. Whenever he was with her, he forgot about everyone else. She liked to be around only just long enough. No lingering, hanging on, invading. She came and left at the right time. She was good. She was hot. A man answered the phone. Staf hung up.

This was frustrating. He decided to make one more call. MJ (an odd name, but he never questioned it). After two rings, there was an answer. It was her; he recognized that raspy, sexy, almost manly voice.

"Hey there, MJ," he said. "It's Staf. How's it going?" he started to count his blessings again. It was going to be a good day all around.

"Staf?" questioned the voice. There was a pause, and he recognized the muffled sound of her talking to someone else in the background. She had her hand on the phone, but he could hear something anyway. She was with someone else. *Shit.* His heart rate went down, and the blood flow eased off, and his whole body went limp too.

"Staf," she said again, "how the heck are you? Where have you been?"

There is some hope, he thought. "Well, I'm over here in …" and he thought about it for a moment. Where was he again? So many places, so much time.

"Oh sunshine, I'm in beautiful Greece, near Athens, I think, or something like that. I think you should come over."

She giggled a little at this, and his hope renewed.

"Come take the next flight over. The shopping is phenomenal."

"How sweet, Staf, I would love to." He felt ecstatic. Maybe he would get to know her and possibly even marry her, he thought. The giggling continued.

"But Staf, honey, I'm married. I have a kid now. I can't just do that, but that's very sweet of you."

Damn, he thought, *married and with kids*. He could just see her mouth the words with her thick, red lips. He missed them. But married with kids? He didn't want to have anything to do with that. He suddenly wanted to get off the phone quickly but felt obligated to catch up on some other small talk. After what seemed like an eternity of listening about shopping, diapers, and the everyday things that kids did, he found an opportunity to escape and gently said good-bye with an empty promise to call or visit when he was in town soon. He forgot to wish her continued happiness, as he had no intention of seeing her or calling her ever again.

He dialed another number and got another answering machine. He didn't leave a message. This was frustrating. Just because he had been away for two years didn't mean that everyone should move on with their lives. He mildly scolded himself for the absurd thought. Then the thought came to him that he could just hang out here, find a bar, get drunk, and find a woman. This was a quaint, touristy town.

He stashed his phone and hailed a taxi to the nearest hotel—a cheap one; he wasn't sure if his credit card still worked. He would have to sort that out very soon. He noted the bars along the way. He checked into his room, oblivious of the cost. Then he finally remembered his friend. *Better call him before I get out and forget.*

"Hey, Staf, it's been a short while. How's it going?" Staf was relieved to hear a friendly voice, someone that he could count on no matter what. It suddenly felt like the last burdens had been taken off his shoulders. His friend would take care of everything. He related burning the mannequin.

"Well, Jake, I've got everything sorted out. I'm free. I'm done," he said. "I can do whatever I want, no more running or hiding. I'm in Greece, want to come over?"

His friend chuckled. "Would love to, but you know I can't; Jenn would kill me. What do you need? Send another postcard too. Near Athens, eh? I'll have to look that up."

"Well," answered Staf, "how is my account? Can I afford to stay here? Do my credit cards still work? Can I charter the yacht again?"

"I don't know how to tell you this," said Jake, lowering his voice with concern, "but you burned through a lot of money during the last two years, and I've been trying to get hold of you for quite a while."

Staf's heart sank. He didn't want to hear it. He was bankrupt, and he knew it, he felt it. He looked up again. If the sun could shine through his room, he knew it would not feel so warm right now. He closed his eyes.

"Well, as you know, you burned through a lot, and there were legal fees, broken contracts. I was able to put some in a special fund for your retirement, but the truth is …" and this lingered on too long. Staf wondered about the hotels he would be staying in. Maybe he should check into the hostel instead. He looked down to the ground. He had no idea what was in his accounts. "We burned through about half of it."

Shit, thought Staf when the reality set in. Half of it. Half of what? How much did he have to start with? He realized that he had no idea what he owned past his clothes. Half of a lot could be a lot; half of a little could be very little. He held his breath.

"Are you sitting down?"

"Yes!" Yelled Staf, impatient, suddenly needing to know how much money he had like he never had before.

"Well, although there was quite a bit from the playing contracts, the endorsements, and the continued royalties, although diminished lately …" This was dragging on, as was Jake's usual style, and Staf bit his lip to keep from yelling into the phone and risk cutting him off or prolonging the speech.

"Well, roughly, you have only 1.5 billion left. You have to understand that …" and the rest just floated past Staf. One and a half billion. He could have imagined worse, much worse. $1.5 billion! He might not have to check into the hostel. Shit, he should upgrade to a suite. $1.5 billion. There was no need to worry; the last possible burden was lifted off his shoulders. It was a glorious day. It barely sunk in that he had lost the equivalent in two years and that potentially this was an amount that would not be adequate for the rest of his life. But for a moment, he had been prepared for much worse.

He was grateful to and for his friend. Jake was the best thing that had ever happened to him, possibly even better than his running career. Possibly.

He heard his friend finish talking but didn't know what he had said. But then he heard, "So? What do you think about that?" Staf didn't know what to say; he hadn't heard the last part at all and didn't care. He was set. He didn't need to know any more, and he smiled,

"What do I think?" he said, and he could just sense his friend's mounting frustration as he knew the conversation was over. "I think that you know exactly what to do. See ya!"

He hung up just in time to hear the start of his friend's familiar rant and cut it short. He loved to do that. He smiled. He was going to keep the Ferrari and his glass house and buy a superyacht. He was going to start living again.

He went downstairs and got some quick directions to some stores for clothes and things. It was a rustic hotel; he presumed there was no such thing as a suite here, and he didn't have time to bother with such a thing today.

He tipped the front desk tremendously to have toiletries brought up to his room as soon as possible, meaning before he got back from shopping. He ran out and went to the first men's store he could find. He couldn't make up his mind on some shirts and pants, and so he bought them all—six different shirts and three pairs of pants in order to go out for one night. He had them altered on the spot. No one recognized him.

He reached his room and found his toiletries as ordered, and as he was about to have a hot bath, he realized that his room didn't have a bath, only a shower (presumably to avoid a strain on the local fresh water supply). After the shower, he shaved and admired himself in the mirror. His hair was a mangled mess. It was late in the day. He knew there was no way to find a barber at this time of day. He found the pomade in his toiletries and put enough of the goop on his head to keep his hair out of the way. *That will do till tomorrow*, he thought and stood back and admired himself. What a transformation that can happen in just one day—from a ragged, rough, dirty, desperate man back to his old confident, smart, stylish self from two years ago.

Jake called back, and in order to get information on the waiting superyacht, Staf had to endure a lecture. A different superyacht was available. It was off shore.

Staf pulled himself away from the mirror and headed down the stairs to the narrow streets below. Passing the counter, he noted the surprised look as the staff tried to connect him with the haggard man that had checked in a few hours earlier.

Staf met the crew and took another Zodiac to the yacht for a tour. It was a luxurious Abeking and Rasmussen. It was monstrous. It had a huge living room where the furniture was accented with polished teak. There was a spacious living room with the latest HD TV. There were several master suites to choose from; Staf's favorite was on the top floor and had a large viewing area that reminded him of his glass house. The crew had just arrived from a long journey, and they decided to stay in his hotel too. He returned to the docks on the Zodiac with the crew, and they parted for the night.

There was an annoying noise, a constant buzzing. As Staf awoke, he hit the alarm at the side of the bed. The annoying buzzing was gone, but now there was a tremendous pain in his head. Staf swung his legs over the side of the bed and let the hangover sink in. He rested his head in his hands and gently rubbed his temples with his fingers. It didn't help; the pain was just inside his forehead, unreachable. He needed some painkillers. It was his first hangover in two years, and it was a doozy. The familiar thought rang through his mind: *I'll never drink again.* What the hell had happened last night? He was trying to remember some of it. Walking out of the hotel was the easy part. The tour of the yacht. The return to the pier. There had been a bar, and then another and another. He had bought drinks, and then others had bought drinks. What the hell was it he kept drinking? Ooza? Ouza? Ooka? Something like that, one after another. He coughed after the first two shots. After that, they slid down easily, deceptively. Wait. The pain was gone for a moment. If he didn't move, the pain might not come back. Just thinking about it made his head hurt again.

Maybe he could sleep some more? He fell back into bed and bumped into something. It moved. What? He looked up across the bed and found a lump covered in a blanket, starting to stir. *You dirty dog*, thought Staf as he tried to remember this part of the night, and a smile tried to creep across his face. But what is the use of a fun night if you can't remember it? He hoped that it was good and that some other part of him appreciated it. He pulled back the cover and saw some long tresses of curly hair. *Cool*, he thought, *back in the game.*

He gave himself a mental pat on the back. He decided not to bother the shapely form beside him, and newly energized, still trying to piece together the night, he slithered out of bed and went to the bathroom. He had a short pee. Short relative to the pee one might have if beer had been involved instead of ouzo, at least, and when he flushed the toilet, he noted that the flusher got stuck and the toilet seemed to be plugged. He watched as the water level rose and then started to spill over the side of the bowl. *Hmm*, he thought and tried to find a shutoff or something. He fiddled with the handle, but that didn't work. He took the lid off the toilet and stopped the flow, but not until a considerable amount had already fallen on the floor. "Shit," he muttered to himself and was grossed out at the dirty water pooled around his feet.

He grabbed his toothbrush while looking at himself in the mirror, but it slipped out of his hand and landed on the wet floor. "Double shit," muttered Staf as he soberly decided not to brush his teeth with the contaminated brush.

He paused at the bathroom mirror and looked at himself. He was free. Life was great. Things were looking up. But he looked like hell. He peered into his bloodshot, mangled reflection and thought about splashing cold water on his face. He was just trying to muster the energy to do it. He finally let an arm go—painfully, for every movement seemed to aggravate that pain in his head—and feebly splashed some drops on his face. It felt great. He turned to leave the bathroom and slipped on the wet floor, splashing in the toilet water. "Triple damn," he muttered to himself. Life was going to be great, but the day was not starting out well. He ambled into the room and noticed the coffee maker. *That's the ticket for a hangover—a cup of java*, he thought to himself. He inserted the grind packet into the cup and plugged it in. A short occurred, and smoke arose from the outlet. Staf rolled his eyes—*more problems at this stupid hotel*—and he wished he had taken the time to check into a better place.

He reached for the plug and burned his hand, probably because of a mild shock from some kind of short circuit. "Damn," he yelled out as he peeled his hand away. The coffee maker crashed to the floor, spilling water and breaking the cantina. The sound woke the woman in the bed. She jolted up, wide eyed. She wasn't wearing a top, but maybe she should have been. Staf noticed that her boobs hung considerably and tried to remember them from last night. She looked around and focused on Staf. She yelled something Greek to him. He didn't understand and just stood there. She yelled at him again. This pissed him off. His head hurt, his hand hurt, and he didn't need this woman to aggravate things. He ignored her and turned his back to get some clothes on and get out for some coffee. That's what he needed: some sun, coffee, and some air. He heard a knock at the door. As he went to the door, he heard some Greek cursing behind him, and a pillow hit him. The alarm clock missed him and hit the wall beside the door and exploded into pieces. He opened the door a crack, and saw the hotel staff.

"Yes?" he enquired. The staff member apparently could speak English and demanded that he turn off the water. "Sure," muttered Staf, and he closed the door, which immediately prompted the porter to start hammering on the door and shouting at him again. He turned and something hit his head, sending him into the closet. It took a moment for the hangover and brief concussion to leave his head, and he looked up. Apparently this woman he had spent the night with was really pissed off, and she hovered over him yelling in Greek, waving a lamp in her right arm. Staf wanted to close his eyes and ears to this, but he dared not take his eyes off this crazy woman. He held out his hands.

"Look, I don't know what happened last night, but maybe you can tell me nicely, and we can sort some of this out. I'm sure it was fun." *Or a mistake,* he silently thought. This angered her more, and she continued to advance, raising the lamp. There was still knocking at the door from the hotel staff. There was a lot of pounding going around—on the door, from this woman, and in his head.

He slowly got up and went carefully to the bathroom and got a towel. He handed this to the woman, whom he realized was not wearing anything, and took note of her, which didn't do much for him, because of the state he was in. He looked away, and this apparently was another mistake. The lamp hit him in the head again and broke. The knocking at the door intensified. *What the hell is going on here?* He turned around to see the woman march off to the side of the bed. She continued to yell at him in rapid Greek as she got dressed. He noted the broken lamp on the floor but felt confident that he could pay for it. He smiled. Everything was going to be okay if he could get past this morning.

The woman saw him smile, came over waving her fist, still half dressed and clearly intent on punching him. He successfully fended off the attack and decided he could escape outside and recruit the help of the hotel staff. They normally see this stuff all the time. He opened the door and stepped outside, followed by a barrage of delicate fists from his Greek friend. But the yelling didn't stop. The concierge pushed him in the direction of the stairs while joining the woman in shouting, waving fists.

Things were getting worse, thought Staf. He made his way slowly down the stairs, followed by the yelling and arm-waving pair from above. As he passed the second floor, he caught sight of movement from his left and noticed a cat. It was black, of course.

Bad Luck. As he faced it, he startled it too, and it arched its back, hissing and spitting with its hair on end. Staf was startled too, and stumbled down the last few steps backward to the first floor. He hit the last step off balance and stumbled into an old couple as they were about to climb the stairs. They fell to the floor.

"Aieeeee," yelled the front counter man, clearly annoyed. Great, thought Staf, the front counter, concierge, some woman, and now an old couple too.

There was Greek flying at him from all angles and all sides. There was malice and hatred all around him, and it seemed to be spreading like an infectious disease.

Staf decided to get out and deal with the bill and damages later. This angered the people in the hotel, and they converged on him. His headache seemed unimportant now. He flung open the door and escaped outside. He nearly ran into another man walking a pair of dogs. He startled them, and the dogs barked at him ferociously, straining on their leashes. The owner was annoyed at this and started yelling at Staf too. Staf straightened himself and rolled his eyes. *What is going on here?* The dog owner was shouting at him, still restraining his dogs, and was able to release one hand to shake a fist at him.

The hotel door behind him was opening, and he decided he'd better start getting away from all this mess. There was a coffee shop down the road. He started to walk that way and noticed that the shouting behind him intensified. The hotel people, along with the dogs and owner, were following him, intent on catching him for something. He noticed this as he turned around and decided to walk a little faster. They sped up too. He passed the coffee shop and as he looked behind, he decided not to stop. He heard tires squeal, closed his eyes, and waited for an impact. He heard a thud and a slight crack instead.

He opened his eyes and looked around him to discover he had inadvertently walked into the middle of an intersection. A bus had avoided him and slammed into a pole. He could hear more voices and shouting. He looked up and saw the bus driver yelling at him, shaking yet another fist, but although the shout must have been loud, it was drowned out because the glass was still in the way. But passengers started to disembark and glowered at him angrily.

Some noticed the hotel crowd also shouting and shaking their fists at him. The woman was pointing at him and yelling something to the rest in Greek. This seemed to really upset the passengers, and they started to approach him, reaching out. Staf was terrified, and on instinct, he backed away. What was that woman telling them? It really seemed to upset them.

As he backed away, they approached faster. Staf's heart raced. Just as an arm was about to reach him, he decided to turn and run. This was an all-too-familiar feeling for him, and instinctive too. For a second, he wondered if anything had changed at all.

He quickly reached the other side of the road with the crowd in pursuit. As he looked back, he noticed a police car already on the scene, and the bus driver was there to describe what had happened. He was waving his arms like crazy as he talked, and the two officers were looking at him with disbelief and then with seriousness.

Staf was still only jogging on the other side of the road when he noticed the police reach for their guns and turn toward him. He decided to bolt. There was now a mob of thirty bus passengers and hotel people (and two dogs) chasing him, and now the cops were unholstering their guns. *Shit*, he thought and just decided to run straight for a while. He heard some distinct shouting above the rest of the din and then heard a pop, and a bullet passed near his head. He sped up and turned down a narrow street. The noise of the crowd behind him was starting to rise.

Some windows opened in the apartments above the street. People started yelling down at him, and some started throwing things at him. At the next intersection, he dared to turn for a second to see what was behind him and was horrified to see an angry mob filling the streets, joined by people from the apartments. Something was being said, and the word seemed to fuel anger and hatred and rile up the throng. What the hell was going on? He had just woken up a few minutes ago, and now he was out in the middle of the streets in pajamas with an angry horde chasing him. This was too much. He needed time, lots of alone time, to sort this out and figure out what was going on. The only way to do that was to lose the crowd and find a quiet space.

He made a quick right down another narrow road, and that seemed to drown out the noise of the crowd. Staf slowed to a trot and tried to think. Some kids playing in the street saw him come up. They could hear the faint noise of the crowd in the background. Staf walked briskly past them and gave them a meek smile. They ran inside. More windows flew open above him. It seemed that word was spreading faster than he could run. He turned again and could see more people coming out of apartments and into the streets. The front of the throng now turned the corner, and the newcomers were apprised of what was going on. They immediately looked at him with malice and joined the chase. Staf realized that there was not going to be a safe place at all here. Instinctively, he headed for the pier; the only way out was with the yacht.

The mob was now a roar behind him, growing like an avalanche. He looked ahead. The pier was several blocks away; he might be able to make the distance without anyone knowing his true destination. Maybe a few quick turns and he could lose them. He was in an all-out sprint again. Was it only yesterday that his chasing days had expired? This thought depressed him. Nothing had changed; he was being chased by people instead of a golem.

The pier was only one block away now. He tried to remember where the Zodiac was. He couldn't. He would have to guess. As he ran to the pier, he tried to look ahead to spot it. There were so many boats out there.

The mob turned the corner and started to spill into the final stretch to the pier. They had figured out his destination. Staf vaguely recognized the pier as he approached it and tried to remember their parking spot. He targeted the fourth pier from the left of the office, but his memory was a bit vague. The angry mob (could there already be hundreds of people?) seemed to be able to keep pace with him, and the faster ones broke away in hot pursuit. But Staf was used to running, and he could run all day.

He scanned ahead and could not find the Zodiac. Then it hit him: it wasn't the fourth pier on the left; it was on the right. He had the picture in his mind backward because he had looked at it as he came off the yacht. It was too late; he couldn't change it now. Without pausing, he reached the end of the pier as the group reached the start of it. Another shot whistled by his head. He ran off the end and dove into the water. He made an immediate right turn under the water and headed for the other side of the dock system. He decided he'd better hold his breath as long as he could. He swam what seemed for ages, and after a minute, he heard the faint splashing of others jumping in the water. His lungs were starting to complain, and he was still a few meters away from the other side. If he came up for air now, someone would spot him. He needed to get to the other side. The people under the water wouldn't be able to see him this far, but he just focused on swimming fast. His lungs started to scream. They wanted to breathe even if it was water.

There were a few feet to go. He was starting to slow down, losing energy. His lungs were begging for air. He bolted for the surface and hit his head on the pier. He gasped for air but had to take in some water too. He struggled to keep himself above water as he gasped, choked, and coughed for air, but the noise of the crowd seemed to cover him. He didn't waste any time and hurried three more piers over and immediately recognized the Zodiac. No one was near.

He swam to the far side and discreetly climbed the side. Staying low, he crawled to the controls. He dared only catch his breath for a moment and took a quick look to the left.

It was incredible. There were hundreds of people out there searching for him, and he was sure most didn't know why. Someone pointed at his Zodiac, and a string of people started pointing and yelling orders. A group of the mob started to make their way over to his pier. *Damn, I'd better get this thing going*, thought Staf.

He still hadn't caught his breath, his lungs still ached, and he still sensed a bit of water at the bottom of them. He stepped to the side and undid the rope. There were two. The mob spotted him, and the shouting and yelling intensified. They were on to him. He figured he had a minute to get rid of the ropes and get away.

The aft side was done quickly, and he raced to the front, trying to calm himself in order to work without stalling. He had about fifteen seconds to start the yacht and get out of there. He jumped back to the controls and reached for the ignition. Nothing. He had forgotten that the keys were in his pants, and they were still in the hotel. Ten seconds to go. His mind raced. Two years on the road did not leave him with no escape.

The spare! They always had a spare, and with a quick lift of the carpet, he found it. He snatched it deliberately, trying to calm himself to avoid fumbling it, and promptly put it in the ignition and smoothly turned the key. The boat started instantly. The lead runners were two yards away. Staf slammed the throttles forward. The noise was deafening, and the front of the boat lurched up.

Chapter 22: Stefano's Perspective

Stefano was running like he had never run before with full patriotism and passion fuelling his legs. Like his parents, he had never left Greece. He had traveled up and down and around the coast but never had any desire to see anything else but his beloved home. And now, it was under attack.

From what he had learned, he was helping the police and the community chase down this man, a foreigner, who had come to terrorize his home. Marco, already well behind him in the mob, had told him part of the story. This morning, hotel staff had made a routine visit to a room where a foreigner was holding a woman hostage. Apparently he had seduced her last night by tainting her drinks. This foreigner was in the midst of arming a bomb in the room when it exploded.

While attempting to flee the scene, he had punched an elderly woman who was in his way, knocking her unconscious. What kind of an animal would do that?

Helena was on the bus that he tried to hijack in order to get new hostages. Ruthless. The man was ruthless. He had been thwarted by the quick, efficient response of the local police.

If he caught up with the foreigner, he was going to kill him, thought Stefano. He gained more speed and left more people behind. He was a young man, strong and healthy with neat, long dark hair combed to the back. He was clean shaven. Mario joined him on his right; he was also breathing only lightly. He updated Stefano on more information.

"I noticed him in the bar last night. What a shady character. I knew he was up to no good, the way he was buying drinks for everyone, just being overly friendly. I warned everyone to keep a close eye on him. And look what he has done! The hotel concierge says that even the dogs and cats don't like him, and we all know about the intuition of animals."

Mario had a short two-by-four in his hand. Stefano thought that was a good idea and kept his eyes open for something that might make a weapon. Someone from up front yelled out, "Unbelievable, he kicked two little boys who were in his way!"

Stefano ran harder. He was running on pure rage. He was going to catch this man. Mario sped up close behind. They were nearing the front of the pack and would overtake them all. He could see the man running to the pier.

The bastard, he thought, *terrorizing my homeland and then running away like a coward.* He would make sure he didn't get away, make sure he couldn't return to terrorize again. He was going to do the world a favor. The first thing to do was break his legs so he couldn't run away, and then slowly kill him, getting all the information. He had to kill him before the police could get him. They would be too easy on him.

"I'm going to kill him," echoed Mario beside him, clearly thinking the same way.

The lead group was on the pier. The man had nowhere to run. It was either a boat or swim, and no one could outswim a local. This stranger was not going to outswim Stefano. Not a chance.

He raced to the entrance of the dock and watched the stranger dive into the water. He looked out into the bay for the boat that he might be trying to swim to. A moment later, some of his pursuers were in the water. He slowed on the dock while Mario charged forward; he was probably going to chase him in the water.

Everyone was on the dock and was looking out for a sign of the foreigner. Tall Antonio made it up to the dock.

"What a character," he added. "Apparently, he is an international terrorist. He has a warrant from our good U.S. friends and our neighbors in the Azores. He came into town disguised as a poor man, almost a beggar. Then he bought new clothes, shaved, and tried to change his appearance in every way. He even tried to get a haircut, but it was too late in the day. He is a desperate, dangerous man."

"Wait a minute!" shouted Gregario. "His boat isn't on this dock. It's on the one over there!" He pointed to a small Zodiac.

Stefano bolted out of the dock and charged even faster to the next one. *What a sly fox*, thought Stefano, but he was not sly enough to outwit Stefano. No one was as sharp and as quick as him. As soon as he heard the words, he knew the terrorist was heading for his boat, and Stefano was going catch him. He was so furious, all he saw was red.

He raced faster than he had ever done before, and no one else was near him. He entered the dock looking at the boat. And there he was! He wasn't going to get away. The boat hadn't even started yet. Stefano prepared himself to jump into the boat. He was steps from the boat when he heard the motor come on, but it was too late; he was within jumping range.

Suddenly, the engine roared, and the boat lurched forward, the front jumping out of the water. The noise and the movement caught Stefano off guard, and a quick calculation showed that he could probably make the jump easily. Probably was not good enough. He decided to play it safe and let the equipped authorities take care of him. They were better armed and trained to deal with this. Besides, stories get blown out of proportion around here. It was a part of daily life. The poor fellow had probably just got up on the wrong side of the bed. Stefano turned and headed to work.

Chapter 23: Back to Mexico

Staf sat in the superyacht in the Mediterranean off the coast of Greece. He was exhausted. He felt unsafe; the police, coast guard, or maybe military would be after him. He was going to call Jake again, but of course his phone was still in the hotel room, lost again. But this was a superyacht, and there was a phone in each room. Jake answered promptly.

"Hello, Mr. Nurren," he said formally.

"Yo, Jake." Staf used an extra casual manner to contrast starkly with Jake.

"Congratulations," continued Jake. "Just when I thought you couldn't possibly break any more laws or get any higher on a wanted list."

Staf thought about it for a moment. The most recent events were incredibly odd. He let Jake continue.

"You apparently tried to take hostages? Blow up a hotel? Hijack a bus? A gunfight with police? And now you have pirated a yacht according to the crew stranded in Greece. You have now been branded an international terrorist. I can't think of anything you can do to get more wanted."

Staf listened. His pulse began to quicken again, and the hair on his neck stood up. Could it be the mannequin had returned? It had been nothing but a pile of ashes when he left it two days ago. There was no mistaking the feeling. The golem was nearing. It was probably about a mile away, if his judgment was right, and it was noticeably faster than before. He looked out on the water and could see something coming toward him. It reminded him of a shark.

He retracted the anchor, started the yacht, and steered westward.

"I don't know what to tell you, Jake. I thought I had him beat, but Pinocchio is about a half mile away now. I can't stop right this moment. I am heading west."

"You can't stay in Europe anymore. You can't come to the states. How about Africa? You are there anyway."

Staf thought about it for a moment. What would he do in Africa? Run around for a while?

"Do you know how these boats work? Maybe I'll just go to South America. The ten-day boat ride will give me a chance to think things over. Do you have any suggestions?"

"The first one that comes to mind is to let the crew return to the ship. But then they will make you walk the plank; there is no way they will let you stay on their boat. Otherwise, I don't have any ideas. Not that you would listen to me anyway. But I do have to advise you to turn yourself in."

"Well, you can reach me on the yacht. I'll call you back when I figure out how to steer this thing, and maybe you can get the crew to South America to pick it up."

The phone rang as soon as he hung it up. It wasn't Jake, so he didn't pick it up. He estimated it was equally likely to be the crew wanting their yacht back or the police. He didn't want to talk to either of them. He sailed full throttle to the straight of Gibraltar and out into the Atlantic. He consulted the map and GPS. The Azores would be too busy too; he needed something more isolated.

He experimented with the GPS routing and coupled it to the yacht and was satisfied that the boat was steering southwest to Acapulco. The tension eased, so he knew he was making some distance. But it had become uncannily fast, and that was going to be troublesome.

It couldn't be stopped, and it was getting faster. Staf imagined himself in a constant run, exhausted, with the golem just steps behind him. It reminded him of his nightmares.

The weather remained cool and overcast, the sun unable to break past the thick layer of cloud. It looked like it wanted to rain but held back. He would often look out at the endless sea, wistfully hoping for the chance to stop and smell the roses.

On day five, he called his parents. His mom answered the phone.

"Hello, son. It's been a while again—"

"How's Dad?" interrupted Staf.

She paused.

Thick clouds continued to block out the sun, and a few brave raindrops fell. A sudden gust of wind shook him, and his bones felt cold. The pause was long enough to give Staf the answer; his dad had passed away. She sensed his understanding in the continued silence. Staf lost track of time.

"The funeral is in two days. Please come home."

There was more silence, and again, it conveyed the answer. He thought about explaining his problem, but it wasn't the right time. He wanted to stay on the phone and share their grief. He also wanted to hang up and hide. He was in the middle of nowhere in the ocean, and it suddenly didn't seem big enough to hide him.

"I'll see you in a few weeks," he offered and hung up. More than ever before, he wanted his life back.

As the coast of Mexico came into view, he realized he had spent ten days on the boat without having come up with any ideas. Ten days alone, but at least he hadn't had to run. Physically. But they had been sleepless, restless nights; he had been afraid he would dream of his dad.

He brought the yacht to a stop about two miles off the coast, and after coordinating the sonar, he anchored the yacht. He took a dinghy and snuck into Mexico.

Surprisingly, there was no one around. He expected the military to be waiting or a plane or helicopter to be looking for him. And his ten days on the yacht had not given him any rest.

As he set foot on land again, he already felt exhausted. He beached the dinghy just down from the main city and left it there.

He was in a rural area; there were a few run-down houses nearby. He found an old paved road, but it had not been kept up, and it almost resembled a dirt road. It was dusty.

The sun came out as soon as he touched land, and it was scorching. *Funny*, he thought; it had been cloudy the whole time he was by the cool water. Now, away from the water, it became intensely hot. The farther he got from water, the hotter it got. He thought about getting back to the boat, but what would he do there? The yacht would need gas soon, and he was not in a position to buy gas. What should he do now? Run? Walk?

Then the familiar feeling came back to him. But how could it be? It was becoming incredibly fast. Staf would need to go from one mode of transportation to another in order to stay ahead. Maybe he could get in a hot air balloon and stay aloft. But even balloons have to land sometime. He started to run. He didn't know where; he just ran. And knowing that the golem was fast and on his heels again, he ran as fast as he could. He suddenly missed his ten days on the boat. Ten days to think, and come up with nothing.

It was the evening of the first day of running, a clear, warm, starry night with distant noises of crickets and frogs. There was a constant fear inside of him; he sensed that the golem was not far behind. Every little noise startled him.

A twig snapped on the left, and Staf jumped to the right, but nothing came. Probably some sort of small animal. There was another rustle from behind, and Staf glanced backward. Nothing. Or maybe not. He stopped to have a look. Could it be? Something shimmered in what little light there was. Was there something darker than night on the road? Staf could hardly breathe in fear. Then it was unmistakable: a stick man, darker than dark, sprinting fast toward him. A slight shimmer of star light reflected on its smooth, featureless face. And even worse, he could hear the haunting clip-clop echoing in the still night.

Staf needed to run and run fast. His body ached. He was tired. He wanted to close his eyes, sit down, and just wait and see what happened. He turned and ran as if running the final Olympic sprint. Staf ran and ran down dusty roads through one village and then another. Many reminded him of towns he had seen in spaghetti westerns. He didn't come across many large centers. He saw one in the distance and decided to steer clear of it.

Once the yacht was discovered, which was inevitable, there would be a search for him in the major centers, so he stayed on the dusty roads and trails and managed to avoid people. It was exhausting. He was going to the United States. He would know his way around better there. He looked up at the sun and tried to figure out which way was north. He ran day and night, the clip-clop constantly behind him. He was at a loss about how to increase the distance. For three days straight he ran. He couldn't seem to increase the distance between him and the golem. It was always about a mile behind him.

It was fast, much faster than the first night two years ago. Thinking about it, Staf had a short chuckle. A deranged, resigned, manic chuckle. There was nothing funny about this, but the irony was beyond sane. A truck came up the road quickly behind him, and he recalled events in the Azores. It was some sort of delivery truck. As it passed, Staf noticed that it had a small sort of ledge on the back. In desperation, he lunged for the handle on the door. He got it and held on, dragged behind the truck. He wanted to catch his breath, but it was tough to hold on while he was being dragged along, so with his final ounce of energy, Staf pulled himself onto the ledge of the truck, where he could finally relax. It was the first time he had stopped in three days.

His legs thanked him for the break. When he looked back, the golem was already out of sight. An hour later, the truck came into a small village and pulled over, probably for a break. Staf hopped off, not wanting to get noticed. It was now midday and siesta time. He found someone on the side of the road and asked for directions to the United States.

"Cientos de miles," said the stranger as he pointed north.

Staf ran through the village. It was typical, with most of the stores lined on both sides of the main street. At what might have been the main intersection of the small town, there was a bar. Cervesa it said, and Staf knew the term well. He decided to run in and have a beer. He promptly ran out as the clip-clop sounds of the golem reached the sidewalk. He was also scared of the bartender.

Staf blindly ran out of the bar and chose a direction away from the clip-clops. It was north. North to the United States. He hitched onto the back of another truck with practiced ease, as if this was his normal way to travel now. A mile from the border, he jumped off and ran to the side of the road. His plan was to reach some section of the border that was unmanned, find a break in the fence, and go through.

It was night again, and the crickets chirped like an alarm to the border patrol, and the stars shone as brightly as possible, as if to illuminate his incursion. He had heard that border patrol had become very adept at stemming migration. The economy had done its part too. He found several sections of the fence that were repaired and then one that he could work with. He peeled it from the bottom and worked his way under it despite the crickets and stars.

His senses told him that the golem was still a fair distance behind him.

He easily slithered under the chain-link fence and immediately bolted northwest toward the coast. He didn't know where else to go but home.

He ran again without stopping. He had now gone four days without sleep, and he didn't dare stop now. He found a rough road that appeared to go north and followed it absently.

In the early morning, a truck pulled over and offered him a ride to the next town, which was more convenient than hopping onto the back. The driver probably couldn't figure out why someone was running out in the middle of nowhere, and Staf looked like someone who needed help. They drove in complete silence. He was dropped off at the edge of town.

Staf was completely exhausted. His legs hurt, his lungs hurt, and four days without sleep had made his foggy head hurt; there wasn't a part of his body that didn't complain. He felt gross, sweaty, dirty; he couldn't remember his last shower or the last time he had brushed his teeth. He would have a few hours until the golem arrived, and although he needed to wash, brush his teeth, and sleep, he didn't know what order to do them. He leaned against a fence post and thought about the evil that was after him. How could a mere person get past this? Could magic do it? He had already tried a psychic. He recalled the brief discussion in the Vatican, and then he had a desperate idea and took off down the road with new energy.

Chapter 24: Meet the Priest

Pastor Roger was in the backyard gardening. He pulled weeds, plucked dead flowers, and watered bushes. *All in a quiet day's work*, he thought contentedly. He was a happy fellow. He was portly, for he loved his blessed meals, yet he was always active, always doing something. He liked to be outside when the weather was nice, mowing the lawn, gardening, washing. On rainy days, Pastor Roger would be in the small church, dusting statues, wiping pews, replenishing water. There was a lot of help available in this small town, but he still liked to do things himself. He left the organization and the planning to the senior group, the elderly ladies. It was customary for them to come over almost daily for a meeting and tea to discuss and to plan. They were always discussing and planning, but they never did anything. But he didn't mind, and he enjoyed having them come over as long as they generally left him alone in his garden.

He had been at the church for twelve years and had presided over countless baptisms, weddings, and funerals. He was happy and liked to think he projected that on his group and therefore the whole town. A whole town was content because he was content. He figured he was destined to grow old here, which meant just a few more years. The central church generally left him alone, and maybe they had even forgotten about him.

He had just finished tending the rose garden. His garden was popular for wedding pictures. The day was sunny and clear; one small lonely cloud drifted to the sun and blotted it out. The change in the air was instantaneous. With the warmth of the rays blocked, the wind, which had been a silent relief, became noticeable.

Pastor Roger looked up at the sun and shaded his eyes. It was almost noon, time to go in and get a glass of water and maybe lunch. The ladies sometimes had an extra sandwich square lying around after tea.

He entered the church from the small door at the back and gently placed his gardening gloves on the floor to the side. With the lights off and the sun blotted out, the church seemed very dark for an afternoon, the result of his eyes not being accustomed to the sudden change in brightness. It was peaceful and quiet in his church, but a mounting tension built in him. He had never had that feeling before. He looked around. A chill went up his spine, and the hair on the back of his neck stood up.

What a strange thing, he thought to himself and forced himself to look around. There was a knock on the large front doors. He proceeded up the aisle. The impatient knock came again.

"Come in," he invited in his quiet voice. The door opened, and a haggard man entered the church. Father Roger didn't recognize him, and considering his strange feeling, he wanted the stranger to leave or at least to continue the meeting outside. Trying as best he could to mask his revulsion, he said, "Welcome. What can I do for you?"

The stranger looked like a wild animal, and a faint odor permeated the air. Pastor Roger couldn't help but wrinkle his nose, but he forced a smile and waited for reply.

"Umm," stammered the stranger, "I need some advice." Then after a pause, he said, "And I need to make a confession."

Pastor Roger avoided rolling his eyes. This was not a Catholic church, and therefore confessions were unnecessary here; clearly this man didn't know what he was doing and was grasping at the end of his rope for some redemption. But he wanted to help, and sometimes he enjoyed these different situations, although not often. He had come across the occasional case of theft or adultery. He hadn't had to deal with a killing yet, and a mild trepidation came over him as he wondered if he would face it this time.

"Please," said Father Roger, shifting into the role of confidant and allowing a more authoritative tone to creep into his voice, "please sit down." He invited the stranger to a pew.

The stranger invited Pastor Roger to sit first. This was a serious thing, thought Pastor Roger. Generally, when a person asked him to sit on the inside, they needed to avoid feeling trapped, needed to have an escape.

He had a good way about him; the church was not a business to him but a passion. He kept his sermons brief, usually taking something in the news and tying it in with a verse from the Bible. The sermon rarely lasted more than ten minutes. The tea ladies had objected to such brevity until he had gently asked them to allow it to continue as long as the growth in attendance continued. The topic lost interest to the ladies, and they moved on to other, more pressing global (town) issues.

Then, when he had decided to change the method of collection (a box in the back versus the tray handed around), they had fought again, a little harder this time, and again, he had gently received their permission to continue on a trial basis. He wanted all to feel welcome without the subtle burden of collection. He was all too familiar with his family's approach to collection. Everyone had to have some change. Was it enough? You never felt like it was.

He gently got his system in place; he was very proud of his welcoming church. Maybe that's why this stranger had chosen his church, even though this was the wrong place for a confessional. He was still willing to listen to him and help if he could.

"Where's the booth?" The stranger looked around.

Pastor Roger explained that it was not part of their system but that he was willing to listen. He dug deep for more patience and understanding. He introduced himself.

"I'm Pastor Roger. What's troubling you?"

The stranger looked down at his hands, clearly trying to find a place to begin a long story. He looked up at the ceiling, and Pastor Roger wondered if he was searching for hidden art, something like the Sistine Chapel. People sometimes liken a nice church to an art gallery. He leaned back.

Pastor Roger sensed that his guest was becoming more relaxed. He looked into his eyes and slouched slightly in the pew.

"Well, when I was young, I wanted something really badly. I sort of made a deal with the devil, so to speak"—he shot a quick glance at the pastor and noticed no change in expression—"and now I find myself being chased or being haunted as a result." He paused.

After a moment in which Pastor Roger waited to see if in fact the stranger was finished speaking, he replied, "Well, generally speaking—and you are a bit vague about this," said Pastor Roger, and he paused after saying this, looking closely at the stranger to indicate that he should elaborate shortly. He continued. "I have generally found that you have to go back to the source. Unfortunately, we can't go back in time and change what we have already done, but we can give back what we have taken and accept the price."

"But I can't give it back," protested the stranger.

"But instead of running from the problem, can you face it?"

"Not precisely."

"Perhaps, instead of running from the problem, you can arrange a compromise and come to different understanding. There might still be a price to pay, but you are young, and providing it is forthright and honest in the eyes of the law and of God, perhaps you can solve your problem."

The stranger did not seem to like the advice, but it seemed to make him think. Then the stranger started to tell him a strange story about his soul, running, and golems.

An hour passed, and the tension in the air started to increase. The stranger felt it too. He fidgeted and looked around as if he were ready to leave, run, or escape. Pastor Roger felt an overwhelming desire for him to leave too and resisted it. He would have liked to advise him to check into the hospital but didn't know how to do that politely.

"I don't know what to tell you," said the pastor. "Perhaps it would be folly going to the source, but I have generally found that the best path to take. Right what you have done wrong. If possible." He added the last part quickly, like a disclaimer. "Please come back any time. I would very much like to know how this all goes for you, and I hope it goes well." He silently hoped never to see this fellow again, but he sincerely wished him well.

They shook hands, and Pastor Roger made a mental note to wash his hands immediately. Staf left the pew and went quickly up the aisle as Pastor Roger went to the rear of the church to his garden's entrance. He turned to see the stranger quickly leave.

A heavy weight was lifted off his shoulders. He shrugged, put on his gardening gloves, and opened the door. It was pouring rain outside, and black birds were dismantling his rose garden. He fought the temptation to curse his recent visitor, and at the same time, he hoped he would never meet him again. He was mad at himself for the thought, and it troubled him for quite some time.

Staf hitchhiked to the outskirts of his old hometown. It was approaching midnight. He wanted to phone Jake and let him know where he was just in case things didn't turn out well.

Phoneless since he left the superyacht, he looked for a pay phone. This was his old neighborhood, and as he walked, he recalled a gas station with a pay phone just around the corner. He wanted to go to the bar, the bar he had visited fifteen years ago on his sixteenth birthday, exactly fifteen years ago today. The gas station was still there, and oddly enough, no one was using the phone.

He crossed his fingers and entered the booth, and his good fortune continued as he noted the phone was not vandalized. He picked it up and listened to the dial tone. Things were changing. He could feel it. He had to dial Jake's number three times, because the number seven wasn't working properly. Jake promptly answered the phone.

"Finally, Staf. You wouldn't believe the shit I've got to deal with here. But at least you haven't added to it. Yet. How is your jogging going? Where are you now?"

"You wouldn't believe it."

"I wouldn't, eh? Well then, my guess is that you would be back in the states somewhere; how about back in the old neighborhood?"

"You just can't stop being a jerk, can you?"

"When we spoke two weeks ago, I gave you a brief summary of your misdeeds. You are on the wanted list. Not high, because you haven't actually succeeded in killing anyone yet. But because of your well-earned status, and as your attorney, noting confidentiality and all that stuff, I suspect my phone is tapped, and they might get a trace on your call. By the way, I don't think I can get you any more cell phones."

"Jake, I just wanted to thank you for all your help."

"Where the hell did that come from? I wish I could say you're welcome."

Staf didn't laugh. "I'll be in touch soon."

"So what are you up to now? Don't tell me, you have to run?"

"I sort of do, but I am trying one last way to fix things up. If this line is tapped, I probably shouldn't tell you how."

"That sounds good to me, Staf, but also too good. And by the way, I am advising you to turn yourself in."

Staf hung up and exited the phone booth. He passed the gas station and was suddenly very conscious of cameras and that sort of thing, but he needed to get on the road. He noticed a police car quickly and silently pull up. Staf entered the station's store and went to the wash rooms at the back. He found an emergency exit and promptly left. He wanted to get to the bar.

Several blocks down, he ducked into a corner store as another police cruiser drove by. He left down another lane and found another cruiser. It seemed suddenly that the police were cruising everywhere, and a few were even wandering on foot. Staf recalled Jake's subtle advice; his phone was tapped, and they had probably traced his call.

But this was his neighborhood, and he knew several back alleys and shortcuts to get where he wanted to go.

The night was silent except for the occasional barking dog. He went another few blocks quickly. He wanted to get out of there at a brisk walk without attracting attention. He tried to think of a way to get to the bar discreetly. Another dog barked, distracting his train of thought. Loose pets were one of his pet peeves. Several dogs barked. It was very annoying. Wait. Maybe police dogs? On his scent? From where? With no time to sort that out, he crisscrossed his way downtown in an all-out sprint again. Did it ever stop? Running from the mannequin was bad enough, but the mob in Greece, the police, and now dogs were just too much. He felt he was running from the world.

The barking got fainter.

Staf entered his old hometown bar, the bar he and Jake had been into fifteen years earlier. The place hadn't changed; the tables were all in the same places, the pool table and darts were in the shadowy area in the back. Staf took a look around.

The bartender was the same too. He was a little older and had a little less hair, and it was now gray. His face was a little more drawn out, but the smart sharp eyes were still there, and he worked at the same steady, smart pace that kept him busy and efficient without exhausting him.

Staf sat down at the same spot as he had decades earlier. He quickly ordered a beer. The bartender looked at him, and a hint of recognition came to his face, betrayed by a look that was just a second longer than normal. Staf knew he had been vaguely recognized. He wondered if the bartender was going to ask for identification. Staf took a long draw from the draft and looked around at the bar.

Everyone looked vaguely the same. They all seemed to have a vagueness about them that you couldn't place; you couldn't quite specify the color of their eyes, the shape of their noses, or whether their hair was long or short. They all appeared about the same, just put in different combinations.

Staf was at the bottom of his drink. He tried to pierce the back room. He ordered his last draft; he would have to leave very soon. There was no serious tension in his gut yet, but it wouldn't be too long.

As he waited for his draft, he heard the old, croaky voice that he was waiting for, and his heart skipped a beat with excitement and hope instead of fear. He quickly looked at the bar, and there he was, hunched over, looking desperate, the gloves with the holes for the fingers, the torn shirt just a little dirtier than before.

"I'll get that," said Staf to the bartender while his eyes focused on his old friend. The old fiend shot him a look, and there was the other peculiar trait, each eye going in a different direction so that

Staf wasn't sure where he was looking. His eyes narrowed and peered at something, presumably Staf. Suddenly, his eyes grew wide with recognition.

"I don't want your damn beer!" he bellowed.

He threw some change on the table and hobbled to the back room surprisingly fast. Staf kept his eyes on him and charged after him. He nearly lost him in the dark shadows and forms of the back room. It was more crowded than he had thought; there were men playing pool, darts, and cards. There was darkness in the back, not because of smoke but because light could not penetrate it.

The patron seemed to glide through the crowd, while Staf bumped clumsily into people. He faintly saw the door in the back open, and he charged for it, catching it before it could close.

The back alley was dark with one small light hanging over the door casting shadows instead of light. The patron was a few steps to the left, deeper in the darkness, and Staf started the chase. Suddenly the patron stopped. Surely, thought Staf, this fellow knew who he was and what he had done and knew he wasn't going to slip away so easily.

Then another thought came to mind. He was alone in the back alley; maybe that wasn't such a good place to be with this man. As if to prove this point, the patron stopped and stood straight. Suddenly he didn't seem to hunch over so much and didn't seem to have that aura of an out-of-luck person. He turned and faced Staf. Staf could barely see his eyes, but they seemed to focus fine now, both looking straight at him instead of in different directions. They were the same eyes, but they were malevolent now. There was a hint of red in them.

He just stood there staring at Staf. Staf was still beside the door, and he thought about trying to escape back into the bar, but he needed to get this done, and he had gone through too much and come too far to give up now.

After a moment of silence, Staf spoke up. He wanted to sound confident, but his voice only came out half as forceful as he wanted it to. "I need to arrange another meeting." *Shit*, thought Staf. This was asking; he had meant to be more assertive. He said it again, louder. "I want another meeting."

A leer flickered on the patron's face in the shadows. Apparently, when outside the bar, the patron had perfect white teeth, a straight back, and perfectly centered vision, as far as Staf could tell from what little light shone from the lonely lightbulb.

"First," he said, "I don't care what you want, or demand, if that is the word you really meant to use, you feeble thing." He leered. "And second, I am not going to meet any of your demands or make any deals with the likes of you. Seems you have a hard time keeping your promises, and you have pissed off many. But there is one in particular that you shouldn't have. I don't want to deal with you. There is a danger about you that I don't dare get involved with, if you know what I mean, and I know you do." The leer morphed into an evil smile. "I think you should start running. But I recommend you go that way." The smile ceased, and the face became hidden in the shadows of his hat.

"Wait!" pleaded Staf, not sounding at all forceful. "I need another job, and I will be willing to do anything." A small smile formed in the shadow, and Staf added, "Almost anything." The smile vanished quickly. "There must be something I can do."

"Why would I take the chance of dealing with you anyway? Have you ever come across a certain red carpet?"

Staf recognized the implication. He thought about it for a moment and realized that he himself wouldn't bother to help anyone if he risked going into the red carpet. The memory of the red creeping up his arms and legs gave him a shudder.

"You must have a price," said Staf quickly, sensing a dead end. "I can do anything, go anywhere. There must be something."

He managed to say it without pleading too much. There was a long silence. The shadows didn't move. It was thinking. Staf held his breath and didn't dare move from his spot.

After a moment, slowly and without a smile or leer, the man said, "I have a small delivery to make overseas to Switzerland, a trip I would rather not take at the moment. The difficulty is that it must not be stopped or delayed in any way."

There was another pause. Staf looked on, holding his breath. He wanted to tell him to hurry up.

"It must be delivered. Understand that I could do it myself, but I am busy here." The sly leer came back.

"I will deliver it! Switzerland, no problem!" Staf was wondering if there was a catch; it was too easy. Were gangs trying to stop the delivery? That didn't make sense. He was a rickety old man, or he had been when he was in the bar, anyway. Staf's gut began to hurt. He started to hear a faint clip-clop. He needed to get this going. He didn't need time for details.

The smile faded again and the patron said in a calm voice, "You mean you wouldn't have any problems getting to Switzerland, no travel problems, no problems clearing customs?"

"No!" interrupted Staf. He saw an opening and needed to take advantage of it quickly.

"I will arrange a meeting." He was talking slowly, deliberately slowly, in the opinion of Staf. The clip-clops where getting louder. Staf tried to have some patience.

"The meeting will allow for a temporary cessation of your predicament, with a permanent result dependent upon the successful completion of your"—there was another deliberate pause for effect—"new assignment."

The term was clearly meant to imply that the previous one was not completed, which was true. Staf quickly thought about it. A simple delivery. The clip-clops where clearly audible; it was probably around the corner. He had seconds to think it over. He could hardly think straight. Was there a possible catch? A delivery to Switzerland. He had been there before. It would be easy enough if nothing was chasing him.

The clip-clops came around the corner. The leering patron grew hideously large. The lips had to part to show the teeth. There was nothing else to see. Staf needed to turn and run soon.

"Okay," he said quickly, "arrange it!"

Staf held his breath. The smile lingered. He said nothing. The clip-clops where only a dozen steps behind him, closing fast. Staf had seconds. He was ready to bolt. He crouched a bit. *This may have been a waste of time*, he thought. *Got to get running. Can't take a chance on getting caught.* He was still beside the back door of the bar; the light above it flickered. He had to squint. The patron was a faint outline in the dark. The golem was steps behind him. He had to run. This was a trap. He crouched more, and the patron said, "Go in the door."

"What?" yelled Staf, and the shadow laughed and blended into the dark.

The clip-clops where so loud he could hardly think. He knew instinctively that one of its wooden hands was reaching out. He had to move. He threw the door open and ran in. It slammed behind him. He took ten strides at full speed, waiting for the inevitable crash of the door behind him. As he focused on what was ahead of him, he realized that it might not happen. He was back on the red carpet heading toward the ornate oak desk. Rial was behind the desk, glaring at him.

Staf ran to the desk, slowing down in the last few strides. This was all too familiar. He began to wonder how this new deal was going to work out. It couldn't possibly be worse than his present situation.

"Sit," ordered Rial as if it would be a waste of air to say more. Staf already knew that a chair would be behind him and sat in it without looking. This was where it had all started, including the golem, and now he knew how the temporary cessation was going to be arranged. His heart rate slowed a little. He heard a padded thumping behind him and knew that the golem had entered and was running after him, but it was a slower thump, and the knot in his stomach wasn't there. It wasn't going after him anymore. That feeling had stopped as soon as he entered the door.

The golem thumped past him. Staf jumped as it passed, never having let it intentionally come that close to him before. It ran around the desk to a spot behind Rial as he continued to glare at Staf. The golem stopped, feet together. The feet and legs merged. The arms shrank into the body, and then the head dipped a little and became rough. It had changed back into an old stick.

As the head shrank, the crystal ball emerged from what had been its face and gently rolled down to the floor and up the desk leg and stopped on the desk to the right of Rial. Staf felt eerily as if he were back in his glass house when he had first met the golem. The air was not as hot. He noticed lots of subtle noises. Black birds circled noisily overhead. Bugs, rats, and other animals snorted, squawked, and slithered in the dark. Clearly, Rial was not as fearsome as the boss, but it was still not a good place to be.

He recalled their last meeting.

"Hello, Rial," said Staf almost cheerfully but not wanting to push it. "Good to see you. A bit of a promotion?" Sometimes he couldn't control his mouth.

There was no friendliness in Rial's demeanor. He was preoccupied with something in front of him on the desk that Staf could not see. Then Rial handed him a small, neatly wrapped box.

"A limousine is outside. It will take you to the airport. A chartered plane is waiting for you. It will take you to Geneva. Customs is taken care of. Another limousine will take you to a building. You will go to the fifth floor, suite 506. Give the package to Dr Eckhardt. Our deal will be done. Do not delay or hesitate in any way whatsoever."

Rial started to write something on the desk. Staf looked at the small box. That was it? Two years on the run for this?

Rial stopped writing and glared at Staf.

The last words echoed in Staf's mind. Do not delay whatsoever. Staf slowly and carefully picked up the package and turned without acknowledging Rial. He avoided looking down at the red carpet, but he could sense tugs on the bottom of his shoes, as if someone was telling him not to go. This was the third time that he had ignored the pleading people trapped in the hell carpet, but the golem wasn't chasing him anymore. That was all that mattered right now. He didn't want to turn and look at it. The sight of even a long stick would terrorize him for the rest of his life. As he neared the door, he sped up. He was on his way to freedom; the first step was this meeting, and the next step would be out the door.

As promised, a black limousine was waiting for him in the alley with the back door open.

They promptly drove off. The divider was already up and heavily tinted so that he couldn't see the driver. Outside, traffic was light.

They went through many intersections, but they didn't have to stop. All the traffic lights were always green for them.

He desperately wanted to call Jake, and a quick search reminded him that he still didn't have a cell phone.

The car stopped, and the back door opened. Staf didn't see anyone. The car door was perfectly aligned with the airplane door. Staf put a foot on the aircraft stairs and then abruptly turned and dove into the limousine before the door closed. He had almost forgotten the package, which was still on the seat. Staf couldn't believe how he had almost screwed up the simplest task.

He boarded the plane. It was a large Boeing 767 and was painted black as if to blend in with darkness, which made it seem invisible. The inside was in a corporate configuration, with several couches, a bar, a large-screen television, and an aft bedroom. Staf sat on the couch with the package in his lap. He was the only one on the plane except for the pilots, who were already behind the sealed cockpit door.

The aircraft door closed, and the plane promptly taxied and took off without delay.

There was no flight attendant. Staf spent the entire journey sitting on the sofa with the package in his lap.

Staf sat like a zombie on the sofa for eight hours. He hadn't slept for over five days now. He had almost forgotten the package already and just needed to get the last few steps out of the way, and then he was free. After he dropped off the package, he promised himself a week of sleep.

Without any notice, the plane started to descend. He heard the landing gear come down and the motors that operated the flaps. Runway lights passing the window indicated that they had landed. The landing was so smooth he hadn't realized that they had touched down. It was night. Perfect to keep the plane invisible. The only sensation he had was a slight feeling of being pushed out of his seat. It struck him that he had never had a seat belt on.

The final leg of Staf's journey was starting.

The plane stopped at the ramp, and the door was promptly opened from the outside. Staf came to the door but didn't see anyone. At the bottom of the steps was the open door of another limousine.

Staf got in and put the package on his lap. The drive resembled his previous one. He even thought it was the exact same car. Contrary to what he had heard, there seemed to be no traffic in Geneva; the ride was smooth and as uninterrupted as the ride in L.A. It was still dark outside, but Staf had no idea what time it was. Light traffic suggested it might be three or four in the morning. After thirty minutes, the car stopped, and the door opened. He wasn't surprised to find no one outside. He expected to be exactly at the front door of a building and wasn't disappointed.

He entered the building and found the elevator on the right. It was waiting for him. He entered, and the door promptly closed, and before Staf could find the button for the fifth floor, he was there.

It was the final step. He couldn't believe it. *Deliver the package, the deal is done, and all is good.* He ran down the hall, promptly found 506, and entered. A receptionist smiled at him, and after a brief conversation on the phone, she showed him to the back office and introduced him to Dr. Eckhardt. He seemed to vaguely recognize Staf.

This made Staf think that the last two years and a week without sleep had taken so much out of him that he didn't look like himself. But the doctor welcomed him warmly. Staf didn't care about meeting him; he was giddy with excitement. This was the end of his ordeal. Staf smiled and handed him the package. It was done.

They had a short, forgettable conversation. Staf listened to none of it, shook the doctor's hand, and left. Just outside the office door, he let out a long sigh. His legs felt like they would never run again. And he didn't want them to. There were no shadows. The sun was rising. It looked bright and happy. He left the building, stood outside, and wondered what to do. He wanted to sleep, sit, walk, eat, drink, and shower all at once. Anything but run. He also needed to tell someone. He found a phone booth and made a call on his credit card.

"Hello again, Staf. So soon this time?"

Staf was used to this now and didn't bother to comment. It was just too nice a day.

"Guess where I am now?"

"Do you really want me to play this game again? Okay, well, clearly not in our hometown anymore, so how about Geneva?"

"Asshole. I have good news though."

"So do I. I've had a team working on your case for quite some time now, and in the last twenty-four hours, we've made amazing progress. Your original DWI case was thrown out for lack of evidence. That issue with the plane in New York was a manufacturing defect, and the DA agrees that you acted as any man would by running away from a disintegrating aircraft. The Azores problem was quietly dropped after we paid the damages. We called it a night of celebration that got out of control. And the yacht crew heard about the misunderstanding that created the mob. They actually laughed at your antics. The long and the short of it is that you have one heck of a good lawyer. You're a free man. Run wherever you want to."

Unbelievable, thought Staf. Could the boss manipulate events as easily as stirring a cup of coffee? Stir a group of people into an angry mob? Make him scared of a running stick? Cut down his routes of escape until it led him back to this point?

"I don't have to run anymore. I completed my end of the deal. The golem is gone, the sun is up, the roses smell lovely. After a week of constant running without sleep, I am going to disappear somewhere and hibernate. Disappear with my feet up, drink in my hand, and work on my French."

"You do that, Staf, and keep in touch."

The phone was already dead.

Staf went to the train station again. He took the next train to the coast, and despite his tiredness, he couldn't sleep on the train. He went to the marina and anonymously rented a yacht for a month. It was not as big as the superyacht he had grown accustomed to, but it was extremely comfortable to sit in the Mediterranean and do nothing but practice happiness.

Chapter 25: A Month after the Drop-off

Staf spent a full month on the boat doing nothing. He had enough supplies, and he simply enjoyed the peace and quiet.

He wasn't sure exactly where off the coast of France he was, but what was important was there were not many other boats around. And the weather was nice. He thought about going into port but put it off every day. He slept in most days, listened to music, watched TV, went swimming, and did some snorkeling.

After a month of bliss, he turned on his phone. It was about time to return to reality. He had been away far too long. He called Jake. Maybe he would know where Amber was. The phone rang. Someone picked it up.

"Staf, get your act together and your ass over here!" There was no greeting.

"Hi, Jake?"

"Just when I thought you couldn't pile the shit any higher."

"Well, let's lower the pile a little then."

"Where are you?"

"I don't know. On a boat somewhere. There's lots of water around."

"Somehow, I don't think you know the trouble you are in."

"Actually, I have been feeling great this last week. And I haven't lost this cell phone. What's up?"

"Well, what do you want first, the bad news or the really bad news? Never mind. You messed up big time, twice."

Staf wished he hadn't made the phone call. He was happy and wanted to stay that way. He wondered if he could stay happy by merely not hearing bad news. Turning off the phone would help. But then the mysterious news would haunt him until he found it out.

"Should I run and hide again?"

"No. And you have nowhere to go. Well, off the top of my head, you could try for Atlantis or Oz till you piss them off too. Are you trying to get banished from the world? That sample you dropped last month, well, it was a sample of that drink you took in high school. Apparently it has been examined and tested and is a new form of performance-enhancing drug. A new class. And they can't replicate the formula in the lab. They did, however, manage to develop a test for it. You don't need many guesses to figure out whether your samples tested positive, do you? With the revelation that you cheated, your entire career will be removed from the record books."

Staf could barely speak. It seemed too much to take in. He recalled the drink. He wondered if there was a bug in the sample, recalling the one that slithered down his throat.

So this was the small problem. He couldn't even make a joke out of it anymore and whispered, "So what's the big problem?"

"Well, you dropped the sample off in Europe. They suspect the United States has been harboring this stuff for years. They're blaming the whole country, not just you. There is a move to erase every record, every medal, and every accomplishment of American athletes in the world arena. Today it's expected that the US soccer team will be expelled from the World Cup. It is doubtful that we will be allowed to send anyone to the Olympics next year. Staf, the sports community is in disarray in every corner just because of you. Do you realize the depth and magnitude of this? You have completely destroyed athletics in the United States and the world. But the effect goes well beyond just athletes. This has affected every person in the world. The whole world, Staf."

Staf was at a loss. He had spent a month of bliss on his boat while everything outside his bubble was crumbling. He didn't know what to say. His mind was a whirlwind, and he couldn't grasp a single thought.

"They have re-opened your files, revived your arrest warrants, and made up dozens of others. Everyone, and I mean everyone in the world, is trying to find you. Staf, you there? You need to get back here. I will call you back in an hour and let you know the terms of your surrender. I will try to get house arrest with a tracing bracelet, and we'll agree to pay the expense of hiring guards for your house. And one more thing, Staf. The IOC wants all the medals back. They are just missing one. That would be the one with you, so don't forget to bring it back too. And Staf, don't run away from this one. You must come back and face this."

Staf hung up. He could not fathom the impact he had had on the world of sports. It didn't settle in. Decimate US sports? Impossible. Worldwide arrest warrant? Just a piece of paper. But give up his medals? That was going to be the hardest thing he ever had to do.

Chapter 26: Julie Karver

Julie Karver stood on the baseline ready, swaying on her legs, on her toes, ready to pounce in any direction. "Like a panther," she repeated to herself as she stalked the tennis ball.

The ball was not her real prey; the prey was the person holding it, the notorious number two. A distant number two.

This was match point at Wimbledon, and this was going to put her in the history books. Three consecutive grand slams, and this year without losing any sets. They didn't know what they were going to call it. Triple grand slam? Diamond grand? Platinum grand? That was for later.

The feat was astounding in the modern era of tennis. But then, not really when you think about the time and training.

Since she was three, she had held a tennis racquet. She played nationally at ten, became the national champion at thirteen. She achieved her first grand slam at fifteen and now, on the verge of her eighteenth birthday, a triple grand slam.

She had lived tennis eight hours a day, seven days a week, three hundred sixty-five days a year for fifteen years. She had taken a day off two years previously when she had the flu and another last year after winning the second grand slam. The days off were painful and restless. All she wanted to do was go on the court. She couldn't stop thinking about it that day.

At night, the ball was bouncing around her mind like a pong game. She dreamed of running down the side and slamming a shot down the line and tossed in her sleep. Then a run to the net for a drop shot. She tossed again. Then to the back to smash a lob. She twitched.

But there was no resting now.

She had never tasted a chocolate bar, never had a soft drink. She had tried a taste of chocolate birthday cake at a child's party long ago and hated it. Halfway through the party, as someone uselessly tapped a piñata, she had begged her mom to take her to a tennis court.

This was the final point at Wimbledon on the eve of a triple grand slam. She was making history. And this was going to be easy. She was not going to lose this point.

Her prey had briefly juggled two balls and selected the slightly smaller of the two with the hopes of using a smaller, faster ball on the first serve. The balls were not entirely new; they had already been through three games. They had therefore lost a fraction of their original air pressure and would be slightly slower. Julie added this to the list of factors in her mind that would tell her what to expect on the serve.

The ball was tossed up and took forever to come down. It was directly overhead, probably a straight serve down the line. She noted the windup, the stance, the left foot pointing slightly to the centre of the court, her opponent's back arched backward instead of to the side; there was an 80 percent probability that it would come down the line. Then came the swing from directly behind her head, not the side. Unless she wanted to make history with the dumbest slice serve in match point history, this serve was going down the line.

She made a short hop and landed on her toes at exactly the same time that the racquet struck the ball. She started to move to the left. The ball hadn't left the racquet yet, but she was on her way.

The server turned, her back sprung forward, her shoulder rotated, her wrist uncocked. The racquet contacted the ball, the shaft bent, the strings stretched, and the ball deformed into the stings. Then the reverse: the arm accelerated forward, the shaft of the racquet whiplashed while the strings sprung back, and the ball rebounded. The swing of the arm and the snap of the wrist accelerated the ball into a bullet.

Before the ball could scream over the net, Julie was on her way. She would be early. She wound up and aimed down the backhand line. She already saw it there, knew how fast it was going to go, and knew her opponent wasn't going to get it. She had already won the match, won Wimbledon, won the third grand slam, and the serve hadn't crossed the net. It finally arrived, and she crushed it down the line for the winner.

Her opponent's flailing racquet was nowhere near the ball.

Julie was numb. It was unbelievable. Warmth spread over her body as the realization sunk in. She stopped. Was it really finished or was it another dream? Was this the night before again, dreaming of the win? Thunderous applause from the huge crowd. The standing ovation proved to her it wasn't a dream. But she was still not sure. Her dejected opponent came to the net. They embraced. She looked into the stands to her coach and fiancé and saw him standing, beaming. She waved to him. It was true.

She slowly raised her hands in victory, and the dams let loose behind her eyes as the tears started to flow down like two small rivers. She was the best ever.

At the press conference with the small sports media group, she answered the usual questions about how it felt and what was next. Then Tom from the Sports Network asked, "How do we know you are clean?"

"Huh?" she answered, confused.

"What drugs are you on? This feat is impossible. All players are training day and night, training as hard as you are. What drugs helped you get to this spot today? Come clean now. We all know what happened to Staf Nurren; you might as well admit it now and save the tennis federation the embarrassment. You have to be on something, regardless of clean test results. That could change tomorrow. Come clean now."

The room fell silent. Julie didn't know what to say. The bubble was burst. She had put everything in her life into this since she was three; tennis was all she knew. She had spent her childhood without cakes, pop, and chips, without playground games or even birthday parties. She had never taken any drugs, not even an aspirin for a headache. This was shattering. She didn't know what to say and sat dumbfounded.

The media sat silent for a moment, and they suddenly took her silence as admission. They sprang to life with a barrage of questions.

"What drugs are they? How long? How did you avoid detection?"

Microphones and faces sprang up from all directions, camera flashes blinded her, but she didn't move; she was stunned.

There was a tap on her shoulder, and her fiancé took her arm and escorted her out of the side entrance. Her publicist stood in and started to say something to everyone, something vague and noncommittal, and the words *no comment* rang out.

This infuriated her; she had a comment. It was a flat-out no, but the scene happened so fast that she didn't have time to respond.

They entered an empty changing room, and her coach locked the door.

"Don't listen to them," he consoled her.

She was still in shock and didn't know what to do or say. She sat there blankly.

"You should be very proud of your feat," he added. "It was a phenomenal accomplishment, and you worked hard for it, and deserve every bit of recognition."

"But there is a shadow over it all." She paused. "I'm just going to keep on going, keep on testing. I'll submit to any test they want. I am 100 percent clean. Arrange it."

"Arrange what?"

"Arrange for a complete test, the most complete test possible. Test for anything and everything. Make the results public. I have the money now; I'll pay for it."

"It won't change anything," said her fiancé. "The news is already out there on twitter, Facebook, youtube. Once the dust settles and the test results come in, it won't matter anymore. People have already made up their minds."

"But this is so unfair. I'm not Staf. I could never cheat like that bastard did and never will!"

She was sitting down and leaning forward, burying her face in her hands. Her long, untied hair hung over her face and partially hid her. She wasn't crying, but whatever she was doing was hidden.

"Can I ask you something before we move forward with this?" He stood solemnly before her.

She looked up trustingly. Something made her feel insecure. It was a vague question, and she hated those; the answer was obviously going to be yes.

They had a completely open, trusting relationship. As a coach, as a boyfriend, and as a future husband, he was the only man in her life. She confided everything to him—her innermost, darkest secrets, ones that she could barely admit to herself. He probably saw some things in her that she didn't even know about. She had never known anyone as deeply and intimately as she knew him. Their relationship was beyond mere likes and dislikes; they knew the subtle nuances, the small things that could make a difference.

Once when she had dragged him out shopping in an Asian flea market, which he protested but gave in to far too easily, he had showed mild interest in a carving. It was the only thing that he showed any interest in during the afternoon of shopping, so when his back was turned, she had bought it quickly. Without having time to haggle over the price, she had paid the keeper what he asked for, unknowingly insulting him at the same time.

She had given him the carving in the taxi ride back to the hotel, and he had feigned a small, seemingly forced interest and gratitude with a predictable "Wow, that's great. Thanks." That was all he ever said about it. The small, insignificant thank-you was meaningless; however, she did note that the carving still stood prominently on his apartment coffee table. That was a far bigger appreciation than he could ever have verbalized.

But in the changing room after a disastrous press conference, shortly after having completed the impossible in tennis, she held her breath as she allowed him to ask his foreboding question. It was impossible that he would doubt her accomplishment; they were best friends and knew everything about each other. They had absolutely no secrets at all. Everything was in the open, and so this question and the manner in which it was asked was like an approaching storm.

"Did you cheat?"

The words floated over and slowly sunk into Julie. She was confused. She heard something, but it was impossible. She tried to figure out what he had asked. Surely it could not possibly be the question she had just heard. She needed to clarify it; there had been too much stress today. Her ears were playing tricks on her. Quietly and seriously, he asked, "Have you ever taken any drugs?"

She heard it clearly this time. He had doubts in her.

A mounting roar built up in her ears. She couldn't hear anymore. It was the storm of rage and betrayal. The indestructible pillar of their friendship, trust, and love was crumbling. Everything in the room seemed to blend together, and she couldn't discern anything. Her coach faded into the mess.

The roar in her mind blocked out all thoughts. Somewhere, there was a need to cry, but it couldn't find its way through. Everything that she thought about, believed in, and trusted in the world was being torn apart by the hurricane in her head.

The coach watched Julie expectantly. He saw her eyes glaze over. He watched her get up, walk out, and disappear from his life. She never played tennis again.

Staf silently and discreetly checked into the French embassy. When he came to the gates, the guards glowered at him. The doors opened silently. No one checked his ID, and no one talked to him. There was no need to.

He met the ambassador inside. They didn't shake hands.

Staf was shown to a room. He stayed there for two hours. Then there was a knock at the door. He was led to a back door in a gloomy courtyard. He got into a limousine with tinted windows. They drove to an airport in the rain.

The door was opened for him at the steps of a plane. He climbed the steps, and the jet promptly took him home.

Staf was immediately put under arrest and put in jail. Jake promptly got him out; there was nothing to charge him with. The product he had used was not a banned substance. There was no evidence that he had lied about anything. He had voluntarily come home. There was no risk of flight. However, there was an inquiry being held in New York. Staf was impolitely ordered to voluntarily attend.

Staf planned to return to Malibu, and his fond memories of his glass house and car occasionally relieved him of his current torment. He had forgotten the state it was in when he left, but that was a blur.

He recalled the cool night breezes through his open window, the furniture and art he had purchased and spread neatly throughout the house, the finely landscaped pool, and his eight balconies, each with a different view; two of his favorites were the front facing the pacific and the rear facing wild foothills dotted with brush and a lonely cactus.

He had roughly designed it. The contractor had enjoyed the challenges.

At one point, it was going to be featured in some sort of home show and magazine, but Staf was glad to be unavailable and enjoy his private time there. Like now. He wondered if this was the lowest he had ever felt. He tried to compare it to the recent past when the wooden mannequin was chasing him.

His house had been repaired in his absence. On his second morning there, after some coffee on the Pacific balcony, he went into his den and sifted through his old medals, badges, and trophies, deciding many had to be stored for now. Some had to be returned.

He found a very dusty piece of paper in a box housing his early high school Medals. It was the plain business card with Rial's name and phone number on it. Staf was fearful of the card, as if this card had started the whole mess. Everything associated with this card was evil. But he was also afraid to throw it out.

The next day, he left for New York.

Chapter 27: The End Is Near

Staf was in Central Park. He needed to get out of the hotel and get air, and this seemed like the best place on a cool afternoon. His mind had not been able to rest since he checked in to the embassy in France. First, the words from Jake had to settle in. Then the reaction of expatriates. Then the disappointment in everyone. When he returned to the United States, the full force of what he had done hit him.

It had seemed easy enough—deliver a small package. He had been their biggest sports hero and caused the biggest crisis.

Before his downfall, everyone had been excited about sports. Not only had Olympic ratings soared, but also football, baseball, basketball, hockey, soccer, tennis, everything sports related. Funding for sports was up. Crime was down.

In every event, people looked for a Staf. Bill had set a new home run record, a feat that almost came close to Staf. Yvonne had three gold medals in the Olympics; if she could repeat it two more times, you might almost put her up there with Staf.

Everything abound sports had been a comparison to Staf; he was the yardstick. The Staf of hockey, the Staf of volleyball.

A decade of this made his downfall tragic. His downfall alienated the United States but unified the world. Everyone agreed to condemn him. His records were erased. He was taken out of the hall of fame. In his high school, his picture on the athletic wall was vandalized. He was not welcome at sporting events. All sports stars, including those who had worked hard, came under scrutiny. "He's probably on something," or, "That record is absolutely impossible to break, he has to be cheating," people said. Everyone lost interest in sports.

Super Bowl ratings were dismal, and the Olympic committee was having trouble finding a host country; there were mumblings about cancelling them.

There was a plunge in sports advertising. Companies like Lightning put all endorsements on hold for fear of another Staf. Sports that were dependent on financing and support were cancelled. His name became synonymous with cheating. Worse yet, no one was interested in doing their best. It was a new fear. If you did well, you were under suspicion, and testing couldn't clear an athlete anymore.

The world became a place where no one strived anymore. You could be the best business man or a famed artist or photographer, but you did not dare to win in sports. It was actually better to come in second.

Staf got up from the bench and continued his walk.

He passed some soccer pitches in the south gardens of Central Park, where several groups of kids were playing organized league games. He paused. It was funny how stark the differences in young kids could be. Some were clearly into the game, while others were easily distracted or uncoordinated. Pressure, age, and experience would wean those ones out. Only the best would continue into adult life, the rest having to abandon sports as fanciful dreams.

Staf had cheated the process. Not many do. Maybe that was the worst part. Some excellent players use drugs to get a small edge, to shave microseconds off their times.

But he had used a drug to get a huge edge. Every edge. An impossible edge.

As he watched one soccer game, one young child stood out, easily weaving in and out of the other group, easily scoring several times. His teammates often passed it to him if they were tired or just wanted to get rid of the ball. He seemed to be at the right place all the time. It looked natural to him.

He drew the other team to him, made smart passes up the field, and then came back impossible distances to stop the other team.

The parents admired his skill, until one parent loudly asked from partway down the field, "Joey's like the next Staf Nurren. Can I get some of those drugs for my kid?"

Everyone laughed. The child's father laughed half-heartedly too, pride vanishing from his eyes.

It was halftime, and the kids came over to their coach for some orange slices and popsicles. The young star's father discreetly came over to him and said something. The young boy looked distraught. The father appeared pained but insistent.

The game promptly continued, and Staf noted a stark change in the young star. He spent very little time with the ball. He kicked it away from himself as if he was afraid of it. He ran slowly and gave the ball away several times and didn't help with defense. He asked to be subbed off. He then went to his father. The discussion was brief, with no disagreement. They left the game.

Staf noticed the general silence and guilt in the parents. It mimicked his own guilt. He couldn't watch the rest of the game and quietly continued down the path.

He found another bench and reflected more.

How could it possibly have gone so bad after having gone so well? Things couldn't continue like this. He needed to have another meeting.

After fumbling in his pockets and wallet, he found Rial's business card with the phone number. It was in perfect shape.

He searched the park for a pay phone, and after finding an unvandalized, operational one, he dialed the number. There was no answer. Frustrated, he slammed the phone into the holder and cursed.

He turned and discovered a smartly dressed man facing him, an agent.

"I need to see him," said Staf fearfully. The memory of the red carpet helped him keep his language respectable.

"He's extremely busy; an appointment is not possible. What can I help you with?" he said in a bored way, is if he were asked the same question by a hundred different people every day.

"Look, why did all this happen? There must be something I can do to reverse this. It wasn't supposed to work out this way."

"I don't know what you are talking about. Everything went as planned, and that doesn't make him less busy. There is no time for this. You made the deal, and you got what you wanted."

"There has to be another way. Please. You can't leave things like this; it's not just my hell anymore," said Staf as his voice slowly trailed off. Then, almost in a whisper, he continued, "The whole world is ..." He couldn't finish it. He had just realized what he had done.

"Hell? Is that what you wanted to say? The whole world is a hell. Or in one? Or whatever the hell you want to call it. Stop wasting my time. Don't call again."

"Wait!" pleaded Staf again, stunned and confused with his new realization. He hung his head, dreading to say the words, and reluctantly, they came out, words he never thought could ever leave his lips again. "I'll offer my ... soul," he whispered.

"Soul?" shouted the agent angrily. "Did you say soul?" He said it with mounting excitement and intensity. Staf felt an anguish in his chest, but he knew this was the right thing to do. He had to make this sacrifice. Then he heard something odd. A chuckle. The chuckle grew into a laugh. The laugh increased to an uncontrollable fit. Staf looked up to see who was laughing. It was the agent. He didn't think it was possible for one of these things to laugh, and here, in front of him, at the worst part of his life out of all the times that he had thought he could sink no further, this thing was laughing at the offer of the thing that meant most to him. What was this all about? There was nothing funny about this. This was going to be the most unfunny thing since the first time. This evil agent saw humor in this?

The agent was laughing hysterically, almost uncontrollably, and was ready to double over. The scene made Staf start to join him in a laugh, and he started a hesitant one, not understanding what might be so humorous.

"I don't think it's that funny," smiled Staf meekly.

"Oh, you mean you were serious?" Said the agent, and he started into an impossibly louder laugh. He finally doubled over. He could hardly breathe through his bellyaching laugh.

"Really, what's so funny about that? I'm serious about my offer."

"Oh, for crying out loud," said the agent, quickly coming to his senses. "You're a bit slow even though you run fast. He doesn't need your pathetic soul; what would he want that for? He's got no use for souls. You watch too many movies." The mood suddenly changed, the leftover smile quickly morphed into a sneer, and he growled, "And don't call about that anymore. We're finished with you. We'll call you if we need anything else."

"But …" interjected Staf as he ran his hands through his matted hair and rubbed his temples, but when he looked up again, the agent was gone. He cursed and looked at the business card. He was going to call again; this was not the end of it. But the card was not in his hand. He checked his pockets. Empty. He looked in his shirt pocket, he searched the ground, and he looked in the garbage can nearby. No card. In desperation, he even asked some people walking by if they had seen it. They ignored him and hurried past.

He searched for five hours in the bushes, in every crevice of his clothes, inside his underwear. He checked again around the phone and widened his circle and looked even more. He looked in piles of leaves, in dirt, under rocks. He tried to recall the number from memory. It was the wrong one. He tried others; they were wrong too.

At the end of five hours, exhausted both mentally and physically, he had to give up. He didn't want to admit that the card had disappeared with the agent. That would be giving up on his last shred of hope. He slumped onto the park bench and mulled the agent's words. They bothered him; things didn't make sense. The boss had seemed to have a very keen interest his soul and in making him one of his agents. His agents were superlative judges of character. They never made mistakes, and the boss was even better. It didn't make sense; how could they pick him, and how could he sign away his soul and then get it back so easily? And he had got it back by merely delivering a small package. That's when it hit him, and it almost knocked him out. He finally realized it. The lightbulb came on. He saw everything as it was and as it was supposed to be. Everything had worked out perfectly the way they had planned it.

They knew he would fight for his soul and make the deal to save it. They knew that his downfall would morally devastate the world. It made sense. They had never wanted his soul; that was never part of the plan. "He's got no use for souls"; that's what the agent had said.

They wanted his downfall. It was all choreographed right from the start. Right to the end. The world despaired, and Staf was singularly to blame every step of the way. He was beside himself in disbelief. He started a sinister laugh. Many more thoughts and possible outcomes crossed his mind. Maybe he could compete against this demon? Maybe he could make a comeback, prove himself clean, restore faith. Maybe he could try again to make another deal?

He needed to leave the park. He needed to be anywhere but the park.

Chapter 28: Staf's Fans

He left the main entrance and waited at the crosswalk. There was a coffee shop on the other side or maybe the bar down the street. He thought about it while waiting for the light to change.

"Hey, aren't you the great Staf Nurren?" came a young man's voice from behind him. Staf turned around.

"Yes," he responded, hoping to finally see a friendly face. There was a small mixed group waiting with him—an elderly lady on his left, a young businessman with a briefcase on his right, a young goth woman with two young men directly behind him. The young woman had a sly smirk as she looked up, and her tall friend stared icily, pretending to look like an uninterested vampire. The other goth man leered, his dangling piercings adding to his sinister costume. The ring in his nose reminded Staf of a doorknocker, and it flapped against his upper lip as he shoved Staf into the intersection.

Staf stumbled backward and heard a great squeal of tires. The squeal was very close. Instinctively, he turned to face it while someone screamed. He heard a car horn from somewhere else as the front of the bus filled his vision with darkness.

Staf slowly opened his eyes. Everything was white. He was lying on white sheets, and all he could make out were fuzzy shapes with white outlines. The lights were white; the sunshine reflected off white walls. He blinked, and this caused a tremendous headache. He wished himself back to sleep.

Staf woke again and could have opened his eyes, but he didn't want that terrible headache. He was afraid to blink. The shapes were clearer. He could hear something too. Beeps and dinging. Someone was talking far away. He was not alone. Sounds made his head hurt now. He closed his eyes but couldn't wish himself to sleep this time. The dinging got louder. Echoing footsteps came into the room, each step pounding in his head. They stopped beside his bed in front of him. After a moment, he heard the footsteps leave. He ordered his eyes to open to see who was leaving. His eyes wouldn't obey. He went back to sleep.

Staf slowly opened his eyes. He was on his left side now, facing a window. He heard a whisper behind him.

"Welcome back, Staf. Good to see you are awake again."

"Stop shouting, Jake," whispered Staf. He hadn't meant to whisper. Staf wanted to know where he was and what had happened, but his mind didn't want to go there. He wanted to sit up, but his body was defiant. Nothing happened. He put more effort into it. His arm moved, and slowly, the rest of his body responded. Everything ached. His chest, his arms, his legs. And his head too, but bearably.

"Whoa," responded Jake loudly, but calmly. "Take it easy, slowly."

A nurse came in. "Hello, Mr. Nurren," she said matter-of-factly as if she were a business associate. "And should I say welcome back? How long have you been awake?"

"Ah," responded Staf, but he was parched, well past thirsty, and his dry lips were like rubber. All he could muster was a whisper through his swollen, lazy tongue, and the effort made his chest hurt too. Jake interjected.

"He just woke up about two minutes ago."

"Very well," said the nurse, and she kindly asked, "Do you need anything for the pain?"

Staf imperceptibly shook his said and barely managed to squeeze the word "no" between his teeth. It was quieter than a whisper.

"Well, let me know if you need any." And she promptly stepped out. Staf watched her go out and was disappointed that her image had done nothing to make him feel better. He must have been in really bad shape.

He couldn't recall anything after watching a child's soccer game in Central Park.

"How long have I been here?" he whispered.

"A week. Do you want some water?" Jake offered. Staf nodded helplessly. "It's on the stand beside you."

Thanks, thought Staf. He didn't want to waste the effort of talking to Jake, knowing that his friend was deliberately taunting him. He was starting to feel much more awake and aware of where he was. He reached for the glass and noticed the cast around his swollen hands and fingers. They looked like purple pickles. "Holy shit," remarked Staf. "What else am I going to find out?"

"Well, you won't be playing the piano anymore," Jake offered. It was a lot less cruel than telling him he wouldn't run anymore.

"And you won't be running anymore either," added Jake as if reading Staf's mind. Staf wondered if Jake could also hear the barrage of profanity coming at him. Jake laughed. Staf's question was answered.

"I'm glad to see you waking up and getting better. I should be going soon and straightening out some, er, stuff. But I'll be back in the late afternoon before heading back to L.A. Maybe then I can fill you in."

The shock of finding the condition of his hands made him forget about his thirst and headache. He felt his parched, rubbery lips crack in places. He reached over with his other hand, also bruised and swollen but without a cast, and managed to fumble for the cup. He put the flexible straw in his mouth and took a long sip. The sip seemed to make him feel full. He could feel the cool water slither down his throat and slosh in his stomach. He was so dry, it must have watered everything on its way down. It was the tastiest water he could remember, but his mouth felt weird.

"Hey, what the hell happened to my mouth?"

"Your mouth? Oh, you must mean your teeth. Well, you used them to stop the bus. Your hands and ribs pitched in to help. You should have seen the bus. You'll be happy to know it's still in the shop too." As usual, he could always count on Jake for the truth.

This wasn't enough to lighten Staf's mood. He loved his teeth. He was a little vain that way. Right away, he wondered if he could get dentures that weren't obvious. He also wanted to see if any teeth had survived. His tongue searched the inside of his mouth and reported that there was something still left in the last two rows of his otherwise empty gums. This made him wake up a bit more. He became aware of fractured bones in almost every limb. His right arm, left fingers, and left leg required pins. The bandages on his chest protected his broken ribs. He had a massive concussion. His head was shaved, and there was a part of his skull that he feared to touch.

He had a short conversation with Jake about some of the related business that was being taken care of today. His headache diminished but was still there.

Later that day, he had a hysterical visit from his mother. She had visited and sat by his side every day during his coma and had just missed his awakening. In response to her query, he assured her that he had been wearing clean underwear at the time of his accident.

He was still awake at dinner, feeling drowsy, but feeling surprisingly well considering his accident. He was most happy to have been interested in the nurse that came in and checked on him. Those related parts did not seem to be broken.

In the afternoon, he insisted on being demoted from the morphine to Tylenol. He didn't want to become dependent. After three hours, the pain snuck back like an ocean tide. If someone had told him he was lucky to be alive, he would have suggested otherwise. He promptly begged the nurse to reverse the order. She took her time. He didn't like her anymore. When she was finally finished, he relaxed and went to sleep again.

Staf was having a dream. Finally. It had been a couple of days. And this one was vivid, too. He was back in the Olympic Stadium. It should have felt good, but he was uneasy. The noise was as he remembered it. Loud. Deafening.

He was assembled with a group in the middle of the field. He recognized his Kenyan friend, but was ignored by him. It was odd to have him here, a marathoner with a group of sprinters. Everyone looked energetic, stretched, and ready to run. He did not feel like running. An announcer called, "Ready. Set."

Staf looked around. No one seemed particularly ready. He didn't know how to stand or where to go. The gun went off.

Dale promptly tagged the Kenyan, called out "You're it," and ran away. His Kenyan friend ran over to Staf, tagged him, and also said "You're it," and then ran away to another side of the field.

Staf started to laugh. A game of tag? Tag was an Olympic event now? What a fun dream. He promptly ran after the Kenyan. He easily caught up and reached out. He was about to tag him and was preparing to make the call, but the Kenyan sped up. Staf ran faster. His friend ran faster too, and weaved. Staf followed him closely. He caught up again and reached out. The Kenyan sped up just a little, enough to stay out of reach. Staf got mad and used all his energy. The Kenyan was able to remain one step ahead, and he made it look easy. Staf was furious. He decided to deal with him later and went after other, slower runners.

The same thing happened. He couldn't reach them. When he did, they sped up. The crowd booed him mercilessly. It was a horrible sound. A horn indicated that the time was up. Staf flopped on the ground exhausted. The other runners smiled, congratulated each other, and all received gold medals. They left the field, and the stadium emptied. He was still on the ground.

Staf woke breathing heavily. *Shit, what a nightmare*, he thought. He had had enough morphine to mask the pain, but he could sense that in his sleep, he had tried to clench his fist, and he could feel the numb throbbing of his hand without feeling the pain. He hoped he hadn't hurt it too much. He looked at the time. He had only been asleep for an hour. It was still early evening. He didn't want to go to sleep anymore. He had another toothless drink (that was a feeling that was going to be hard to get used to). He fought off sleep for another twenty minutes and then succumbed.

He had several other dreams during the night, all about running. He ran down endless corridors, going nowhere. It was a boring nightmare that he couldn't wake up from.

He woke again and looked at the time; it was early morning. He had another toothless drink, received another shot of morphine, and went back to sleep.

He was in his glass castle. He was in the living room in his recliner, watching his flat-screen TV. He was watching replays of football's phenomenal year. The typical cool evening breeze was coming in through the southwest window near the kitchen, fluttering the light drapes gently. Staf looked at the kitchen patio door, and a small bundle of fur rolled in. He watched as it came around the counter and walked up to his recliner. It was a small, white kitten. It jumped into the recliner with him and, curled like a cotton ball by his hand, and seemed to doze off. He numbly stroked it.

Staf wasn't that crazy about animals, and no pets were allowed in his home; however, this small fur ball was too cute to evict. He turned his attention to the TV again. He was watching a soccer game and wanted to turn up the volume. Then the clip-clop sounds came out of the television. He couldn't get out of his chair. His body wouldn't respond. He looked at his hands and legs; he was bandaged to the chair. The television exploded, and the wooden mannequin broke through and charged at him. In two strides, it was almost on him and reached out. Staf didn't have time to react. His reactions were slow. His heart rate hadn't gone up yet, and his breathing was low. He hadn't moved at all from the chair. He was not going to get away this time. The mannequin reached out with an arm without breaking stride, and Staf did nothing except watch, helpless as he squirmed in his chair.

There was a movement at his side, and the small kitten launched itself at the wooden mannequin. As it flew through the air, it grew and transformed into a massive white tiger with fangs. Wings sprang from its side, and it accelerated as it flew into a blinding white flash. The impact sent the mannequin backward (which Staf had never seen before), and then the mannequin exploded.

Staf woke up again and felt rested. Somehow, he hadn't jolted awake this time. He looked at the clock on the left. It was three in the morning. He was not alone. He slowly looked right. There was a woman beside his bed. Or was it a man? He or she was not very tall. Young with a smooth complexion. Peaceful eyes. Curly, shoulder-length hair. He or she vaguely resembled someone he had seen in paintings, and someone he had seen fifteen years ago.

"I thought I might see you again before I died," mumbled Staf, slightly scared of his premonition. She held out her hand, and he reluctantly took it. The cast melted off his right hand, and his fingers shrunk to a normal size and turned pink. The metal pins eased out of his arm and clanked on the floor. The bandages on his left arm and chest slid off. He tested his legs. The clinks in the bed suggested that the pins had come out of his legs too. The bruises didn't hurt. He slowly swung himself to put his feet on the floor and sat upright, thinking that dying was very peaceful.

They walked out of the hospital room hand in hand. Staf didn't feel like talking anymore, but he was about to remind her about his teeth, and noticed they were already in place.

They were walking slowly, and Staf felt the need to say something. "I'm going to do my best to figure out what to do to make things right. Perhaps you have some ideas?" He continued looking ahead. Then he couldn't resist. "Am I dead?"

There was no reply. They continued to walk down the hall. Then he added, "If I am not, providing you are not taking me to purgatory or something worse, maybe you can swing by when my time is up?" Still no response. They walked in silence. He was afraid to bring it up again.

They stopped at the nurse's station. He was alone.

Chapter 29: The Reporter's Perspective

It was just another job that someone had to cover—Staf's hospital story. The top reporters (the ones with the closest desks to the editor) had already been here, had already talked to the doctor, the nurses, Staf's lawyer. Their job had been to find anybody coming in or out of Staf's room and talk to them, because talking to Staf would be impossible. Apparently, he had come out of his coma, but was sleeping most of the time, sedated on morphine. Reporters were not allowed to see him. For two weeks, Staf had been at the hospital, and the reporters gradually gave up. She was the only one left; the assignment had progressed down the row of desks until it had landed on the last one, which was hers.

She was generally the feel-good reporter; she covered the rescued cats, the crazy fundraisers, the happy reunions. She liked those easy, straightforward reports, but she wanted something a little more, just one small big story, and then she felt she could go back to the usual.

She had done her research. Staf's mom had visited him briefly. She had already been interviewed. She would have liked to be the one to get that interview. He had no friends, unless the lawyer was one, but who can be friends with a lawyer?

He lived in Malibu in a unique glass house and had one fancy car and lots of medals, trophies, and records. And one blemish. And now, both of his arms and legs were broken, one of each requiring pins; he had three broken ribs, one punctured lung, a severe concussion, few teeth left, and two crushed vertebrae. He would walk again but not run. At least he had his eyes; she herself would have given up lots of body parts in order to keep her eyes. She wondered if he felt the same.

It was early morning. She had been home during the evening, couldn't sleep, and had decided to go for a drive. Her drive brought her to the hospital in the middle of the night, and she decided to check up on her story. Nothing. Of course she wasn't allowed to see him.

The nurses recognized her. It was a quiet evening, and so they didn't mind her invisible presence. She joined them for a coffee at break time.

She was still sipping her coffee at the nurse's station when a patient walked up. He looked remarkably similar to Staf, except that he was in good condition. She studied him and gave him a brief smile. She returned to her magazine but had to look at him again. He stopped in the area and looked confused, as if he was expecting to find something. Since she was the only person in the area at the moment, he approached her.

"Are you a nurse?" he asked. His gown was not securely tied to the back. She hoped that he wouldn't turn around.

"No, I am not. You look remarkably well, Mr. Nurren." She took a chance on his identity. He nodded.

"Are you a doctor then?"

"Reporter for the *Post*," she answered honestly, despite the inclination to be evasive to get more information. To her surprise, he didn't flinch. Maybe she could get a short interview? No one was around. *Play it safe*, she thought. *Don't be too aggressive.* "Out for a stroll?" she asked. It was an awkward question, considering other more pressing things, such as his accident and the impending inquiry. The word on the street was that he had staged the accident in order to avoid the inquiry. She was in a good position to answer that question. But that was for later. She wanted to be gentle with this recently comatose patient.

"I was looking for something, but I'm really not sure what. Are you here to find some dirt about the shit I'm in?"

"If you have time. We could go for a coffee, but you are a little overdressed. Have a seat." He took a seat a little more quickly than she would have thought. She had an image of chasing him with a throng of reporters, trying to squeeze in a question. She studied him quietly. It was as if they had an appointment. She decided not to dive into anything too quickly. Maybe they could just have a conversation and save the interview for next time—tomorrow, if she played her cards right. "How are you feeling? You look remarkably well, considering the accident that I heard about." She was certain the rumors were true. He was avoiding the inquiry. What a report this was going to be!

"To tell you the truth, I felt like a bus hit me until about ten minutes ago. I think I could go for a run now; care to join me?" He paused. She didn't laugh. He started again more seriously. "I should be able to make the inquiry. Hopefully I can put all this behind me, behind everyone. Get everything back to normal. Or the way it used to be."

She recalled the picture of the bus. The witnesses. He had been hit by a bus. She decided to move on from his injuries. She was already going to make the front page by declaring that Staf would attend the inquiry as scheduled. It was already a success. She was going to find out more about him. Then she could follow more of the human interest angle that she was used to dealing with.

"This will probably be one of the first questions that they ask you at the inquiry, and everyone else wants to know. Did you ever take a performance enhancing drug?"

"I don't know. I didn't know what it was I took. It happened fifteen years ago. But to be honest, I knew it would help my performance; I just didn't know it was a drug. I heard, after the fact, that it wasn't one of the banned ones, although I am sure that will change soon."

The admission of taking something would be another revelation. The fact that it wasn't banned at the time had already raised interesting problems.

"Do you think you would have been so successful without it?"

"I would like to think so, but I doubt it. I could barely make the high school team until I took it." Staf looked off into the distance.

"Would you still have taken it if it had been banned?"

"I don't know. I think I would, especially if other runners were taking it. And someone else always is. For sure if I couldn't get caught. Yes, I think I would." Staf was clearly thinking deeply and replying honestly.

"Sounds like you think the present system is ineffective. Do you think they should allow drugs in sports? Do you think that would level the playing field?" She didn't know why she asked that question. It wasn't really relevant.

Staf didn't answer. The silence was awkward. Jaymie didn't push for an answer. Several minutes had passed. Staf stared off into the distance. She didn't interrupt his train of thought. She figured the interview was over. She needed to negotiate the next one. Could she get an exclusive?

Staf interrupted the silence.

"Let's talk about it another time."

Jaymie handed him a business card. Staf excused himself and went back to his room. She let him leave in silence.

She drove home and spent the rest of the night writing a report. She submitted it to the editor. The editor scoffed at the report and then checked the hospital for Staf's updated condition. He immediately ran the story, Then he moved her to a desk closer to his office.

Chapter 30: The Inquiry

Staf was at the hotel getting ready for the inquiry. It was a dumb system, he thought to himself; everyone knew it went on, and they pretended to do some sort of inquiry, as if they are going to solve something. There had been many cases like his—in baseball, football, soccer, track and field. Whenever a record was broken, whenever someone excelled, there was an investigation, and if something was uncovered, an inquiry. It was a nuisance. A farce. He didn't care.

Some athletes were afraid to take cold medicine when sick for fear that something would show up on a test. Eight cups of coffee was about the limit before caffeine limits were exceeded.

But there was equal effort in hiding it—a battle between detecting performance enhancement and hiding it, a game of hide and seek. Maybe everyone should be home free.

When blood doping was first discovered, injections were hidden between toes. Athletes took steroids during training and stopped taking them in time to pass the test. Players, coaches, trainers, and doctors all worked to beat the system.

Then there was the effect of egos. "I couldn't possibly lose a race unless the other side cheated." A record broken? There had to be something, anything. The latest drugs? Injection points? Cold medicine? Too much caffeine? Anything? People asked around in the locker room, and if they couldn't find anything, they made it up.

But what if you really were on drugs? It didn't matter. All you had to do was pass the test. You were not on drugs if you passed a test. Your personal doctor could give you a confidential pregame test. If you failed, you could withdraw. Injury was the easiest excuse. Your doctor could help with that too.

What if you got a positive test? You could say it was just cold medicine; the doctor said it was okay; it was a misunderstanding. You had overactive glands.

But what if you were caught red handed? You just had to say you didn't know. And if they proved you did know, you had to apologize. And if they didn't believe you, you could cry. If you were really good, they would let you play anyway as long as you passed the next test. As long as you passed the test, you were not on drugs.

Staf was a little tense about the upcoming inquiry. He had a nicely pressed suit on. Jake was waiting at the inquiry, but they both knew that the media was going to be out in full force, and so they were going to arrive separately; Staf was going to make his entrance alone, one small man going up against the mountain of organized sports—the athletes, the coaches, the schools and universities, the endorsements, the market, the media. He was alone in this. He just had to tell it like it was.

He had nothing prepared. He took the familiar elevator down to the lobby and headed for the door. Someone jumped off the couch in the lobby and ran over.

"Hello, Mr. Nurren. Dave, from the *Times*. Can you answer a few quick questions?"

Damn, thought Staf. *How did he find out I was here? Probably took a chance.*

"Well, as you know," said Staf, not breaking stride, "I have a very important meeting. I'm afraid I haven't left any time for a quick interview; perhaps I can answer a question on the way to my ride?" He decided to stall a bit and cut off the reporter as he opened his mouth to ask something. "You know how traffic can be, and after all"—he drew it out like his old neighbor Mrs. Wilson would have— "it is a very, very important inquiry, and we all hope to ..."

By this time he had reached the door and opened it just enough to pass through. The reporter had to quickly decide to open his door, or follow Staf through the other. He chose to open the adjacent door, and was one step behind. He quickly caught up. Staf continued, "I am looking forward to it."

The reporter stepped into stride beside him.

"Will you admit to using drugs at the inquiry?"

The limousine was waiting curbside in front of the hotel. It was the same, familiar driver.

The driver rolled his eyes. Staf wondered if he was the only driver around. The door was open, and Staf hopped in, and once seated, he looked at the reporter and said, "As you know, there has been a lot said in the media lately …"

The door closed, and Staf merely mouthed some words. He had said nothing. He hoped that he had appeared to cooperate, or else there would be more bad press, more to pile on the mountainous heap. Everyone was trying to do their jobs well, and he didn't want to make it entirely impossible. But he had fun trying to stall. He recalled Mrs. Wilson and wondered if he would wish for someone to talk to when he was seventy. Even a reporter.

The drive to the enquiry through stop-and-go traffic seemed endless. The outside just seemed to pass him by, the busy streets numbed by the quiet inside of the limousine. He couldn't concentrate on anything with the inquiry on his mind, and although he had rehearsed many of his answers, he had every intention of coming clean and telling the truth about everything except for the nature of the boss and the general description of his office, particularly the red carpet. He was going to describe him as a person who sold performance enhancers in the back alley.

His hospital conversation was on his mind too. However, he needed a diversion, and looking at the chauffeur, he realized that it was no accident he had been hired. This was done intentionally by Jake.

He promptly took out his phone. He wondered who to dial, and then he decided not to dial anyone.

"Hello, may I speak with Dr. Connor please?" he said loudly into his phone. Staf noticed a small twitch in the driver's ears. He continued his imaginary conversation. "Yes, you may. It's Staf Nurren, and it's very important, an emergency."

He waited quietly on the phone for about the time he thought it would take to forward the call to an office.

"Hello, Dr. Connor. It's Staf Nurren. As part of the diagnosis, you had asked me to call you if there were any significant changes." The ears twitched again, and the driver leaned back slightly.

"Well, I thought it was worth mentioning that the diarrhea had turned from an almost black to a very light shade of brown, and also, there is a noticeable change in the stink." The divider window was starting to move up. The window was halfway up. Staf had to hurry. "And about the experiment with corn …" The window was up. Staf laughed and stashed his phone.

The New York streets reminded him of being on the run in the Azores, the shop windows flying by like life in general.

They reached the conference building, and he snapped out of his daydream. As agreed, the reporters were all kept fifty feet away, and he climbed the lonely steps with the din of the reporters, onlookers, and camera flashes around him. It struck him how different this noise was from a stadium. The noise felt like additional pressure on him, surrounding him, pushing in, compressing him. He felt small and vulnerable, but he slowly and deliberately went into the inquiry, ignoring the crowd.

Because he didn't stop and say something, even "no comment", he was sure something bad would be written.

The large wooden door in front of him reminded him of other doors that he hadn't wanted to enter. It was heavy and seemed to require a lot of energy to move. He had never been in this building before.

He mindlessly took a few steps into the large foyer and was horrified to see a red carpet under his feet. It wasn't the red carpet he had come to fear, but it still had an effect on him, and he jumped to the side. The heavy doors closed, cutting off the outside. He took several steps, and his shoes made a loud clip-clop noise that echoed in the large room. It didn't help his nerves.

A woman at the end of the hall was motioning to him. The attendant at the door had a small earpiece in her left ear. She spoke into a hand piece, and after a moment, she opened the door and motioned Staf to enter. It was a large, spacious forum. It was incredibly quiet except for the sound of squeaks as people turned in their seats to watch him enter from the rear of the large room. It was surprisingly sparsely filled. Most of the people there were reporters or relevant spectators. Some detectives were likely there, as well as some physicians and maybe some coaches.

Staf didn't look at them and focused on the front. There was a table, some microphones. A panel of three people sat at an elevated platform. Staf's knees felt weak as he tried to walk calmly and deliberately to the front without hesitation. The clip-clop of his shoes loudly announced his presence. He tried unsuccessfully to walk softly.

He recalled the many times his knees had felt weak and his heart had pounded. Track finals, meetings, the red carpet, the golem. He didn't notice the stares, the heads slowly turning in unison as he walked down the aisle. Staf did become momentarily distracted by the sound of hushed whispers echoing around the hall like the calm before the storm.

He took his seat and resisted the temptation to turn around and see who was in attendance. The three panel members were all stiff and glum looking. There were two men and one woman, but they all looked the same. They were all over fifty, of average build, and wore glasses, although the woman had them hanging around her neck suspended on a tether. The wrinkles were just starting to form on their faces. They didn't smile, and it looked like a smile might be beyond them. It might break the mold. They were hunched over the desk and looked like gargoyles.

There was a lengthy pause. *For effect*, thought Staf. Intimidation. Formalities. To make it look serious.

As Staf sat there, he regained his composure. He started to get pissed off. The man at the left leaned over and said something to the woman. They seemed oblivious to the fact the he was there. At length, he decided to take matters into his own hands. He got up, and proceeded to leave. More silence. At length, there came a voice from the front.

"Mr. Nurren, where are you going?"

Staf turned around in mock surprise. He walked back to the front and tapped on the microphone. It was working.

"It seems that you have nothing for me, and so I will continue on with other things. Good day."

"Mr. Nurren," continued the man on the right, his moving lips the only thing to show that he was not a statue, "this is a serious inquiry, although it is not a criminal trial. You must realize that there are extremely important issues involved here. I would think with the gravity and impact here, you could afford a little time and respect."

This pissed off Staf, but he kept himself calm.

"Sure," he replied with feigned sincerity. "Take your time. When shall I come back? Clearly you need more time to prepare. Just let me know when you are ready, and I will come back."

Someone laughed in the forum. The woman replied, "Please have a seat, Mr. Nurren. We will begin momentarily." This annoyed him more. He found a pen and started to twirl it in his fingers. It flew out of his hand, and clanked several feet away. He decided not to retrieve it.

The dispassionate panel sat at the podium and continued their gargoyle impersonations. Staf was not sure why, but he had had enough with these people. They expected respect without earning it. He had no respect for them. He had already decided on the action he was going to take, and he looked forward to it, considering this poor start.

The man in the center finally cleared his throat. Something was going to happen. Staf made a point of not giving him any attention at his motion, even though the forum became alert with anticipation.

Either make it boring, or make it interesting, thought Staf. It reminded him of a German saying, "Schwetz oder Scheiss Buchstabe," which meant, "speak or shit letters." He laughed inside.

"Hello, Mr. Nurren," the man in the center said stiffly. "Thank you for taking time to come to this inquiry." He paused and peered at Staf over his glasses.

Staf guessed he was supposed to reply, so he didn't. Was everyone going to thank him in turn, or did they expect a thank-you in return?

The man cleared his throat again and looked at his paper. "You've had quite a career."

Staf noted that this still wasn't a question, so he still did not respond. He did give the man his undivided attention. Staf started to wonder if that's why these inquiries lasted so long and cost so much—windy, unimportant questions. Perhaps they were milking the overtime. He started to daydream. It suddenly occurred to him that he had not desired to run for quite some time. He tried to remember the last time he had wanted to, and it was over two years ago at his final Olympics. Why had he not wanted to run since then? The answer was obvious, considering how busy he had been.

He was snapped out of his dream when the man spoke again, and Staf wondered if something useful was going to be said this time.

"We have a problem here. You brought a sample into the hands of a doctor three months ago. Testing on this sample has determined it to be a type of drug capable of improving athletic performance. It had never been seen before. Although no test previously existed, they were able to form one, and your samples tested positive. Many times. In fact, every time." This guy obviously wanted to be heard, so Staf let him talk; he couldn't incriminate himself if he didn't talk.

"Mr. Nurren," the man continued, and Staf hated the way he said it, sort of like *new wren*. "The IOC has the most stringent anti doping rules in sports. How did you hide this for so long?"

Uh oh, thought Staf, *finally a question I have to answer. Keep it simple.* He paused for a long moment before responding. "I didn't hide it at all; I submitted to all the tests completely and answered all questions about drugs honestly."

"So you didn't take any performance-enhancing drugs?"

"I took something, but to the best of my knowledge, it wasn't banned."

"How so? Either you used performance-enhancing drugs, or you didn't. Did you use them?"

"Which banned drug did I take?"

"We are hoping you could tell us."

"The United States Anti-Doping Agency has a list of banned and controlled substances. I couldn't find mine on the list."

"That's not the issue here. Whether it was or was not on the list, the issue here is whether or not you used something to improve your performance."

"Yes"

"Please elaborate."

"There have been many instances when I might have had an aspirin on the day of a run." The gargoyles leered.

"Did you take anything else to improve your performance?"

"Yes."

"What was it?"

"I don't know."

Pause. "When did you take it?"

"Fifteen years ago."

"How often did you take it?"

"Once." There was laughter from behind.

"Who gave it to you?"

"I don't know."

"Mr. Nurren, are you being evasive? I find it hard to believe that you only took this illegal drug once fifteen years ago, and that it still shows up on your samples. Let me remind you that you are under oath."

"What illegal substance was it again? I can't remember the name."

The panel could see where this was going. It was going to be some sort of loophole. If the product was not listed as illegal and did not fall into the category of growth hormone, blood doping, adrenaline, etc., then what could they do? But there were other problems involved.

"Standard forms ask about the history of drug use. Clearly you lied on them. Why did you not come forward with your drug use years ago."

"I did."

The room suddenly hushed to silence. A bird crowed outside. Staf was sure it was a black one.

"Please elaborate."

"My application to college specifically asked that question. I answered yes. During the medical, I answered the same. I couldn't give the name of the product, because I don't know what it was. I've never been asked again since."

The silence was broken by whispers from the back. One whisper can be quite subtle, but lots of whispering can sound like a storm.

The gargoyles leaned in together and talked. This had clearly taken them by surprise. He knew they were going to subpoena his college records and have a closer look at them. Someone was going to get in trouble for this incomplete investigation.

At length, the panel came back with a much friendlier tone.

"Mr. Nurren, the problem is, although there is now a test for this substance, the lab hasn't been able to reproduce it. It seems this is decades from being created in any lab. It would be very helpful to know where it came from."

"It quite literally came from a back alley. I'm sorry I can't help you more," he said insincerely.

"I'm sorry to hear that," replied the panel, also insincerely. It was an antagonistic atmosphere. "Is there any other information you can supply or comments you would like to make?"

Here was Staf's moment. This is what he was waiting for. It struck him suddenly. The years running on the track and from trouble, the thinking, the meeting. Everything had come down to this.

"Yes", he said quietly. They all looked up from their papers expectantly. The last few whispers faded. Outside the right window, the bird crowed again. On the other side, a break in the clouds allowed some sunlight to filter in.

He gathered himself up, and loudly, and clearly, said, "You need to level the playing field."

The gargoyles leered. One interrupted. "That's precisely what we are trying to do here."

Staf continued. "But you are failing as did prohibition and the war on drugs, such as marijuana and cocaine. You need to take a new approach. You have arbitrarily chosen one aspect of performance enhancement and made a crusade out of it. A witch hunt. It has become McCarthyism." It sounded like the right word for his train of thought, but maybe it was too rash. He wanted to draw comparisons. "Prohibition failed to regulate alcohol. The war on recreational drugs is not being won. Drugs in sports are the same. The more you regulate it, the more people get around it. Athletes want a fair game, and you cannot provide that under the present system." It wasn't coming out as planned. He should have written it down. It sounded like he was saying it was only a crime if you got caught, but that wasn't it at all. He was worried that he was not explaining himself properly and tried to clarify.

"Get rid of the rules, and there won't be a battle of trying to find the offenders out there. No one will be offending. Instead, work with sports medicine to define optimal uses, optimal levels and treatments. Athletes will be better for it instead of using back-alley pharmacists. It will also level the playing field. Right now, when a sprinter breaks a world record, we first wait for his test results. If they are negative, we wonder how he cheated the system.

"When athletes first took drugs there was nothing wrong with it. Then it became illegal, and a test was made. Then there was a drug to mask the test. Now there is a test to detect masking drugs, which indirectly implies guilt. It's a seesaw battle in science between detecting and hiding. Stop the battle. It will continue. Make a compromise. Work together to find acceptable levels that are healthy, even optimal. Don't force weight lifters to buy locker-room drugs that lead to shorter lives and dangerous temperaments. Sell legalized ones and monitor their use and quality; help athletes perform better and more safely. Let's work together to allow all athletes all over the world to be confident in their victories and defeats. Let accomplishments stand. Let's remove the rules that have taken the fun and challenge out of sports. Ironically, the challenge in sports is to be able to win without the assistance of drugs, but if everyone used something to enhance performance, then a personal accomplishment would still stand. In short, level the playing field. The present system has failed and will continue to do so."

The hall was quiet. The storm of whispers started again. The whispers grew louder till a full-blown gale of talking erupted. The gargoyles were unmoved. At length, the man in the center called for order, and when the room returned to silence, the man on the right spoke sarcastically. "Thank you very much for your thoughts, but what you are asking for really amounts to the legalization of cheating. I hardly think that would be in everyone's best interests. We are on a mission here to bring respectability back to sports. Specifically in this case, to identify the latest method of outright cheating so that everyone can have a fair chance regardless of where they are from or which back alley they visit."

Staf had had enough. He had used his opportunity to speak, and he was finished.

"Then thank you for your time." He turned and walked down the aisle. Through the eruption of talking and questions, he could hear the gavel and the command for silence and the command for him to return and complete the inquiry. He left, pretending not to hear them.

Outside in the hall, the security guard tried to get him back. He declined and left her standing as she spoke into her mike, trying to relay the response and ask for instruction. Staf went outside, and the steps down to the waiting limo were still clear. It was a refreshingly cool day. Funny how a nice cool day can feel so good; the same day on the way to the inquiry had felt so glum.

The throng of reporters had obviously heard the result. There were flashes everywhere and questions and demands fired from all sides. Staf deliberately got into his limo, and they left for the hotel. Staf's phone rang. It was Jake.

"Clearly we are going to have to meet later on today." Staf noted that nothing was said about his comments. It wouldn't have gotten anywhere anyway.

"Sure, tonight at what time?"

"Try fifteen minutes. Plaza Hotel room 2215. You're checked in already. And Staf, we're going to have to hire you a personal assistant and public relations person to stay with you at all times. I can't handle your shit anymore." Staf laughed. "Just don't go to your hotel unless you are ready for the zoo that's on its way there. Someone will get your things later."

The divider was still up. Staf called the limousine company and was forwarded. In the front seat, the driver picked up his phone.

"Hello, let's go to the Plaza Hotel instead." The driver hung up without speaking.

Chapter 31: Recovery

It was done, and Staf was exhausted. He didn't want to complain about it; it was different this time. For the two years he had been on the run, he had been past exhaustion out of necessity. This time, it was voluntary.

It started with a series of exclusive reports with Jaymie at the *Post*. He had been going around non-stop doing talk shows and interviews. He had created quite a controversy with the idea of permitting drugs instead of banning them. He promoted the concept of regulating drugs in sports to optimize and improve performance. He said they should be used safely, not banned. He wanted to regulate quality so that optimal and safe amounts were used instead of ad hoc or experimental amounts. The debate continued even among athletes. Staf figured it was the current users who wanted to relax the rules.

He was back in his glass house in Malibu. He had snuck in to avoid Mrs. Wilson, and in the morning, he snuck out to the car. On his way out, he glanced casually next door and noticed that he had new neighbors. Reluctantly, he went over, and after a short discussion, he learned that Mrs. Wilson had passed away. He didn't know why, but he felt horrible, as if his bad thoughts had caused her death. He wished she was still around so he could try to avoid her. He might have been willing to make himself slightly visible in order to procure a pie. He recalled that he had yet to visit his father's grave and vowed to call his mother later that day and go together.

These new neighbors were nice but boring and characterless. He grabbed a drink and went out to his private deck on the third floor overlooking the pool. He looked out over the southbound Pacific

Highway in the distance. He decided to turn on the phone. It rang immediately.

"Where are you?" It was Stephanie, his personal secretary. No pleasantries. He might have to fire her.

"Upstairs on my balcony." He was going to say something smart but was too tired.

"I don't see you." He heard steps coming up the stairs. This was his personal balcony, where he could be alone. No one else was allowed. She was fired for sure.

"I've been trying to reach you for two days," she berated him.

"Go away," he said flatly, almost meaning it. She softened.

"Can we meet up here?"

"I'll meet you beside the pool," he offered.

"Okay," she said but didn't move.

"I'll be down shortly."

She got the hint, thereby retaining employment.

Staf slowly got up and sauntered downstairs. The glass floors felt nice and cool on his bare feet, almost refreshing. It made him want to take a cold shower or maybe a dip in the pool. The day felt like it was going to shape out quite well. On his way through the sliding doors onto the sunny deck, he grabbed a chair. Stephanie was waiting there, somewhat impatient although perhaps also enjoying the sun, the view, and the atmosphere on the deck.

"I've been trying to reach you all day," she started again. He was tired of the same routine.

"So I heard," he replied dryly.

"If we're going to move forward, you are going to have to be more accessible."

"Then let's not move forward." His assistant sighed impatiently

He took off his sunglasses to look at her more directly. "If there is something to work on, let's work on it, but I am not desperately looking for contracts, and I am not interested in being scolded for my availability like a child coming in late for dinner. So cut to the chase professionally, or get out. And when you do get out, I don't want to see you again. Ever." He was going to call Jake and get a new assistant very soon.

She ignored him. "The top pharmaceutical companies are going to have a commercial steroid out within the next few months. They want you to promote it. Of course, because of conflict of interest, you will only be able to promote one."

"Of course," muttered Staf, and he looked out into the distant hills toward Los Angeles. And then it came to him. This might be another step in the process of righting things. He thought about it further. If he could represent a company quickly, get a product to market soon, he would force the hand of the government, of the public. It would have to be a company with the product out the fastest. And maybe one overseas. She now had his attention. But he had to wait; he didn't want to show it. They spent the next three hours going over the initial proposals. One was local, and one was overseas in Europe. He asked for short-term contracts, of course.

Sports doctors and coaches developed enhanced training programs that included quality and standards. The result might be improved performance, but there would be fewer long-term health problems in their athletes. A few records were being broken; however, oddly enough, there were not as many as people thought there would be. The reasons were kept to locker-room whispers.

A debate raged about the next Olympics, and to break a deadlock, it was proposed that there would be two events, one for persons using performance enhancers and one for persons without. Although this produced a tentative agreement, the general public was certain the latter group would become corrupt. It would be like a continuation of the old way.

Several years later, Staf was alone again on his personal balcony thinking about the changes in his life. He had become a star in running and the richest man in sports. He had destroyed sports and then started the healing process. He was unsure what direction it was going to take and wanted to stay as far away from it as possible. The drug battle in sports continued. He became reclusive.

New stars emerged, and the drug companies jumped on the wagon. Staf had enough money to maintain his house, car, and comfortable lifestyle. On a positive note, he could not afford his secretary anymore.

Chapter 32: Staf's Last Night in His House

Staf hadn't been feeling well lately. He was well aware that heavy steroid use could cause premature hardening of the arteries. He was up at night, feeling cold but sweating. He had to change his sheets and pajamas at least once a night. He couldn't make up his mind whether to leave the windows open or closed. Open, and it was too cold. Closed, and it was too hot. The same with blankets. He had extras on and was shivering and sweating. It was just another little cold, he thought, although he never got them often. It just seemed like there were more lately. But he refused to see a doctor, and he refused to admit that age might be a factor.

For three days, he rarely got out of bed. He did so only to go to the bathroom. He had eaten nothing except a few crackers. On the third day, he had trouble getting out of bed and felt generally weak but thought he had rounded the corner on his ailment.

In the morning, he got up and then fell back into bed with dizziness. When he got up again, he could hardly catch his breath in the bathroom. He sat on the toilet much longer than usual. He couldn't focus anymore. He didn't know how much time had passed on the throne. It might have been an hour just sitting there, leaning against the sink. Perhaps he had temporarily passed out or gone to sleep again. It was late afternoon. It was hot again. He didn't have the energy to open the windows.

At least all the curtains were shut, he thought. He had another shiver, got up, and labored back to bed. There was no need to go down to the kitchen. It was too far. He wasn't hungry anyway. He had a cup in the bathroom, but he wasn't thirsty either, although his lips were like rubber. He went to bed and slept through the afternoon. The same sequence recurred four times a day for a week.

He heard the phone ring a few times but didn't answer it. A few times he checked the numbers just to see who had called—some agents and a few fans and friends.

After a week, he had a very restless sleep again. He didn't even have to go to the bathroom, although there seemed to be very little to dispose of. By the next evening, sleep came more easily and more often. His dreams became more vivid and tied into his feelings of cold and sweat. He dreamed of running often—the Olympics, the Saharan Marathon, and the Northwest Passage Marathon. He was immune to heat and cold when running.

Just after midnight, in the very early hours of the morning, he woke and finally felt much better. He opened his eyes wide. His fever had broken. His pajamas were no longer damp. In fact, the temperature was quite nice. He looked at the time, and it was 1:00 a.m., but he decided to get up and maybe watch a movie or something.

He sat up and suddenly realized he wasn't alone. He hadn't noticed a form beside his bed, and with a start, he looked around. He focused and recognized the familiar form of the angelic person.

"Hey there," said Staf cheerfully. "I haven't seen you in a while; what's it been, thirty years? You look great, not a day over twenty-four. Man oh man, time treats you well."

She looked at him kindly.

"And thanks for your help at the hospital." He searched his body for something requiring repair, but he had to admit that at the moment he was feeling quite well. "Well, to what do I owe the pleasure?"

She looked at him again, silently, possibly with sarcasm.

"Hey," said Staf as if talking to an old friend, "I really didn't think I was going to see you again, until …" He paused and looked around. He swallowed, and quietly whispered, "until I, um, die?" It had started as a statement and petered out into a question. She looked at him solemnly and held out a hand.

Staf thought about his life. Maybe he could just ignore the hand and stay a while longer. He tried to think of the things he had yet to do. Nothing came to mind. Nothing but little things like get groceries and trimming the hedges; there was nothing that he really needed to hang around for or accomplish.

He thought of his friends. He hadn't said good-bye to anyone. But there really wasn't anyone to say good-bye to. He shrugged; the realization was easy to take. He took her hand and was led away.

"This must mean we are going to take the stairs going up, right? Elevator to the top floor? The penthouse? We'll meet your pals at the pearly? You wouldn't be messing with me, would you?" He had another thought. "Do you take bribes?" He laughed. He thought about his house, his car, and his medals. There was no need to bring them; they should already be there. Then he wondered if he would meet Amber again. It was his last thought as his tenure in the physical world ended.

Epilogue

A black sedan drove slowly up Folling Avenue. The driver, an elderly, gray-haired lady, did not entirely know where she was going. She was looking at numbers on the houses and the names of streets. She pulled over and looked at a map. She looked up again and turned the map upside down and looked out again. She pulled out and drove another block and found the entrance to Folling Cemetery. There was no parking area, so she pulled over to the side of the long driveway, neatly parked behind another car, and hobbled out of the car.

She seemed to have the energy to move about easily, but she was clearly near the age where one might consider suspending her license. She used a cane, but it appeared she might need a walker soon too.

She walked around the cemetery for two hours, crisscrossing the area, careful and respectful of the resting places, patiently admiring the headstones and tombstones. She carefully peered at the faded ones and gently shook her head in sadness when she came across ones that indicated babies and young children. She took advantage of several benches scattered around the grounds.

It was a nice fall day; the leaves were changing colors, and many had already fallen and scattered about.

At the end of two hours at the far corner, she came across one hidden among overgrown weeds and dead flowers. The groundskeepers clearly felt that this one did not require much attention, perhaps because it was not often visited.

She cleared some of the dead debris, and seemed satisfied with what she had found. She stood confidently and then delicately leaned over and spat right into the middle of the faded, pathetic tombstone. She carelessly but delicately walked over the middle of the grave to the tombstone, and with the best effort that a seventy-year-old woman could muster, she kicked it and mumbled, "Rot in hell, Staf!"

Julie Karver, the disgraced tennis star, paused at the grave to regain her delicate composure and then slowly walked away, noting a few more headstones as she passed them. She sat on another bench for a rest, got into her car, and drove away.